I ran through the tall, dead grass, eager to read the note,
to get one step closer to Henry, to escape a forest adventure
that was starting to feel far too Grimm for my tastes.

Right before I reached the stick, I thought,
The ground here feels soft.

I reached for the note. It said,
YOU'RE SAFE.

And then the ground gave way below me,
and I fell into a deep, dark hole.

The Last Place on Earth

SQUARE
FISH

HENRY HOLT AND COMPANY | NEW YORK

The Last Place on Earth

CAROL SNOW

For Andrew,
who took me camping once

SQUARE
FISH

An imprint of Macmillan Publishing Group, LLC
175 Fifth Avenue
New York, NY 10010
fiercereads.com

Square Fish and the Square Fish logo are trademarks of Macmillan and are used
by Henry Holt and Company under license from Macmillan.

Our books may be purchased in bulk for promotional, educational, or business
use. Please contact your local bookseller or the Macmillan Corporate and
Premium Sales Department at (800) 221-7945 ext. 5442 or by e-mail at
MacmillanSpecialMarkets@macmillan.com.

Library of Congress Cataloging-in-Publication Data
Snow, Carol, 1965–
    The last place on Earth / Carol Snow.—
        pages   cm
    Summary: "Daisy's best friend Henry has mysteriously disappeared, leaving behind
only a cryptic note"—Provided by publisher.
    ISBN 978-1-250-10436-6 (paperback)   ISBN 978-1-62779-040-6 (ebook)
    [1. Best friends—Fiction.   2. Friendship—Fiction.   3. Love—Fiction.
4. Survival—Fiction.]   I. Title.
    PZ7.S6807Las 2016   [Fic]—dc23   2015003266

Originally published in the United States by Henry Holt and Company
First Square Fish edition: 2017
Book designed by Liz Dresner
Square Fish logo designed by Filomena Tuosto

10 9 8 7 6 5 4 3 2 1

One

ONE DAY HENRY was there, and the next he wasn't.

I assumed he was home sick. Well, playing sick, more likely. When it came to faking an illness, Henry was a master. True, he'd had his slipups, like the time he gargled hot tap water before taking a thermometer from his mother, only to have his temperature come in at 109 degrees. But that was an exception. (To Henry's credit, his argument about the thermometer's "defective engineering" was so convincing that his mother wrote a letter to the manufacturer.)

Most of the time, Henry managed to convince his parents that his cough, headache, nausea, and/or fever were reason enough for him to stay out of school ("I'd feel really bad if I gave it to the other students"), but not serious enough for him to see the doctor. His parents would phone the excuse into the attendance office and head off to their Very Important Jobs in pet insurance and contracts law, while Henry would pass the day downloading music onto his MP3 player and teaching himself the guitar.

Had it been a normal day, I would have sent Henry a text—Hope it isn't fatal—and Henry would have replied right away with something like, Pray for me. And bring me my homework. (Please.)

But there was nothing normal about this day, because there had been nothing normal about the night before. I was all set to act like nothing had happened, if that was how he wanted it, but I wasn't prepared to find an empty desk in our first-period class (Spanish II) or in any of our shared classes that followed (AP European history, honors chemistry, dance, advanced geometry, honors sophomore English). Henry might be lazy, but I had never taken him for a coward.

"Where's Henry?" the girls in dance class asked, as they always did.

"The usual," I said.

Henry was the only boy in dance class, which was exactly why he'd signed up. Anyone who didn't play a sport was required to do two years of physical education or dance.

"I'll take the one where the girls wear spandex shorts and tank tops," he had said.

As for his own clothes, he'd talked the teacher into letting him wear basketball shorts and a T-shirt. Of course he had.

"You want to take one of these for Henry?" our chemistry teacher asked, giving me an extra packet. Only a month into sophomore year, and our teachers had figured it out: Henry would be absent a lot. I'd take his work. Henry would catch up without any problem.

It made me crazy, how easily Henry pulled As without even trying. Sick or healthy, I never missed a day of school. I never forgot a homework assignment. I never left a paper till the last minute. And yet my GPA was lower than Henry's. Not by a lot, but still.

Henry, Henry, Henry.

"I think you're secretly in love with him," my mother said back in ninth grade, when we first started partnering up for school projects, sharing inside jokes, and exchanging endless texts.

"We're just *friends*," I told her.

But we weren't *just* friends. We were *best* friends. And best friends don't disappear without saying anything. Which must mean that our best-friendship was in jeopardy.

By the end of the day, after checking my phone during every passing period and lunch, I still hadn't heard from him. *I won't be the first to text*, I swore.

And then, of course, I thumbed a message before I had a chance to talk myself out of it: I have your chemistry packet.

Text sent, I had nothing to do but wait for a reply. Because there was *no way* I was going to text him again.

Well, unless a whole hour went by without a word.

Will you just answer already?

Still no word.

You promised things wouldn't be weird.

Nothing.

Things are weird. Let's call a do-over. Last night didn't happen. OK?

Nothing.

Finally, at five o'clock, with my mounds of homework not yet begun, I called him and got a recording: "I'm sorry. But the number you are trying to reach is not in service."

I felt cold all over. And then I laughed. No wonder Henry hadn't returned my texts—his phone wasn't working! I should have known there was a good explanation. Henry wasn't a coward. Our friendship hadn't turned weird.

In my room, I found my laptop buried under last night's pajamas and booted it up, positive I'd find a message waiting. I didn't.

"I'm taking some homework over to Henry," I told my older brother, who was sticking three frozen burritos into our vintage microwave. Our kitchen, also vintage (which sounds so much better than *old*) was red-and-white tile. It looked like an In-N-Out Burger.

"Mm," he grunted, pressing in too many minutes. Peter was the king of the exploding burrito.

"Yeah, so tell Mom when she gets home."

"Mm."

Chemistry packet in hand, I let myself out the rickety gate that led to the horse and jogging trail behind our house. The trail wound around a murky pond and then led to a street that led to another street that led to Henry's house. By the time I reached what Henry called the Fortress (picture light sensors and triple locks and a security system with video cameras), I was sweaty and dusty and out of breath.

Though it was big, Henry's house was not what I would call pretty. In fact, it was what I would call ugly. All hard angles and sharp lines, the Fortress was painted an icy white and roofed in blue metal. The gray-blue trim helped, but not much. The one soft touch that Henry's parents had added, red roses under the windows and salmon bougainvillea along the sides, had been planted for security purposes only. An intruder would think twice before braving those thorns. The bees were a bonus.

I climbed the familiar steps to a front door so big that it never failed to intimidate me. Or maybe it was the discreet video camera mounted above the door that made me squirm. I ran a hand over my sweaty forehead and pushed the doorbell. Chimes echoed: *Ding-DONG. Ding-dong-DING.* Averting my eyes from the video camera, I looked instead at the weatherproof sign planted among the red roses: A-1 SECURITY. ARMED RESPONSE.

It did not make me feel better.

I waited for footsteps. *Don't let it be his mother.* I was still wearing what I'd worn to school: a rock band T-shirt, denim miniskirt, and artfully torn black tights. Mrs. Hawking would not approve.

No one came. But maybe Henry had his headphones on. Maybe he was watching TV.

I pushed the doorbell again, listened to the *ding*s and the *dong*s. Still no answer.

The late-afternoon sun reflected off the windows. Not that I could have seen inside anyway; Henry's parents kept the blinds drawn at all times. A flash of color caught my eye. A stained glass suncatcher, shaped like a shooting star and attached with a suction cup, hung between the blinds and a living room window. That was new. Or maybe I'd just never noticed it before. How like Henry's parents to put something pretty (well, pretty-ish; actually, it was kind of tacky) behind the window blinds, where they wouldn't even see it.

Finally, I pulled my phone out of my pocket. In all the time we'd been friends, I'd never called Henry's home number. There had never been any reason to. Besides, I wouldn't have wanted to risk talking to Henry's parents. ("May I ask who is calling? . . . Oh. *Daisy.*" Here his mother or father would insert a disapproving silence. "Henry is rather busy right now.")

But Henry's parents were clearly out of the house. The phone rang four times, and just when I expected a machine to pick up, it rang a fifth time. And a sixth. After eight rings I gave up and slipped the phone back into my pocket. Despite the heat, I shivered.

I shuffled down the steps, paused, and turned back one last time in the hopes that Henry would appear. But the door remained shut. The house appeared deserted, but then it always looked like that: mean and lonely.

As I made my way down the front walkway, I glanced over at the driveway. Not that I expected to see a car there—Henry's parents would never leave their vehicles potentially exposed to thieves and vandals and *goodness knows what*—but . . .

I froze. A newspaper, wrapped in orange plastic, sat in the middle of the gray pavers. I crept toward it as if it were something alive. Something that might bite. A lizard, maybe. Or a rabid possum.

I tried to quiet my mind. Maybe it wasn't the daily paper. Maybe it was some kind of free circular tossed there during the day.

But no. Hands shaking, I picked up the bundle, reached inside, and pulled out the *Orange County Register.* I checked the date: today.

That was when I knew: Henry was gone.

Two

A DAILY PAPER in the driveway. So what? It doesn't seem like much, I know. But Henry's parents believed that a newspaper left out was an advertisement that no one was home. In other words, an invitation to thieves.

The Hawking family left town at least once a month to go camping or fishing or something else nature-related. Whenever they were gone, they paid a neighbor kid to take the paper away by seven in the morning. One time a kid didn't get it until eight thirty, and they fired him. How did they know he was late? Video footage, of course.

You'd think they'd just put their mail or newspaper on vacation hold. But no: Someone who worked at the post office or newspaper might have ties to a crime ring. Before you knew it, intruders would be crawling through their windows. (Assuming they could get past the thorns and bees.)

Henry thought it was funny that his parents were "bat-crap-crazy paranoid." Up till now, I had done my best to laugh along, but it was hard. Henry was the best friend I had ever had. I wanted to like his parents. I wanted them to like me. So far, it wasn't happening.

Now I had to wonder: Were they as crazy as we'd thought? Or had they known something all along?

"I'm worried about Henry," I told my mother, back in our red-and-white kitchen. She had just come in from her day job and was scarfing down a cup of soup before she headed off to teach a jewelry-making class.

"I'm sure he's fine," she said when I told her about the newspaper. "The universe will look after him."

That was one of my mother's favorite sayings, right up there with "Everything happens for a reason" and "Things have a way of working themselves out."

Peter wandered into the kitchen. "We're out of toilet paper again."

"Did you put it on the shopping list?" my mother asked.

"Yeah."

She shrugged. "Last time I went to the store, I forgot the list."

———

The next morning, my mother agreed to swing by Henry's house on the way to school. There were now two newspapers in orange plastic sitting in the driveway.

"I'm sure there's an explanation," my mother said.

I was, too. But I was terrified the explanation would be something awful.

By second period, AP European history, I was in such a frenzy that I broke down and spoke to Gwendolyn Waxweiler. "Have you heard from Henry?" I tried to sound casual, but my voice cracked.

Gwendolyn, sitting on the other side of Henry's empty chair, dropped her gaze to the ends of my hair. Bored one day last summer, I decided to see whether cherry Kool-Aid really works as a hair dye. It really does, especially if you have previously lightened your hair with Sun-In. And the color doesn't come out. So now I know.

She said, "I haven't tried to make contact with Henry." That was the way Gwendolyn talked, as if she were from outer space and hadn't quite figured out normal human speech. She had known Henry for longer than I had—they had gone to the same small, private elementary school. Their parents were friends, and the families did stuff together. Like barbecues! And campouts! And . . . killing defenseless animals!

No matter what I said, Henry would defend man's right to hunt: "At least these animals had a good life until they were shot. Unlike the cow that died for your hamburger." (Perhaps it was growing up in that In-N-Out kitchen, but as much as I wished I had the inner strength to go vegan, I loved nothing more than a Double-Double and fries.)

Still, whatever Henry's arguments about man-versus-animal, he seemed to fall suddenly ill every time his parents scheduled a hunting trip.

"He's just got a cold or something, correct?" Gwendolyn said, as our teacher, Mr. Vasquez, began his daily PowerPoint presentation.

I shrugged and turned my attention to the first slide:

THE BLACK DEATH
"The Plague"
1347–1351 first struck Europe
Death estimates: 1/3–2/3 of European population
Bacterial infection: now curable by antibiotics

Henry found history fascinating, but even though Mr. Vasquez was cool, I always left his class feeling slightly depressed, and not just because it involved a good two hours of homework a night. If our lesson wasn't about disease, it was about war. The kings and queens may have had a good time (as long as they kept their heads), but for the rest of the population in medieval Europe, life was miserable, and death came early, often, and in a whole bunch of disgusting ways.

Two seats away, Gwendolyn took notes with one hand. With the other, she fiddled with her thick braid. Gwendolyn's hair was strawberry blond. It would take Kool-Aid really well.

Usually, Gwendolyn ignored my existence entirely, but she kept glancing over at me. Finally, a few slides later (**"Forms of the Plague"**), when Mr. Vasquez paused to let us copy down some more depressing facts, she leaned over Henry's desk. "Does he not respond to your phone calls?"

"Phone's disconnected."

I copied the first line from the slide:

1. **Bubonic Plague: Most common variant. Carried by rats; spread by fleas. Swellings (buboes) on neck, armpit, and groin. Mortality rate 30–75%. Typical life expectancy: one week.**

"Have you been to his house?" Gwendolyn whispered.

I paused. Should I tell her about the newspapers? No. I wanted someone besides my mother to tell me that I was overreacting.

That everything was going to be fine. Gwendolyn's family was just as bat-crap-crazy paranoid as Henry's. She'd tell me that the abandoned *OC Registers* were a sure sign of calamity.

"Yesterday afternoon," I said. "No one answered the door. But it was kind of early—his parents wouldn't even be home from work yet. And Henry could have been sleeping or listening to music or something."

She nodded, looking less than convinced.

I copied down the next line from the slide.

2. Pneumonic Plague: Attacked respiratory system. Spread by breathing infected air. Mortality rate: 90–95%. Typical life expectancy: 1–2 days.

"When did you last talk to him?" she asked.

"Night before last."

"And everything was normal?"

That was a weird question. Especially since Henry was so *not* normal the last time I had seen him. But how could Gwendolyn know that? Oh no. Now I was getting bat-crap-crazy paranoid. Maybe it was spreading, like the plague. Were there any flea-bitten rats around?

"Sure," I said. "Everything was normal. I guess." I copied down the third plague variant.

3. Septicemic Plague: Attacked the blood system. Mortality rate: near 100%.

"I'm sure everything is fine," I told Gwendolyn, willing my words to be true.

She didn't say anything, just twisted her strawberry-blond braid with renewed vigor.

"The universe will look after him," I added.

At that, she dropped her braid. "Are you kidding me? The universe looks after no one. We're all on our own."

———

Peter's beat-up little car, pale yellow with gray doors, was waiting in front of the school when I got out. Most of the time I walked home—it was just over a mile—but if it was hot outside, my mother would tell my brother to get me.

I grabbed the handle and pulled hard. The door creaked open. I slid into the bucket seat, which was black vinyl laced with pink leopard-print duct tape. The duct tape had come with the car, as had the Jesus stickers on the rear fender. Henry and I had spent a lot of time trying to visualize the previous owners.

"Need to stop for coffee," Peter mumbled, pulling away from the curb. His eyes were puffy. He needed a shave.

"Did you just get up?" I asked.

He shrugged. "Not *just* just, but—whatever."

Another one of my mother's mottoes (there were hundreds) was "I trust my children to make the right choices." That worked okay for me. I chose hard work and responsibility. Which sounds incredibly boring, but there you go. Then there was my brother. After finishing high school in the spring, Peter had mostly chosen to binge on Netflix and sleep through lunch.

I stayed in the car while Peter ran into the grocery store, emerging with a large cardboard cup and a four-pack of toilet paper.

"That TP is not going to last long," I said.

He smirked. "Mom'll buy more. It's on the list."

As we approached the turn to the Fortress, I said, "Can we drive by Henry's house?"

Peter gave a single-shoulder shrug (when it comes to conserving energy, Peter is a master) and flicked on the blinker. We turned off the main road and wound around to Henry's mean-looking house. Peter stopped the car.

I was prepared for the two orange bundles still sitting in the driveway. Still, when I saw them, a fresh stab of disappointment hit me in the stomach.

"You getting out?" Peter asked.

I shook my head. "Let's go home."

In my bedroom, I unloaded my books and notebooks. I booted up my laptop, an old model that my mother had bought for next to nothing when her office updated the equipment. I meant to research some stuff for English but wound up checking my messages instead (nothing from Henry). I stared at the wall. I stared at my laptop screen. Finally, I gave up. I had to go back to the Fortress. Maybe I'd missed something. Maybe there were clues to Henry's whereabouts.

I let myself out the back gate and hurried down the dusty horse and jogging path until I reached the pond. It was usually busy here during the day. Today, a mother walked near the edge, a toddler clutching her skirt. A bicyclist zipped past several old men in camp chairs, fishing rods in their hands, tackle boxes by their feet. Coots and mallards paddled across the green-black surface, while dragon flies hovered among the reeds like tiny helicopters.

I would never again pass this pond without remembering that last night with Henry. He'd known something was up, I was sure of it. He'd known he was going away.

But where? And why?

Three

IT WASN'T UNUSUAL for Henry to show up at my house on a school night, but he usually texted first, and he almost never came this late, just past ten thirty. He had been in school that day. In fact, he hadn't staged an illness for over a week, which I might have found strange if I hadn't been so glad to have him around to challenge me to "power pirouette" contests during dance class or to doodle stupid cartoons in my history notebook when I was supposed to be copying down disgusting facts about medieval Europe. (One word: leeches.)

"You up for a walk?" he asked, hands in his jeans pockets, narrow shoulders angled forward.

I almost said, *No, let's just hang in my living room.* I was in my pajamas already (flowered boxers and a tank top; it was a warm night), and I still had a good half hour of math homework left. But there was something about Henry's expression. His eyes, so dark brown they were almost black, were always sharp, but tonight they looked strained. His jaw muscles twitched.

So I said, "Yeah, sure. Let me just tell my mom and put some clothes on."

Five minutes later, we were out the back gate and onto the trail. Something rustled in the bushes. My arm tickled; I swiped away a spiderweb that might have been imaginary but probably wasn't. The path, so familiar during the day, was kind of creepy at night.

"We going to your house?" I asked.

"*No.*" (Had his voice really been that forceful? I couldn't remember. Mostly, I was just relieved that I wouldn't have to deal with his parents.)

We said almost nothing until we reached the pond, which wasn't as weird as you might think. Henry and I were not only close enough to tell each other everything (at least in my mind), we trusted each other with our silences.

At the pond, Henry stopped as if entranced by the glassy surface. The night was clear. The moon cast a ribbon of light across the water. The air smelled of eucalyptus and wild sage.

I studied his profile: the straight nose, the strong jaw. Henry was better looking from the side than he was full-on. His face was a touch too narrow, and his eyes, dark and deep-set, were a little too close together. But I liked his face from any angle—not in *that way*, not really, but because it was Henry's face. It was so familiar, I knew just how to read it. At least, I had until this night.

"If you knew you only had one day left on earth, what would you do?" Henry asked, his gaze still on the water.

Coming from someone else, this question might have seemed odd, but all the time we launched conversations with things like, "Would you rather be a free-range chicken or a farmed salmon?"

Or, "If you could only bring one book to a desert island, what would it be?" (My answers, in case you're wondering, were farmed salmon and an e-reader. And I don't care if that's cheating.)

"Depends what you mean by last day on earth," I said. "Are we talking solar flare or alien abduction?"

Henry chewed his lower lip. "More like aliens."

"I'd hide," I said.

He shook his head. "No, no, no. One day left and there's no escape. They've got you, I don't know, microchipped or something. And they've got a Daisy-finding task force. And if the aliens don't get you, they'll take out your entire family."

"They could have Peter."

"You can't sacrifice your brother! Peter is my role model." Henry laughed but in a sad way, which I hadn't even known was possible. And then he did this weird whimper-hiccup thing. I let it pass.

"Fine," I said. "If I knew it was my last day on earth, I'd shut myself in my room with a box of cookies. And I'd cry."

"Would you come see me to say good-bye?"

"Sure. Maybe. I don't know. I wouldn't want to make you sad. And besides, I hate good-byes."

There was a long pause. Finally, he spoke. "What kind of cookies?"

"Girl Scout. Thin mints. And those coconut thingies that are like a thousand calories each, but if I'm going to die tomorrow, who cares?"

"That's two boxes. And I didn't say you were going to die tomorrow, I just said . . ." He sighed.

"Is something wrong?" I asked. "You seem weird."

"I'm always weird. It's my natural state."

He held my eyes for a moment. *Henry's taller than I am*, I thought with surprise. When did that happen? We'd been more or less the same height since I'd known him. And then, before I could ask how he'd snuck a growth spurt past me, he did something that was undeniably weird, even for him. He yanked off his sneakers and ran into the pond.

"Henry! Are you crazy? It's gross in there!"

But he didn't answer, just waded through the muck until the water got to waist level and dove under. He remained submerged just long enough to make me worry that he'd gotten caught on something or that his waterlogged jeans had dragged him down, and then he burst through the slimy surface.

"Join me for a swim?" he called.

I stared at him in horror. "That water is disgusting. There is duck crap and fish crap and algae and probably a million kinds of bacteria."

"So that's a no?"

"I think you're going to need antibiotics. I'm serious, Henry."

"Fine," he said. But instead of slogging back through the muck, he turned and dove under the scum again. With choppy strokes, he splashed his way to the center of the pond, where he floated on his back and gazed up at the moon.

If it were anyone else, I would have walked away. But I stayed, of course. I would never desert Henry.

Finally, he backstroked to the shallows, where he stood up and made his way to shore, his feet making sucking sounds in the muck.

"I've always wanted to do that," he said when he got to me. His breathing was heavy. Henry was not one for physical exertion.

"How was it?" My voice was flat.

"Not as fun as I expected. Plus I think I stepped on a turtle." A cloud drifted in front of the moon.

I hugged myself, even though it wasn't cold. "I should get home. Do my math homework."

"I'll walk you."

"No, I'm fine. You should go shower."

"Do I smell that bad?" He tried to smile.

I tried to smile back. And then I gave up and let my gaze fall to the ground. "I'll see you at school. Don't forget that chemistry thing is due tomorrow."

"There's something else I always wanted to do," he said.

I looked up just in time to see his face closing in on mine. "Henry, no!" I took a step backward and stumbled on a tree root, just managing to steady myself before falling.

"I'm sorry," he whispered. "I never should have—"

"It's okay," I said, though of course it was anything but. "I'm just tired. And you're wet. And a little . . ." I caught myself before I said *stinky.*

His eyes glistened. "You mean so much to me. I didn't mean to make things weird."

"You didn't," I lied. "Everything's the same as it always was. Let's just blame tonight on the full moon." (The moon wasn't full.)

"Deal," Henry said. "Things will never be weird between us. I promise." He held my gaze for about two seconds more than was comfortable under the circumstances. "You sure you don't want me to walk you home?"

"Positive." I forced a smile and gave him a quick wave. Then I made my way around the pond, to the trail, past the spiderwebs, through the gate, and into the safety of my house.

I never looked back. Not once.

Four

I KNEW THE house was empty, but I rang the doorbell just in case. At this point, I'd even be happy to see Henry's parents. Well, relieved, anyway.

Ding-DONG. Ding-dong-DING. Nothing.

I raised my eyes to the video camera painted the same ice white as the house. It stared back at me, unblinking. I stuck out my tongue. It did not react.

I rang the bell again because I didn't know what else to do. Finally I gave up and trudged back down the front walkway. Peeking through the narrow slot of the locked metal mailbox, I spied a pile of envelopes and circulars.

Justin Kim. Just like that, I remembered the name of the boy who took in the mail and paper. Henry and I had run into him once while walking around the pond. Later, Henry had pointed out his house, three doors down.

As I hurried away from the Fortress, I prayed that Justin Kim had messed up. That the Hawkings had called him. That he just hadn't showed.

The Kim house also had a sign from A-1 Security planted in the front yard. Perhaps there was some kind of neighborhood discount. No video camera, though—at least that I could see—and unlike Henry's mother, who refused to open the door to strangers (UPS drivers were forced to show credentials beyond their big brown trucks), a petite Asian woman with perfect makeup answered my knocks. She wore a silk tunic, gray leggings, and terry-cloth flip-flops.

"I'm Daisy Cruz," I said. "A friend of Henry's?"

"Henry. Yes. Nice boy." She smiled. Piano notes drifted from farther back in the house.

I tried to keep my tone casual. "Henry and his parents have been gone a couple of days, but their newspapers and mail are still out there." Saying it like that, it didn't seem so ominous. "Do you know if Justin was supposed to get them?"

In a flash, Mrs. Kim's smile transformed into a scowl. "Justin!" The piano music stopped. *"Justin!"*

Justin Kim, a lanky eleven-year-old with a sharp gaze and black hair that stood up like feathers, padded into the front hall.

His mother glared at him. "You forgot to do your job for the Hawkings!"

"No, I didn't."

"You go over this morning?"

"No, but—"

"Then you forgot!"

"They may not have called him," I said.

"They didn't call me!" Justin's voice cracked. He turned from his mother to look at me with something stronger than dislike.

Disappointment clenched my stomach. "Sorry, I was just checking. Mr. and Mrs. Hawking must have forgotten to tell Justin they were going away." My words sounded less than convincing, and not just to me.

Mrs. Kim raised her eyebrows. "Mr. and Mrs. Hawking forget nothing."

I left the Kims' house feeling even more panicked than before, and not just because Justin looked like he might hunt me down and strangle me in my sleep. Even if the Hawkings had neglected to call Justin before they left town—something they would never do—they could have called him from their car on their way to . . . wherever they were.

Unless they didn't drive away at all? Maybe they'd been kidnapped. Or murdered in their sleep (though probably not by Justin Kim; he was saving his strength for me). There was one way to find out.

On the right side of the Hawkings' garage, a keypad glowed like a telephone handset that had lost its way.

"My parents made me promise I'd never tell anyone our security codes," Henry had said one day after school, when we were standing right here, about to go inside. "Yeah? So what are they?" I'd asked.

"What do you want to know—the garage code or the alarm system?"

"Both," I'd said. "I want you to tell me both."

My hands shook as I punched in the numbers. A green light flashed twice. The door lurched and lifted. The family had two cars:

a Mini Cooper for Mr. Hawking, who, since he worked on the far side of Los Angeles, needed something with good gas mileage, and a giant black SUV with tinted windows for Mrs. Hawking. The SUV was roomy enough for camping gear. Also intimidating enough for doing drug deals, though Henry's mom didn't seem the type.

I didn't even realize I'd been holding my breath until I saw the Mini, alone in the vast garage, and let out a huge sigh of relief. They had taken Henry's mom's car, that big, bad wilderness machine. Up in the mountains or down in a valley, cell phone reception would be so sketchy, they wouldn't even know that Henry's phone wasn't working. And they couldn't call to check on whoever they had hired to take in their mail and paper. Justin Kim had obviously been fired without notice.

Nothing to worry about.

I was still worried. The Hawking family did not take off in the middle of the week on a whim. The Hawking family did not do anything on a whim.

The garage was huge, with enough space for three large vehicles if not for the deep floor-to-ceiling cabinets that lined the walls. Around here, pretty much everyone used the garage for storage. My mother's and brother's cars hadn't seen the inside of our garage since . . . ever. But these cabinets were enormous. How could they need to store that much stuff, especially when their house was already too big for three people?

My eyes flicked around the space: no video cameras. Behind me, the garage door remained open like a giant, screaming mouth. I peered around the corner; the street was empty. I pushed the garage door button, and the door lurched back down, sealing me in with the car.

It was hot in here. Blood rushed in my ears. I grabbed the nearest cabinet handle, took a deep breath, and pulled, half expecting to find a weapons arsenal or a body stashed inside.

Toilet paper. I couldn't believe it. The rolls were jammed into the cabinets four deep and six across, stacked all the way to the top. The next cabinet was the same. The Hawkings, family of three, had several hundred rolls of toilet paper sitting in their garage, while in my house we couldn't even keep a spare in the bathroom. I broke into laughter, the sounds echoing around me.

"My parents are gearing up for the Big One," Henry had said whenever the topic of earthquakes came up. I'd assumed he meant stocking jugs of water and some granola bars—enough to get through a few days without power. But this! This was bizarre.

I pulled open the next cabinet, expecting to find yet more toilet paper, but no. This space was jammed with cleaning supplies: dish soap, sponges, window cleaner. The next cabinet was filled with bleach. Just bleach.

I worked my way around the walls, uncovering sacks of rice, bags of beans, canned vegetables, canned meat, canned fish, bouillon cubes, salt, pepper, sugar, more salt. There were flashlights and flares, no-drip candles, and an entire cabinet of batteries, in every imaginable size.

Clearly, the Hawkings expected the Big One to be very big indeed. Of course, if an earthquake was severe enough to merit all these emergency supplies, the odds of the family surviving it were pretty slim.

Unless the universe looked after them. That could happen.

I'd seen enough. I opened the garage and slipped back out into the dazzling sunshine. Hands trembling, I keyed in the code, and the door slid back into place. I took a deep breath and exhaled with a sigh of something approaching relief.

I had just reached the street when a huge white pickup truck pulled up to the curb. The back door opened, and Gwendolyn climbed out. "Did you see Henry? Is he here?"

A minute earlier, and they would have caught me coming out of the garage. Yikes.

I shook my head and tried not to look freaked out. "I just stopped by to give him his homework, but no one answered the door."

Gwendolyn's gaze flicked down to my hands, which were not holding homework. Before she could interrogate me further, her parents got out of the car. Both of them were fair skinned and light eyed, like Gwendolyn, but Mrs. Waxweiler was short and plump, while her husband was a great big bear of a man. And not a cute bear, like a panda. More like a big scary one that comes out during the spring thaw to maul hikers nibbling sunflower seeds. He had brown hair and bushy red eyebrows that looked so much like caterpillars, I half expected them to crawl across his face.

Mrs. Waxweiler, on the other hand, was a blond bubble: one of those moms who look so stereotypically mom-ish that she could be on a commercial for laundry detergent. She wore a pink T-shirt and flowered capris and a superfake smile.

"You are Daisy Cruz," Mr. Waxweiler said, which would have been helpful had I forgotten my name. His voice was surprisingly high for such a large man.

"Yes," I said.

"And you are unaware of Henry's whereabouts."

"Yes."

He appraised the cherry-red ends of my hair, the four earrings, the T-shirt I'd hand-decorated with Sharpies. Though we'd only been acquainted for thirty seconds, I instinctively knew that

Mr. Waxweiler was not the kind of man to appreciate a custom T-shirt.

And then, suddenly, it was like I wasn't even there.

"We'll try the front door," he told his womenfolk. They headed for the walkway.

"They're not there," I said. "I rang the bell twice. And—" I caught myself before I said, *their SUV is missing.*

Mr. and Mrs. Waxweiler didn't even pause, but Gwendolyn spun around and shot me a look as if to say . . . something. But what? *Be quiet? Go away? Watch out?*

Something bad. Her look definitely conveyed something bad.

She spun back around (I'm not just saying that; as a member of the school drill team, Gwendolyn can spin with the best of them) and followed her parents to the front door. Mr. Waxweiler pushed the doorbell and waited, hands on hips.

As if she sensed my eyes on her family, Mrs. Waxweiler turned around and stared at me, her fake smile gone.

Face hot, I gave her a limp wave and hurried away. But after a few paces, something made me glance back. The three of them were still standing side by side on the front stoop, but now Gwendolyn was pointing off to the right. There was something in the landscaping or . . . no. She was pointing at the window.

Her parents stepped up to the very edge of the rosebushes and peered at whatever it was that Gwendolyn had spotted. There was no way they could look into the house. The blinds were shut. There was nothing to see except . . .

The shooting star sun-catcher. That was it. They were staring at that little bit of stained glass, dangling from a suction cup, as if its blue and yellow rays could reveal the secret of life.

Five

"HENRY'S STILL OUT?" Mr. Vasquez, our history teacher, asked.

"Yeah."

It was Friday: test day. Mr. Vasquez put a sheet facedown on my desk.

"Whatever Henry has, it must be catching." He nodded at the empty desk on the far side of Henry's. Gwendolyn was absent, too.

"Must be." I shivered.

Friday was the worst day to miss school because so many teachers gave tests. Besides, there was a football game tonight, which meant that Gwendolyn would have to forgo a halftime performance. Almost as bad, she didn't get to walk around all day wearing tiny blue shorts and a bright yellow T-shirt that said DRILL.

"'Drill,'" Henry had said, the previous Friday, when a girl

wearing the shirt had passed us in the hall. "You think that's meant to be a noun or a verb?"

I considered. "Verb. So if a girl is all, 'Wait, what was I supposed to be doing?' she can just look at her shirt and be like, 'Oh yeah—drill routine.'"

"Sensible." He nodded. "It's a trend that should catch on, kind of like casual Fridays, only this would be verb Fridays. The dancers could wear T-shirts that say 'Dance,' and the math geeks would go with 'Calculate.' The teachers, of course, would wear shirts that said 'Teach.' Yours could say 'Paint' or 'Draw,' depending on your mood."

"How about you?" I said. "What would your shirt say?"

He looked off to one side for a moment, thinking. And then he smiled. "'Sleep.'"

Had that conversation really happened only a week ago? I still couldn't believe how much had changed.

History tests distributed, Mr. Vasquez returned to his desk. "You may begin."

I flipped over my paper and read the first question: **How did the Black Death get its name?**

I wrote: *The Black Death got its name from the black swellings, or buboes, that characterized the disease, along with the black spots that followed. The buboes appeared on the armpits, neck, and/or groin. If the buboes were lanced, the blood that came out was black, thick, and foul-smelling.*

Around the room, students shifted in their seats and cleared their throats. It was hard to write this stuff without squirming.

Next question: **How did the bubonic plague epidemic (the Black Death) affect communities in Europe?**

The epidemic destroyed communities. Families broke apart when the well rejected the sick. Essential services collapsed. In some areas, there was little law and order because the enforcers had died. People panicked as they struggled for their own survival. Properties stood empty. Corpses were dumped in the street or buried in mass graves. Crops withered in the field, and untended cattle wandered in the streets.

This test was not doing wonders for my mood. I'd be happy when we finished the chapter on the Middle Ages and moved to the Renaissance and beyond. I was ready to hear about great art and guillotines. Let me eat cake.

Before I had a chance to answer the third question (**How did the pneumonic plague spread?**) Mr. Vasquez let out an enormous, wet sneeze. Thirty-two heads shot up at once.

"Bless you," someone murmured from the back.

The pneumonic plague spread through droplets in the air, primarily from coughs and sneezes, I wrote, suppressing a giggle.

———

I'd never paid enough attention to Gwendolyn to notice who her friends were, so the DRILL shirts were a big help. During nutrition, I walked up to a girl I recognized from my chemistry class.

"Do you know Gwendolyn Waxweiler?"

"Yeah."

"Do you have her cell number?"

She thought for a moment. "No."

"Do you know anyone who would?"

She thought for another, slightly longer, moment. "No."

I had no more luck with the next two girls I asked, but before the bell rang in math class, I hit pay dirt.

"Are you friends with Gwendolyn Waxweiler?" I asked a pinch-faced drill team girl I'd previously managed to avoid.

She narrowed her eyes. If she didn't watch out, the line between her eyebrows would become permanent. "Why do you want to know?"

"I need her phone number."

"What for?"

I stifled several sarcastic responses. "She's out today, and I need to give her the history homework."

She straightened the notebook on her desk. "Most teachers post assignments on the school website."

"This one doesn't." (Actually, he did.)

The bell rang, and she still hadn't turned over the number. Defeated, I trudged to my seat across the classroom. At the end of class, however, the pinch-faced girl surprised me by slipping a scrap of paper on my desk.

"Just don't tell her where you got it," she said.

Gwendolyn won't answer, I thought, punching in her number after school. She'd see my unfamiliar number in her display, and let it go to voice mail. Fine. I'd leave her a message.

Cars crowded the pickup line in front of the school. I stood just outside the main door, in the shade of the overhang. It was another hot afternoon. Surely Peter would come get me.

When Gwendolyn's phone picked up on the first ring, it suddenly hit me that I had no idea what I was going to say. *Henry's been out, and then today you were out, and that just seemed weird since you seemed fine yesterday, so I thought I'd call and—*

"The number you are trying to reach has been disconnected."

I didn't even realize I'd made a sound till a guy from my Spanish class appeared at my side and touched my arm. "Are you okay?"

Everyone was looking at me.

"Not really," I said. "No."

Peter didn't show up at the school, and he didn't answer his phone (which, being typical behavior, didn't worry me). After waiting fifteen minutes, I gave up and walked home.

By the time I staggered into the house, I was out of breath and drenched in sweat. After dropping my bag in the kitchen, I went through the living room and down the hallway. The worn blue carpet needed a good vacuuming, but right now that was pretty low on my list of priorities.

In my room, I booted up my laptop. A few clicks later, I had the information I needed.

I pushed open the door to Peter's gloomy bedroom, where he sat slumped in his armchair, playing a game on his phone.

"Why didn't you answer your phone?" I asked.

The room looked better in the dark, which may have been why Peter hadn't bothered to change the overhead light since it burned out almost a year ago. As usual, the shades were drawn.

"Huh?" The phone cast a ghostly glow over his face.

"I called your phone like five times, and you didn't pick up."

"What? Oh. Yeah."

"It was really hot, and—oh, never mind. I need you to drive me somewhere."

He shifted his weight in the chair and thumbed his phone. "I'm kind of busy."

"It's an emergency."

"I very much doubt that." With an index finger, he scratched his stubbly chin. Peter had been cute enough in high school, when he played on the basketball team and exposed his skin to sunlight on a regular basis. But too many microwave burritos and not enough activity was making him soft and pale and scruffy. At least he wasn't dirty. A combo aroma of body wash, deodorant, and plug-in room freshener wafted into the hallway.

From past experience, I knew that begging didn't work on Peter.

Nor did threatening to complain to our mother, who wouldn't do anything, anyway. That left bribery.

"I'll buy you hot Cheetos," I said.

At last he perked up. "Deal."

———

Gwendolyn lived in a unguarded gated community, which meant that we had to wait maybe fifty seconds before someone who lived there punched in the magic code, after which we followed them into the development. So much for security. If Peter's crappy car could get through, anyone could.

"Tax records," I told Peter, when he asked how I'd gotten the address. "It's all online."

If I had expected him to be impressed by my cleverness, I would have been disappointed.

Gwendolyn's house, beige stucco with a red tile roof and wood trim, was just as pretty as three identical houses on her street. I don't mean that in a bad way. Unless decay and neglect come into style, no one will ever want to live in a house that looks like ours.

No one answered the door at the Waxweilers' house. I tried the bell twice and then went back to the car.

"No one's there."

"Which proves what, exactly?" asked Peter.

"Nothing." With a sigh, I fastened my seat belt. "I wanted to come because I don't know what else to do."

"I don't get why you're freaking out," Peter said, starting the car. "So Henry went on vacation without telling you. So what?"

"Henry never does anything without telling me." I took one last look at the closed-up house. "Peter—wait."

Something colorful flashed in a front window. I hurried over the tidy lawn and got as close to the window as I could. (Like the Hawkings, the Waxweilers favored thorny plants.) It was close enough. Dangling on the other side of the windowpane was a shooting star sun-catcher, just like the one at Henry's house.

Breathlessly, I told Peter the news.

"And this is significant because . . . ?"

"I don't know! But it has to mean something. And if we can figure out what that something is, then maybe we'll find Henry."

Peter pulled away from the curb. "You said Henry and Gwen have been friends a long time, right?"

"Gwendolyn. No one calls her Gwen. Their *families* have been friends a long time. Henry and Gwendolyn went to that private school together. It's not like Henry would hang out with her if he didn't have to."

"Whatever. If their families have been doing stuff together since Henry and what's-her-face were kids, isn't it possible that they did crafts together? Or that they made the sun-catchers in school?"

"It's possible. But why hang them now?"

He shrugged. "Gwendolyn's could have been up all along. Maybe Henry's mom saw this one hanging and got craft envy and decided to hang hers, too."

"Henry's mother would never get craft envy."

We'd reached the edge of the development. We didn't need a code to get out; a sensor triggered the gate.

"Know what's even better than elementary school craft projects?" Peter asked.

"What?"

"Hot Cheetos."

Soon afterward, we pulled into the chain drugstore that doubled as our neighborhood convenience store. Inside, it was refrigerator-cold. In the chip aisle, Peter didn't hesitate before choosing a jumbo-sized bag.

"Where's Henry's dad's office?" he asked, cradling the orange bag like a baby.

"Far. Like Burbank."

"So maybe that's where they are. Since his hours are long. Maybe they're staying someplace nearby."

"Maybe . . ." It still didn't explain the disconnected phone and abandoned newspapers, but it was an angle I hadn't considered.

"Have you tried calling his dad's office?"

"No," I said. "That's a good idea."

"I have my moments." Peter strolled off for the refrigerator section, where he plucked a big bottle of Dr Pepper from the case. I paid for it without complaint.

Six

SO THEN I went home, found the law firm's number online, called Henry's father, and cleared everything up!

Ha. Kidding.

Mr. Hawking was "unavailable," his secretary told me.

Unavailable like in a meeting? I asked. Or unavailable like not there?

"I'd be happy to take your name and number," the cool-voiced woman on the other end told me.

"Just let me know if he's in the building," I pleaded. "Just let me know if you've seen him since Tuesday."

"I am not at liberty to divulge that information," she replied.

I started to explain the situation, that I was a friend of his son's and—

Click. She put me through to voice mail. I left a garbled message and hung up.

I went back to my good pal Google. In the search box, I typed in Henry's mother's name and "pet insurance." There were a couple of hits but no phone number or employer name. On the plus side, I learned that pet insurance wasn't just for dogs or cats anymore. Rats, mice, chinchillas, goats, geckos—they could all be covered. It was unclear whether rat and mice owners paid higher premiums if they also had cats.

Despite Mrs. Hawking's job, or maybe because of it, Henry had never been allowed to have a pet. "She says they carry diseases," Henry explained. Children carry diseases, too, but that hadn't stopped her from having one.

I used to beg my mother for a cat, but she said that it was wrong to adopt an animal if you're going to leave it alone all day. If Peter didn't get a job soon, I might reopen negotiations.

For now, Peter was back in his gloomy room, propped up on the unmade bed with his own cast-off laptop, surfing the Internet with one hand and shoveling hot Cheetos into his mouth with the other.

I said, "I called Mr. Hawking's law firm, but it didn't get me anywhere."

"Urm," he grunted.

"Do you know if Mom's home for dinner?"

"I-uh-oh."

"Okay. I'm gonna take off. See you later."

"Urm."

I headed out the back gate and toward Henry's house without any real plan. I knew there would be three newspapers in the driveway now, and there were. Still, the sight made my heart race.

This time, I didn't even bother ringing the front doorbell. Instead, I went straight to the garage, punched in the code, and slipped inside. I hit the button for the garage door. It slipped back down, sealing me inside with the Mini Cooper—aka the car Mr. Hawking drove to work every day. Of course he wasn't in Burbank. I should have realized that before calling his work.

I didn't bother going through the big cabinets that lined the garage walls. *Toilet paper.* It wasn't even funny anymore. With Henry missing, nothing was funny anymore.

Well, except goat insurance. That was still funny.

At the back of the garage, three steps led up to a door that could be unlocked using a security pad just like the one outside the garage. I climbed the steps and punched in the same numbers. With a click, the door opened.

Now came the race against time. The door opened up to a small hallway that led to the kitchen. I hurried around the corner to the laundry room. There, on the wall, a red light blinked on the white security pad. Digital numbers counted the seconds left to key in this code, which was different from the one in the garage: forty-seven seconds to go.

Just like that, my mind went blank. I knew the code. I knew I knew it. But the sequence was jammed somewhere in the back of my brain, buried beneath pop song lyrics, important dates in medieval Europe, and the price of a Dr Pepper.

The Hawkings had paid extra to have a security system that would alert the local police in the event of a break-in. That meant that if I didn't come up with the code in—oh no, thirty-two seconds!—I was in huge trouble.

Thirty-one seconds . . . thirty . . .

Got it. I keyed in the number sequence and held my breath. A tone sounded, and the red light turned green.

Heart thumping, I left the laundry room and went into the kitchen. The black granite counters were clear, and no dishes crowded the deep sink. I opened the dishwasher. Inside were plates and mugs and bowls: all clean. So they had taken the time to do dishes before leaving. That was good, right? They hadn't fled in a panic. They hadn't been abducted. Or, if they had been, their kidnapper was unusually tidy.

I opened the refrigerator. There was some salad dressing, butter, pickles, jam, and a package of individually wrapped slices of cheese. In other words: nothing that told me anything.

Next I checked the living room, which the family barely used, and the television room, which they used a lot. Nothing seemed out of place. Not that there was a lot to get messed up. Mr. and Mrs. Hawking did not believe in "nonessentials." So they had couches and coffee tables, TVs, and a few framed family photos, but no books, art, souvenirs, knickknacks, or clutter of any kind. It was so clean, it was creepy.

Again, I thought about the sun-catcher in the front window, the one Gwendolyn's parents had peered at so intently. It had to mean something beyond "we have no taste."

A closed, locked door led to the home office. I'd never been in there, and it didn't look like I'd start now. That left the upstairs bedrooms. The master suite was the first room on the right. It seemed wrong to invade Mr. and Mrs. Hawking's privacy, but hey—I'd already gone through their garage cabinets and broken into their house.

Their king-sized bed was made—not as precisely as I would have expected, but the olive-green spread had been pulled up.

There were two shiny wood dressers, one tall, one short. The tall one had a wedding picture of Mr. and Mrs. Hawking. Henry looked like his mother when she was young. Immediately, I wished I could undo that realization.

Their walk-in closet, filled with clothes and shoes in subdued colors, all neatly arranged, appeared undisturbed. The bathroom was likewise tidy, dark green towels hanging stiffly from a rod.

There were two more bedrooms between the master and Henry's. One was used for storage and the other was supposedly for guests, though the family had had no visitors since I'd known them. School portraits of Henry lined the walls. No one else: just Henry. He had a few relatives in other states, but he never saw them. Not even on his walls.

Henry's door stood open. Weirdly, going in there felt like a bigger invasion of privacy than checking out his parents' bedroom. I'd been in this room so many times, but never alone. Henry would sit in his desk chair, spinning this way and that. I'd lounge on his bed, hanging my head over the side till the blood rush made me dizzy. We'd talk about school or music or movies or friends or teachers or where we wanted to live when we grew up or what jobs we wanted to have.

Well, I talked about jobs I dreamed of: children's book illustrator or film editor or travel photographer. Henry maintained that he was going to "marry well and be a kept man." But we both knew it was a joke. Henry was brilliant. He just hadn't figured out how to channel his energies. But he would someday. Of course he would.

Henry's room was as tidy as the rest of the house, but it had more personality. Unfortunately, the personality was "eight-year-old boy." His bedspread was blue-and-orange patchwork, dotted here and there with ball, glove, and bat appliqués. "Art" signs (quotes important) on the wall said SLUGGER and HOME RUN and GO TEAM.

Henry had never played baseball. He didn't even like watching it.

The biggest nonbaseball touch, Henry's guitar, stood in its usual spot, in a stand in the back corner of the room. For someone who'd never had a formal lesson, he was really good. Of course, he practiced all the time, especially on days when he was supposed to be in school.

If Henry had left for good, he would have taken his guitar with him. At once, I felt relieved and embarrassed. What would he think if he could see me sneaking around his house? What would his parents think?

Henry was fine. He hadn't been taken by aliens or invaders. His communications freeze stemmed from embarrassment over my reaction to his attempted kiss. He'd be back any day now. His family had taken one of their wilderness trips. Or, who knows? Maybe his father had to fly off somewhere for work, and he'd taken his family with him. The big black SUV could be in a parking lot at LAX. Henry could be in London or Paris or Hong Kong. It could happen.

A piece of paper lay on the middle of Henry's desk. I'd already invaded his privacy this much; a quick peek wouldn't hurt. And then I'd leave: set the alarm, sneak out through the garage, and wait, wait, wait till Henry came home to me.

I'd tell him about my fears. I'd confess to breaking into his house. We'd laugh. At least, I hoped we would. And then we'd talk about the thing that started all this madness: our almost-kiss in the murky darkness on that night next to the pond.

The paper had been ripped out of a spiral notebook, the edges rough and curly. In the center, in blue ink, Henry had written two words in his precise, tiny printing: *SAVE ME.*

Seven

"I DON'T UNDERSTAND why you're so worried," my mother said, filling a pot at the kitchen sink. She hauled the pot over to the stove and placed it on a front burner. My mother didn't cook very often, and when she did her brow clenched in such concentration, you'd think she was about to perform an organ transplant.

"Henry's in trouble. Why else would he leave me that note?" Sitting at the kitchen table, I tapped a pen against a blank page of my English notebook. I had an essay outline due on Monday, but I couldn't focus.

"It wasn't a note. Henry wrote a couple of words on a piece of paper and left it on his desk. Could be anything. A song title, a poem . . ."

My mother turned a knob. The stove made a clicking sound but didn't light. "I thought this burner worked."

"Nope," I said. "Only the front left and the back right."

She moved the pot and turned the front left knob. Immediately, a flame leapt up to lick the bottom of the pot. She jumped back as if shocked to discover that something in this house actually worked.

"I think we should call the police," I said.

She turned. "And say what?"

"That we want to file a missing persons report."

She shook her head. "You don't know that they're missing."

"I know it in my gut."

"That won't be enough for the police to go on."

It was awful when my mother made actual sense. It didn't happen very often, and it always threw me. I swallowed hard. My eyes stung. At least she hadn't given me any grief when I'd told her about breaking into the Hawkings' house. My mother believes that anyone who installs an alarm system deserves to be broken into.

Softening, she said, "I can ask Randy for his law enforcement opinion." Randy was my mother's latest Man-Fran. That was what Peter and I called her relationship objects, because when the parade began, I was too young to pronounce "man friend" properly.

"I thought Randy was a security guard," I said.

"He is, but he attended the police academy. Applied, anyway— there were issues. But he understands how the system works." She opened the pantry door. "Do we have pasta?"

"Peter finished it yesterday."

"Oh." She closed the pantry. "Huh." She stared into space, increasingly baffled by the dinner challenge. Then she stared at the not-yet-boiling water, wondering what she could possibly put in it. "Maybe I'll just send Peter out for Mexican."

I shrugged. Normally I'd push for burgers, but tonight I didn't care.

"Speaking of Randy," my mother said. "He invited me to go on a cruise. Mexico. Leaves a week from Saturday."

"That's kind of soon."

"I know it may seem that way, but Randy and I have been together almost two months and—"

"No, I mean that's not a lot of time to plan a cruise."

"Oh! Yeah, it was a last-minute bargain—leftover cabins sold at a huge discount. That's the only way Randy could swing it. You're okay with me going, right?"

"How would I get to school?"

"Peter will drive you." When I raised my eyebrows, she amended, "Or you could walk. Or . . . maybe you can get a ride with Henry."

"Henry is missing," I reminded her.

"Surely he will be back by then. The universe will look out for him. Now . . . about dinner. Do you want Peter to get you a burrito or some tacos?"

Eight

PEOPLE WERE DISAPPEARING. First Henry, then Gwendolyn. Now Mr. Vasquez, our history teacher, was gone. "I hear he is quite ill," the substitute told us when we walked into class on Monday.

"Probably the plague," someone joked.

The substitute frowned and pointed to the assigned reading listed on the board. I opened my textbook and flipped to the necessary page. Around me, people sniffled and coughed. It was too early in the year to be catching a cold. I slid down in my seat and tried not to inhale.

In math class, I looked around for the pinch-faced drill team girl, hoping to pump her for more information about Gwendolyn, but she was out, too.

Walking across the classroom, Hannah Branson caught my

eye. If she wore a verb T-shirt, it would say, GOSSIP or SUCK UP. "What's the deal with Henry? He's been out forever." Hannah was a good five inches taller than I was, plus she had this habit of tilting up her pointy chin, which meant I got a view up her nostrils that I could have done without.

"He's . . . I'm not sure."

"Is he camping?" She tilted her chin up a notch higher. It bugged me that Hannah knew that Henry's family liked to camp, but then, pretty much everything Hannah did bugged me.

"I don't know. Maybe."

She raised her eyebrows. "So . . . did you guys break up?"

I blinked at her. "We were never going out."

"Really?" Her chin finally dropped, and her eyes popped a little.

"Truly." I forced a smile.

"Everyone thought you were."

"Everyone was wrong."

"So . . . you're not going to Homecoming with him?"

"No. I'm not." I had no intention of going to the dance with anyone, not that it was any of her business. Homecoming was the last thing on my mind right now.

"Oh." Hannah pressed her lips together and flitted to her seat.

We had two schoolwide dances every year: Homecoming and Winter Formal. Last February, during biology lab, I was partnered with a small, intense boy named Rudy (verb T-shirt: STUDY) when the whole dance and dating thing first crossed my radar.

"You going to Winter Formal?" Rudy had asked. We were sharing a microscope. Examining bacteria. Love was not in the air. The only thing in the air was the smell of rotting leaves and hand sanitizer.

"Nah." I squirted some goo on a slide. Going to the dance had never occurred to me. It would require tickets, a dress, shoes . . . all kinds of stuff that cost money. Plus, aside from a particularly gorgeous senior water polo player whom I worshipped from afar, no boys in this school interested me. And also, I didn't like being in large groups of, you know. People.

Rudy took the slide and stuck it under the microscope. He peered through the viewfinder and adjusted the lens. "I was thinking the dance might be fun. You want to go together?" His tone was super casual, like he was asking me to join a study group. He kept his eye on the bacteria.

"No, thanks." I jotted down a couple of notes. "I'd rather just stay home. Watch movies or something." I would have said no to a study group, too. I only liked doing homework with Henry.

It wasn't until Rudy looked up, his face bright red, that I realized that he had been asking me out. Like on a date. While examining bacteria.

"I thought he meant in a group of friends!" I later told Henry. He thought the story was hilarious. Of course he did. "Why does Rudy even like me? I hardly know him."

It's not like I wanted to go to the dance, but I felt bad about being so rude.

"Oh, Daisy," Henry said, still laughing a little. "You don't get it."

"What?"

"You're cute. Guys notice you." He kept his tone completely matter-of-fact, like he'd said, *You're right-handed* or *You have brown eyes*.

"All guys?" I asked.

He gave me what can only be described as a Dad Smile. "Only the ones with good taste."

The Dad Smile actually made me feel better. If Henry thought

I was cute, if Henry asked me out—ugh. It would be worse than awkward. I'd be out a best friend.

The day before Winter Formal, a Thursday, I was checking Netflix on Henry's smartphone. (He had a better phone than I did. . . . Well, he had a better everything than I did.)

I said, "We on for a Friday night movie? My turn to pick."

"Can't do tomorrow. Let's say Saturday. And just so you know, I refuse to watch *Message in a Bottle* again." (I wasn't going to make him watch *Message in a Bottle* for the second time. I was going to make him watch *The Vow* for the third.)

"You got something going on with your parents tomorrow?" I asked.

"Uh—no."

"Then why . . ." I met his eyes. My stomach dropped. Just like that, I knew. "The dance?"

He tried to smile, but he got this weird embarrassed look I'd never seen before. "Hannah Branson kept hinting that she wanted to go with me. You know, saying things and texting. So I asked her. Why not."

"You're going to Winter Formal. With Hannah Branson." I had to say it to believe it. And still I didn't believe it. Hannah was in our English class. She had highlights and a fake laugh and . . . that was pretty much all I'd ever noticed at that point. Her gift for gossiping and sucking up to teachers caught my attention later.

I was angry. I had no right to be angry. And yet . . .

"Was this before or after Rudy asked me?"

"Around the same time."

"*Henry.*"

He wouldn't meet my eyes. "After."

I nodded, too afraid I'd cry if I tried to speak. Why would I cry? It wasn't like I wanted to go to the dance with Henry. But still. I didn't want to share him.

"So are you and Hannah . . . a couple?"

His brown-black eyes bugged out, and then he burst out laughing because the idea was so absurd. All at once, I knew it was okay. Hannah would get him for one night, and then he'd be mine again.

That was how it played out, too. He texted me five times throughout the evening:

Bored.

Still bored.

Was I supposed to buy a corsage?

No one told me you had to dance at a dance.

This is no fun without you.

We never mentioned Winter Formal again.

———

Forty-five minutes later, I had absorbed approximately no new math knowledge, but I found myself wondering about the latest missing person. I didn't even know the pinch-faced drill team girl's name.

When the bell rang, I sprang from my seat and caught Hannah on her way out the door.

"You know the girl who sits behind you? She's on drill? She's out today?"

She thought for a minute. "You mean Bethany?"

I said, "I don't know her name. She's kind of . . ." I made a sour look with my face. Which wasn't very nice of me, I know, but it was all in the name of saving Henry.

"Yeah, that's Bethany."

"You know her last name?" Hannah knew everyone and everything, a quality that I normally did not appreciate.

"Bratt," she said. "Two *t*'s."

"Thanks." I turned.

"Why do you want to know her name?" she asked, not missing a beat.

"Henry wants to ask her to the dance," I said.

Nine

"SUPERSIZE ME," PETER said, grabbing a huge bag of chicken-and-waffles-flavored potato chips.

We were at the drugstore, standing in the junk food aisle. Peter's chauffeuring charges were putting a dent in my babysitting money.

"Don't be greedy." I tried to snatch the giant bag out of his hands, but he pulled it away with a loud *crinkle*.

"This Bethany girl lives like two towns away," he said.

"And you have something better to do?" As soon as the words were out, I regretted them. It wasn't Peter's fault that he had no life. Okay, it kind of was, but it was still a sensitive subject.

I looked away so I didn't have to see the hurt in his eyes. "Fine. I'll get you the big bag. But I'm not buying you a soda."

"Don't have to. Mom already gave me grocery money for when

she and the Man-Fran are on their cruise." He trotted over to the soda aisle. After some consideration, he got an orange Fanta.

I opened the next fridge case over and plucked out an iced green tea. "Think this thing with, what's his name, Randy, will last?"

"You mean *forever*?" Peter looked like I'd asked if he believed in fairies.

"Don't be ridiculous. I mean for the length of the cruise."

He considered. "Seven days. Small cabin. Not looking good."

I didn't have to use tax records to track down Bethany's address because her last name was unusual—either there weren't a lot of Bratts to begin with, or the rest had enough sense to change it—and I found her parents listed in at least ten online directories. Thanks to Google Earth, I was able to view a satellite picture of her large house and pool. It's too bad I would never want to spend time with Bethany, because the Santa Ana winds were blowing hot and dusty, and I could use a friend with a pool.

The drive took maybe fifteen minutes—not long enough to justify Peter's supersize chip upgrade, but enough time for every sweat gland in my body to go into emergency mode. The car's air conditioner worked, at least in theory, but it had run out of coolant over a year ago, and Peter couldn't be bothered to get it refilled.

At least there was no community gate to deal with. We pulled right up to Bethany's house, which looked smaller from the street than it had from the satellite.

Peter pulled over to the curb and turned off the car. He hauled the potato chip bag onto his lap and ripped it open.

"She's not going to be home," I said, peeling my legs off the seat. A droplet of sweat slithered down my neck.

"How'd y'know?" Peter asked through a mouthful of salt, grease, and artificial flavors.

"Because people are disappearing. One after another. Without a trace. Like . . ."

"They've been abducted by aliens?" *Crinkle, crinkle.* Peter reached back into the bag.

"Well . . . yeah."

"Awesome." Peter peered at the house with sharpened interest. His face shone with perspiration and perhaps the first infusion of potato chip oil.

At last I got up the courage to leave the car, walk down the path, ring Bethany's bell, and face . . . silence.

Alien abduction. Come on. There had to be a better explanation for why people kept disappearing. But what?

I was squinting up at the hot, bleached sky, looking for evidence of other life forms, when Bethany opened the door. The house's air-conditioning hit me like a bucket of cold water.

"You're here!" I blurted out.

"I live here." She looked awful. Red nose, dirty hair, circles under her eyes. She was wearing pajama bottoms and a faded pink T-shirt. But at least her hair wasn't stringy with sweat like mine was.

"You weren't in school," I said.

"I'm sick." It came out like *Ibe zick.*

"Is Gwendolyn sick, too?"

She shrugged. "I wouldn't know. Did you bring my math homework?"

"Um, no."

She looked at me funny. "Then why are you here?"

"Um . . . I mostly just came to see if you knew where Gwendolyn was."

"I don't."

"Okay."

We gawked at each other in an agonizing silence.

"The math homework is in the book," I said. "I can't remember the page, but if you give me your cell phone number, I'll text you when I get home."

"I'll get it from someone else," she said.

"Okay." I forced a smile. "Hot day today."

"It's kind of weird," she said. "You coming here."

At a loss, I said, "It's not weird. My brother drove me. Um. We have potato chips if you want some? Chicken-and-waffle-flavored. Which sounds kind of gross, but—"

"I'm going back to bed." She shut the door in my face.

There are reasons why I don't have a wide social circle, only some of them having to do with my impeccable taste.

"No aliens?" Peter said when I got back in the car.

"No." I strapped in my seat belt.

He handed me the potato chip bag and started the engine. "I'm disappointed."

I stuck my hand in the bag and met air. "They're almost gone!"

"I'm a growing boy." Peter gave his tummy an affectionate pat.

"We could go back to Gwendolyn's. Check for aliens." I shoved the chips in my mouth, trailing greasy crumbs down my shirt. They tasted odd but not in a bad way.

"Sure." Peter started the car and pulled away from the curb. "Not like I have anything better to do."

We followed a gardener's truck through Gwendolyn's community gate and drove through several streets of almost-identical stucco houses. I thought, *If Gwendolyn's home, then maybe Henry is back, too.*

But her grass needed cutting, and several home service flyers had been left outside the front door. I rang the bell and waited, waited, waited. I didn't think about aliens. I just thought about Henry.

By the time I climbed back in the car, Peter had polished off the chips. "Henry's house next?" he asked.

I nodded.

———

The newspapers were gone from the driveway. Was it possible Henry's family had come home? I opened my car door before Peter had come to a complete stop. I raced up the front steps, rang the bell, and . . .

Nothing.

I swallowed hard, so sick of this nothingness I felt like crying. I rang the bell again and pounded on the door until I felt tears mix with the sweat on my face. I was going to need some serious rehydration later.

You cried? I heard Henry say in my head, his voice shocked and amused. Because surely that was how he would respond once he came home and heard about how I'd grilled Hannah, stalked Bethany, and stoked Peter's belief in aliens.

I wiped my face, turned back to the car, and shook my head to let Peter know that there'd been no answer. I trudged across the overgrown grass and over to the driveway. At the very end, a white plastic gate that was supposed to look like wood opened up to an enclosure where the Hawkings kept their city-issued garbage cans out of sight. (At our house, the garbage cans stood on the side of the driveway, in full view of the neighbors and occasional hungry raccoons.)

I lifted the lid on the green recycling can. Sure enough, the discarded *Orange County Registers*, presumably disposed of by a vigilant neighbor, sat on top of a jumble of soda cans, plastic food containers, and magazines. I checked the black trash can. The smell of old garbage made me shudder, but nothing inside seemed especially strange, not that I took time to investigate.

Back in the car, Peter pretended not to notice the anguish, panic, and fear on my face. He's good that way. Or maybe he just had his mind on more important things.

"Can I see the toilet paper?" he asked. I'd told him about the Hawkings' supply cabinets somewhere between Bethany's and Gwendolyn's houses.

We left the car at the pond, where it wouldn't look suspicious, and strolled back along the quiet roads. At the Hawkings' driveway, we scanned the street to make sure no one was watching and hurried to the garage. I punched in the code, and we slipped inside.

"This is an incredibly clean garage," Peter said.

"Everything in their house is clean. And there's no clutter at all. It's creepy."

Peter's first instinct was to take some of the toilet paper home with us ("I'll replace it"), but I talked him out of it. We admired the cleaning supplies, agreeing that the volume and variety rivaled Target's.

And then we went into the house.

The surfaces had acquired a thin layer of dust since my last visit. Not surprising, given that we were in the middle of an especially bad Santa Ana season. And yet—

"The cleaning lady didn't come."

"They weren't here to let her in," Peter pointed out.

"Yeah, but she normally comes on Saturdays. That way, they can watch to make sure she doesn't steal anything. But Henry's mom can't stand a dirty house, so when they are going away, they have someone at the security company let her in, then they turn on the nanny cam."

Immediately, our heads popped up. The nanny cam was

mounted in a fake light above the pantry door, but there was no telltale red light blinking, thank goodness. The video camera was off. I'd forgotten all about it on my previous visit, but if the Hawkings ever saw me on the feed, breaking into their house . . . I shuddered.

"You think the housekeeper would know anything?" Peter asked.

"Dunno. And I wouldn't know how to get in touch with her, anyway." I ran my hand along the dusty countertop. "Maybe they're just on vacation somewhere."

"That would be disappointing," Peter said.

"Why?"

"No aliens."

"There could still be aliens. The aliens could be holding them hostage in a poolside cabana. Or taking them to the mother ship to do experiments—though ten minutes with Henry's mom, and they'd send them all back."

Peter considered, "I don't think we need to worry about aliens."

"No."

"But zombies are a real possibility."

"Too bad the office is locked," I told Peter. "There could be a planner or something that could tell us where they are."

Peter rattled the knob. "I saw some tools in the garage. . . ."

For someone who had never displayed any practical skills, Peter was remarkably handy with Mr. Hawking's power screwdriver. Within minutes, he had removed the doorknob.

"Voilà." He pushed the door open.

I expected to fall in hate with yet another boring, beige room, but the office was worse: brown plaid couch, green floral chair, a chipped white laminate desk, a fake wood file cabinet with the facing peeling off. The room was like an ugly furniture graveyard. No wonder they kept it locked.

If the room held any secrets beyond its ugliness, it wasn't giving them up: no calendar on the wall, no planner on the desk. I started to open the desk drawer and then stopped myself. This was invading the Hawkings' privacy too much.

Peter had no such qualms. Before I realized what he was doing, he was hauling manila folders out of the filing cabinet and rifling through their contents. "They keep their old electricity bills. Who does that?"

"This doesn't feel right," I said.

Peter frowned at the paper and shook his head. "You want to know what's not right? The Hawkings use more energy than ninety-eight percent of their neighbors."

"The security system uses a lot of juice." I opened the desk drawer. There were pens, paper clips, staples, Post-it notes, and a whole bunch of packs of chewing gum, but no planner. I shut the drawer.

Peter handed me a folder labeled, simply, HENRY. I opened up to a fifth-grade progress report and began to read:

Henry is an unusually bright and creative child. He exhibits abstract thinking abilities and advanced problem-solving skills rarely seen in a child this age. His curiosity and gentle sense of humor make him a pleasure to teach.

Henry does, however, continue to struggle socially. He prefers to eat his lunch in the classroom and resists group activities. His frequent absences may be contributing to his sense of separation from peers.

"Did you find something?"

"Huh?" I looked up to see Peter staring at me.

"No." I closed the folder and walked over to the file cabinet. "It's just school stuff. Do you remember where you found it?"

"It was under *H* for Henry," Peter said.

"What folder are you looking at?"

"'Bills Paid.' Filed under *B*. Though you could argue that it should be 'Paid Bills' and filed under *P*. Whoa! Check it out!"

"What?"

"They've got premium cable *and* Netflix!"

I slipped the Henry file back into the cabinet, between GARAGE DOOR OPENERS and HOUSE REPAIRS. I was about to tell Peter to put his file back, too, when a label farther back caught my eye. SHOOTING STAR SOCIETY. Unlike the other folders, this one was bright yellow, and its label was handwritten in blue ink.

Inside the yellow folder was a single slip of paper. A small graphic of a shooting star, similar to the sun-catcher in the front window, was centered at the top. Below, it read:

Shooting Star Society

National Headquarters

1137 Hemlock Road

Big Bear Lake, California 92315

USA

Facilities for members' use only. Do not share address or information!!

"Look at this." I handed the paper to Peter.

"What is it?"

"I don't know. But maybe that's where they are."

"In Big Bear? But what's the Shooting Star Society?"

"Beats me." I copied down the address and put the file back in the cabinet, checking the other labels to see if anything else seemed out of place.

"Found their cleaning bill," Peter said. He handed it to me.

The Hawkings used Tidy Time Cleaning Service. The bill displayed the company's address, phone number, and website.

"You gonna call them?" Peter asked.

"And say what? That I broke into one of their customers' houses and—"

"Oh, please." He took the bill, checked it, pulled out his cell phone, and punched in the numbers.

"Peter, you can't just—"

He held up a finger to shut me up.

"Helloooooo . . ." He looked up, realizing too late that he had no idea what to say. "I'm, um, a customer? You clean my house? Well, maybe not you yourself, but . . ." He cleared his throat.

I gave Peter a thumbs-up: *Smooth going, dude.*

"I was wondering . . . the thing is . . . I had a question about . . ." He blinked frantically, and just like that, everything fell into place. He should blink more often.

He started over, speaking with confidence this time. "My wife went away for a few days. Weeks. I thought our house was scheduled for a cleaning on Saturday, but no one showed up."

Peter gave the Hawkings' name and address. "They're checking," he mouthed to me.

Finally the person on the other end came back on.

"Oh." Peter's eyebrows shot up. "Really?" His mouth dropped. "No, that's . . . maybe she's planning to stay away longer than I thought." He paused. "Yes. I know these things happen all the time. I should have seen it coming." Another pause. "Uh, not for now. If things change, I'll call you."

He turned off the phone and gazed off, puzzled.

"What?"

"I don't think they've been abducted by aliens."

"What did they say?"

"That Mrs. Hawking left a message on their machine. She said that her family was leaving town, perhaps for good, so she wanted to cancel her service."

"Peter . . ."

"Guy said women leave their husbands all the time. I think he felt sorry for me."

"What do you think happened?" My voice was small.

He shook his head. "I don't know. But it's not good."

Ten

RANDY SHOWED UP at nine thirty Saturday morning. He drove a
silver pickup and wore a Hawaiian shirt. Of course he did.

When it came to Man-Frans, my mother didn't have a type.
She just reacted to whatever type came before, assuming that
different was always better. Like, there was this one guy who
wouldn't stop talking, followed by another who was so quiet that I
was never entirely sure he spoke English.

The Man-Fran who came before Randy was about as far from
a regular, Hawaiian-shirt-wearing Joe as you can get: a poet and
performance artist. I'd be cool with that, but this guy was a *bad*
poet and performance artist. About a month into the relationship, my mother bribed me with promises of éclairs and lattes to
accompany her to a performance in an arty little café downtown,

where her Man-Fran read a poem called "Crows" while gluing black feathers to his black unitard.

Not even kidding.

And then one day Crow Boy just . . . flew away.

All things considered, Randy wasn't that bad. But no way was I going to get attached.

"No wild parties while I'm gone!" my mother chirped as Randy carried her suitcase out to his truck. My mother is not normally a chirpy sort, but she doesn't know how to talk to us when her Man-Frans are around. Which is too bad. For all her faults, she's pretty fun to talk to when she's alone.

"Who would I invite to a party?" Peter said. "My friends are all away at college."

Peter was out of bed at nine thirty in the morning. If Mom had been paying attention, she would have known something was up.

I said, "I only have one friend, and he's missing."

Mom opened her mouth to say . . . something. That Peter should enroll in community college? That I could make more friends? That Henry was not missing, he had simply gone away without telling me?

But any of those discussions would have taken more time than she had to spare, so she closed her mouth. And she smiled a little smile, though her eyes looked kind of nervous.

She crossed the kitchen and threw her arms around me. She smelled like coffee and baby powder.

"I'll stay if you want me to," she said, her voice low and right next to my ear.

"No. You should go."

She took a step back and checked my face.

"I want you to," I said. When she still looked uncertain, I added, "You deserve this."

"Randy's a nice man." It sounded like she was trying to convince herself more than me.

"Good."

"Do I look all right?" She had on an Indian print sundress and one of her hundreds of pairs of dangling mosaic earrings.

"You look great."

"I don't really know what people wear on cruises. . . ."

I shrugged. "From what I've heard about the buffets, elastic-waist pants mostly. But that dress is loose, so you should be good."

She gave my arm a squeeze, put on a bright smile, and then she was off.

From the kitchen table where he sat slumped over a bowl of Cocoa Puffs (I said he was awake; I didn't say he was alert), Peter watched out the window as Randy opened the passenger door. Mom climbed up to the seat. As soon as Randy shut the door, she let the smile drop.

I thought, *She is starting to look old.*

And then I chased the thought from my brain.

"Seven days," Peter said.

"Small cabin," I added.

"Poor guy." Peter slurped his cereal.

"How long till you're ready to leave?" I asked, my thoughts already back on Henry.

Peter shrugged and slurped some more cereal. "I'm ready now."

"You're not wearing pants." His boxers were blue, faded, and a little tight.

"Oh. Yeah. I guess I should put something on."

An hour later, we were on the road, headed for Big Bear. At the last minute, Peter had decided to take a shower, and since I was scheduled to spend about five hours in a car with him, I wasn't going to argue.

The Hawkings probably weren't at the Shooting Star Society's headquarters, but it was possible. In any case, it was the only lead we had. We took my mother's car because it was less likely than Peter's to break down and also because it had a full tank of gas. Besides, the temperature was supposed to hit a hundred degrees today, and Mom's car had working air-conditioning.

Peter started the car, turned on the AC, and stroked the worn velour next to his thigh. "I love how the seats aren't ripped."

I fiddled with the dial. "I love how the radio works."

It's sad when a twelve-year-old Honda Civic is your family's luxury car.

Peter put the car in reverse and zipped down the driveway. "Let's do this."

———

In a few months, day-trip skiers would clog the roads that led to Big Bear, but today traffic was light. We made it out of town and onto the 57 freeway without any problem. We got a little swamped in truck traffic heading through Ontario on the I-10, but that was about it.

As we passed Ontario Mills, Peter said, "Wanna stop at the outlets? I still have that Tilly's gift card I got for graduation. Could use some new T-shirts."

"No."

"Wow. You are worried."

"I don't have any money. But mostly I'm worried."

Peter knew better than to say I had nothing to worry about.

Instead, he just turned up the radio, and we continued our journey across the flat terrain rimmed with soaring mountains, which kept the thick, hot, dirty air down near the valley floor.

Even with the air-conditioning going full blast, it was warm in the car. Outside, the hazy smog blurred the mountains and lent the sky a yellow tinge. On a day like this, the air actually *looked* stinky—and if you don't think that's possible, you've never driven through Ontario during Santa Ana season.

At last, we made it to the base of the mountain, where blackened trees told a stark story of an earlier season's wildfires. Not that that would keep people from building more houses. Or traipsing around the forest on hot, dry days. But it's good to be reminded that yes, when it comes to man versus nature, nature wins every time.

The scorched trees gave way to dry grass and thirsty vegetation. Our radio station fizzled out. I played around with the dial till I found something else.

Before long, the dense, dark forest enveloped us. We forgot about fires and even, for a moment, why we were here in the first place. The second radio station sputtered out. After twisting the dial from country to Latin music and back to country, I gave up and turned it off.

I rolled down my window, and clean, almost-crisp air rushed inside and chased out the lowland heat. "I love mountain air."

"We keep going on this road for how long?" Peter asked.

Since the car lacked GPS and we didn't have smartphones (not that there was reception up here anyway), I'd printed directions before we left home. I'd also checked the address on Google Maps, but the tree cover was so dense, I couldn't see what the building underneath looked like.

"Five-point-three miles. Then turn right."

The narrow road twisted and turned in the dark hush of the towering pines. We passed country stores, a café, a gas station. We were going up, of course. Otherwise, it was hard to get any sense of direction.

At last we reached the turnoff.

"You sure this is it?" Peter eyed the rutted road.

"It's what it says." There was no street sign, but I'd been following the route on my printed directions. This had to be right.

We turned onto the road. Peter watched his speed. Still, the car lurched and bounced. This could not be good for the Civic's shocks.

We passed one cabin set far back from the road. Then another. And then . . . nothing. Just lots of trees. And more bumps and ruts.

"I wish I had a smartphone," I said. "Then I could double-check the directions."

"I wish I had a pony," Peter responded.

We passed a cabin set close to the road. It was all roof, shaped like an upside-down V. A painted wooden sign out front said 1135 HEMLOCK ROAD—THE MURPHY'S (which, by the way, is an incorrect use of the apostrophe).

The Shooting Star Society was at 1137 Hemlock Road. "It should be next." My pulse raced.

We passed an empty lot before coming to the next cabin: 1139 HEMLOCK ROAD—THE JONES' (also wrong). Where was 1137? Did the numbers go out of order? We traveled down the road, checking the house numbers, and they all went up. We turned around and parked in front of the lot. Perhaps the building was set too far back to see from the road.

I opened my door. The air smelled of pine trees and wild grasses. Around us, birds chirped and branches clicked with the sound of little critters hopping around the canopy. Cute little critters. Like squirrels. Or raccoons. Or rats or snakes.

I was going with squirrels.

The dry ground crackled underfoot. It was much cooler up here than on the valley floor, but still the air felt heavy. And also, there were bugs. I swatted at the air and worked my way around the brush. The trees grew thick and tall. A pricker stabbed my toe. It stung again when I pulled it out. And I'd thought flip-flops were the perfect shoe for every occasion.

Peter, in sneakers and basketball shorts, strode ahead of me. When I finally caught up to him, I saw what he did: a vista opening onto wilderness. There was no headquarters building here. There never had been.

"You sure you got the right address?"

"Positive."

"And there's no other Hemlock Road in Big Bear?"

"Nope."

Peter wiped sweat off his brow. "Well, this blows."

I was all set to agree. Instead, I burst into tears.

"Oh, Daze. It's gonna be . . . Henry's gonna be . . . I'm sure we'll . . ."

"I'm hungry," I sobbed.

"That's why you're crying?"

"No-oh-oh." I sobbed a little more. Peter looked majorly uncomfortable. I don't cry all that much, and when I do, it's almost never in front of anybody. Besides, Peter had had very little human interaction over the last few months, so he really didn't know how he was supposed to behave in the face of human emotion.

"Sorry." I wiped my hand across my face and sniffled. "Even though I knew he probably wouldn't be here, I kept hoping."

"He's got to be somewhere," Peter said. "People don't just disappear."

"I never thought so before, but—"

"We'll find him."

Peter turned around and headed for the car, and I followed him, not even stopping to pull out my prickers.

After grabbing a snack at one of the little country stores, we wound down the mountain, past the burnt-out trees, and down to the flat-lands that led back home.

Nothing made sense. Nothing. Why would Henry's family run away like that? Who were they hiding from, and what was the Shooting Star Society? Were they in the federal witness protection program or something? I thought stuff like this only happened in the movies.

Now that we were off the mountain, I had service again. I had a text waiting from an unknown number.

I pushed a button and there it was:

34.451431

-119.347873

HURRY

Eleven

WHAT DID THOSE numbers mean? Were they some kind of code? Or a math puzzle I was supposed to solve? I was more confused than ever.

The text was from Henry; I was certain. It didn't come from his old cell number (which was still out of service; I had checked every day), but the area code, 714, was right.

I thumbed a quick reply—Where are you?—before calling the number, only to receive an automated voice mail recording. The phone was turned off.

"How can you be so sure it's him?" Peter asked. "It could be anyone. Or even a wrong number."

"Because he's telling me to hurry. Just like he left me that note saying 'Save me.' It's him. I know it."

"If you really think he's in trouble, we should call the police," Peter said.

"No. Henry would have called them himself if he wanted their help." I stared out the window as the brown, flat landscape whizzed by. "If only we knew where he was. I feel like these numbers are some kind of puzzle that only I can solve."

"Let me see the numbers," Peter said.

"I already told you what they were."

"Yeah, but I need to see them." He looked away from the road and over at me.

"You're driving!"

"Would you just—"

"Fine." I held up the message and let him look at the text for a full second before taking the phone away. "Like you're going to be able to figure out this math problem—or whatever it is—just like that."

"They're coordinates."

"Huh?"

"Latitude and longitude. He's telling you where he is."

"Oh my gosh, you're right! But . . . how did you *know* that?"

His smile was small but smug. "Video games. It's amazing how much you can learn from them."

Now that I knew what the numbers were, the message made sense, at least sort of. But I still didn't understand why Henry had left in the first place. What kind of trouble were the Hawkings in?

———

At home, I raced to my computer. A quick search on the phone number only told me that it was an Orange County mobile: not very helpful. I dialed the number again and got automated voice mail.

It was easy to find a website that matched latitude and longitude coordinates to a location. I typed in the numbers, not really sure what to expect, and hit return. In response, the website connected me to Google Maps and a spot deep in the Santa Ynez Mountains.

Baffled, I stared at the dark green image, trying to figure out how we would possibly get there without a helicopter. Or a Sherpa. But zooming in, in, and more in revealed a narrow, twisty, possibly unpaved road. No problem for an Expedition, but Mom's Civic wasn't going to like this.

"What time you want to leave in the morning?" Peter asked, looking over my shoulder.

"Why wait? Let's go now."

"No way," Peter said. "This place is going to be hard enough to find in daylight."

He was right. It was already almost dinnertime (frozen burritos were in my future), and even the easy part of the drive—if you can call getting through LA, up the coast, and into the forest easy—was going to take us a good three hours. Maybe more.

"Six a.m.?" I suggested.

Peter scratched his stubble. "Let's say nine."

"Fine." No point arguing. If we got out of here before eleven, it would be a miracle.

———

The next morning, I got up, showered, and dug through my closet for the kind of thing I'd wear if I ever went camping. In the end, I went with cutoff denim shorts, hot-pink sneakers that only clashed with my hair a little bit, and a My Little Pony T-shirt with the sleeves chopped off.

We left at ten thirty and even remembered to lock the doors since it could be dark before we got back. At my request, Peter drove to Henry's house. This time, we didn't bother leaving the car at the pond but instead parked right in the driveway. While Peter waited in the car, I punched in the security codes and slipped into the house. If anyone asked, I'd say I was housesitting. But really, who was going to ask?

I raced up the stairs to Henry's room, where the *SAVE ME* note still lay on the desk. But I wasn't there for the note. Instead, I got down on my knees and yanked the hard black plastic guitar case out from underneath Henry's bed, coughing a little when it brought up dust bunnies. I retrieved the guitar from its stand in the corner, secured it inside the case, and clomped back down the stairs.

"His guitar?" Peter asked when I opened up the backseat and strapped it in.

"It's Henry's most important possession. He'll be missing it."

"But isn't the plan to bring him home?"

"I don't know what the plan is. But there has to be a reason they left. Or were taken. Maybe Henry can't come back." I slammed the back door and climbed into the passenger seat. "Let's get out of here."

As Peter drove down the street and around the pond, I checked my phone, but there were no new texts.

I pulled up the mystery message and thumbed a reply.

I'm coming.

———

On the freeway, we made good time until we hit downtown LA, which is pretty much always a parking lot. Beyond downtown, traffic sped up, then slowed down, then started moving at an okay pace. We passed the Hollywood sign, the Scientology center, and the Hollywood Tower. In the San Fernando Valley, traffic slowed again to almost a halt. We pulled off to get a couple of In-N-Out burgers. It's always hotter in the Valley, but today the heat was so brutal that I had no choice but to add a chocolate milk shake to the order. Mom's grocery money was going fast.

Back on the road, we passed through the brown and thirsty Santa Monica mountains. Then it was back to flatland, farmland, and a brief stretch along the ocean. We opened our windows and let the cool, salty air wash over us.

"You sure those coordinates don't take us to the beach?" Peter asked.

"Not even close."

"Too bad."

We turned onto the Maricopa Highway and drove up and inland, past subdivisions and farmland and chunks of open space. In the other direction, traffic was heavy with recreational vehicles, overstuffed minivans, and cars pulling boats.

Outside of Ojai, we stopped for gas and Twizzlers. Because sometimes you just need Twizzlers. Back in the car, following my printed directions, we turned off the highway. We passed leafy housing developments and more farmland before reaching Lake Casitas. Powerboats bobbed on the deep green surface, and pop-up trailers half filled the adjacent campgrounds.

"Take a right on Route 150," I told Peter. "And then take your first left."

The two-lane road was smooth. Away from the lake, traffic was sparse—as were trees. The land shone a thirsty autumn yellow, dotted here and there with defiantly green bushes. Soon we turned again, onto a rougher, narrower lane—a two-car road only if both cars were small. Fortunately, there were no other vehicles in sight.

We drove in silence until I saw the sign. "Entering Los Padres National Forest," I said.

"You were always a really good reader," Peter said.

"Thank you."

As if knowing nature had higher standards to uphold on forest land (or maybe there was just a water source nearby), the vegetation immediately became greener, denser, taller.

"All this undeveloped wilderness . . . ," Peter said. "It makes me nervous."

I handed him a Twizzler. "Chew this. It helps."

Although it was narrow, the road was nice and smooth, all ready for suburban campers looking to pitch a tent and cook their dehydrated camping food over . . . whatever campers cook over (not an open flame; warnings against campfires were posted everywhere).

But the route was high and the curves perilous, and when I looked over the edge, my stomach churned. I closed my eyes. That helped. Good thing I wasn't driving. On the plus side, worrying about what would happen if the car careened off the edge of the mountain took my mind off worrying about what would happen once we reached the mystery coordinates.

Henry must have sent the text. Right? I'd received no reply to my last message. And now that I was up here, deep in the forest, I'd lost all cell phone reception.

And then it hit me: If there was no reception up here, how had Henry sent the text in the first place? Either he hadn't been in the middle of nowhere when he'd sent it, or someone else had sent it for him.

Or maybe the text wasn't from Henry at all. Maybe it was a wrong number from some outdoorsy type giving directions to a camper friend. That would be bad. Also embarrassing.

Slowly, carefully, we bumped along and up, navigating curves and switchbacks. The road's surface went from smooth to rutted to barely paved. It had been over four hours since we'd left Henry's house. It would still be a while before we hit the coordinates. We definitely had to get out of here and back to civilization before darkness fell.

"Thanks for doing this," I said, my voice barely a whisper.

"Huh?" Peter glanced away from the road.

"Thanks for driving me here. And up to Big Bear. And . . . everything. I know you have better things to do."

Peter snorted. "No, I don't."

"Yeah, but it seemed like the thing to say."

Just when I thought the road couldn't get any worse, it gave up any pretense of being paved. At least the dirt was packed enough to drive on without too much risk of a flat tire. I examined the map I'd printed out, but without street signs or landmarks, I couldn't tell how far we were from our destination. There would be a clearing off to the right, at the very curve of a sharp turn; I could see that in the satellite pictures. We couldn't possibly miss it. Could we?

The terrain lurched and curved too much to see far ahead. Every once in a while, I checked my phone on the off chance that I could get a signal, but of course there was none.

And then, finally, it was there, to our right—the small dirt clearing. Peter pulled off the road. There was no one waiting, not even some random camper who had mistakenly sent the coordinates to my number.

"Um," Peter said.

"You can say that again." My voice cracked.

"You're not going to cry again, are you?"

I shook my head, trying hard to keep it together.

"You can cry if you want to." Peter sounded unsure.

I laughed (with, okay, a tiny sob thrown in). "Might as well look around."

I got out of the car. The air was warm and sweet, with an undertone of decay. The forest here was prettier than in Big Bear—the trees less dense and more varied, with some wildflowers peeking through the underbrush. Ahead, a stand of trees loomed like something out of a fairy tale, sunlight dappling bark, twisted branches reaching out to embrace you. Or abduct you. One of those.

There was no path, no way anyone could wander into the trees without getting hopelessly lost unless they left . . .

Pebbles.

I blinked. Surely I'd imagined that they had been left there by design? But no: A trail of ghostly white pebbles led around a bush, through a dried patch of wild grass, and to a tall oak tree.

Something fluttered against the tree. I ran to get a better look. It was a folded note, nailed to the trunk. I pulled it down and read

D–

You came! I knew you would. My parents enrolled me in a wilderness education program. So boring, but they said you could visit. My dad has to go to work later in the week, so he said he'll drive you home.

I've marked some trees ahead. Just follow them till you reach me.

H.

My laughter came so fast and high, I sounded like a crazy person, even to myself. I ran back along the pebble path to the clearing, where Peter stood leaning against the car, arms crossed over his chest.

His face and posture relaxed when he saw me, but when I showed him the note, he said, "Daze, this is weird."

"Henry is weird. That's why I like him. This is his handwriting. He's here." I opened the back door and unstrapped Henry's guitar.

Peter squinted at the note. "Are you sure this is Henry's writing?"

I hauled the guitar case out of the car and shut the door. "Positive. Tiny and spiky. No one else writes like that."

Henry was going to be so happy when he saw his guitar. Hopefully, he'd be happy to see me, too.

Peter shook his head. "Who takes their kids out of school to learn about wilderness?" My shoulders tightened with irritation. Here I was, all relieved and happy, and Peter was still looking for a conspiracy. I said, "Henry's parents are weird. They don't trust normal schools. They let Henry miss class all the time."

"But why wouldn't he have told you he was going away? And why not invite you to visit him in a normal way? Why the drama?"

"I think he knew I'd be upset about him going away, and he didn't want to tell me."

I hadn't told Peter about the awkward night at the pond and how Henry had tried to kiss me. And I wasn't going to tell him now. It was none of his business. Besides, I didn't want to waste any more time. Henry was waiting for me.

"So you're really going to stay up here?" Peter asked.

I slung the guitar case strap over my shoulder. "Of course not. Henry can miss a week of school, but I can't. I've got a pile of homework due tomorrow as it is. But I need to see him. And bring him his guitar. Wait here. I'll be back within the hour so we can get back to the main road before dark."

"You don't want me to come with you?"

"It's not that." It was that. I wasn't sure what it would be like when Henry and I first saw each other, and I wanted to be alone. "What if we go into the woods together and something happened? This way, if I don't come back, you can go for help."

"You said that like getting lost in the forest is no big deal."

"Henry marked the way. I won't get lost."

Actually, I almost did. I followed the pebble trail again, but without the note fluttering from the oak tree, I found myself momentarily disoriented. But then I spotted the bush with the purple berries and beyond it a sapling with a yellow ribbon fluttering from a low branch. I worked my way over. The ribbon was actually a piece of caution tape. Most people would have taken that as a bad omen.

Next to the sapling's skinny trunk, I scanned the forest until I saw another flash of yellow. This time the caution tape was tied around a big old tree that reached high into the air.

This was like a treasure hunt—super fun!

No, it wasn't. It was like a strange, anxious dream. But if this was what it would take to find Henry, then okay.

From there, it took a few moments longer to spot the next ribbon, behind a bush and down a gully. My feet slipped on some dead leaves, and I almost dropped the guitar. In the time it took to regain my balance, a wave of panic washed over me. What if I really did get lost out here? How many more ribbons did I have to follow before I found Henry?

But then, almost as if he knew I'd be getting nervous at this stage of the creepy treasure hunt, the caution ribbons came in a steady and almost-straight line of shrubs. Shrub number four . . . shrub number five . . . six, seven, eight. At the ninth shrub, another note fluttered in the breeze. I pulled it off. Immediately, the sight of Henry's tiny, spiky handwriting made me feel better.

Almost here! Now look to your left and follow the pebbles.

H.

Sure enough, there was another pebble trail, this one denser than the last, though the stones were difficult to spot against the tan, dusty earth.

The pebbles led me around a boulder, along a dried-out streambed, and over a log. At the far side of the streambed, I looked back to see if I could spy any of the yellow ribbons, but they were out of view. It would be difficult to retrace my steps.

If I got lost . . .

No. It wouldn't happen. And if it did, Henry and Peter would have a rescue squad out in no time. *Follow the white pebbles.* . . .

A bramble bush scraped my thigh. Sweat drenched my T-shirt. My heart pounded all the way down to my swollen fingertips. I should have brought water.

Pebbles . . . pebbles . . .

For one terrifying instant, the path seemed to run out, but the forest gave way to a clearing that in spring would be green but was now a parched yellow. In the middle of the clearing someone had planted a big stick, a note speared through the top.

I ran through the tall, dead grass, eager to read the note, to get one step closer to Henry, to escape a forest adventure that was starting to feel far too Grimm for my tastes.

Right before I reached the stick, I thought, *The ground here feels soft.*

I reached for the note. It said, *YOU'RE SAFE.*

And then the ground gave way below me, and I fell into a deep, dark hole.

Twelve

I WAS ON the ground. On my butt. My ankle hurt. Otherwise, I seemed to be pretty much okay—if you consider being stuck at the bottom of a fifteen-foot hole okay.

"Henry? Are you up there? Help!"

A patch of brilliant blue sky bloomed above, but the dirt walls muffled my voice. Panic bubbled in my throat. I struggled to my feet, favoring the good ankle, and wiped the soil and rocks from my hands onto my shorts. I pulled out my phone. The good news was that it hadn't broken. The bad news was that of course it had no signal—and the battery was almost dead, anyway.

The guitar had taken a few hits on the way down, but the case protected it. Plus, I had at least partly cushioned its fall, which probably accounted for the soreness in my ribs.

My elbow stung. I stepped into a patch of sunlight and twisted my arm until I got a look at a big, dirty scrape that started just above my elbow and ran along the forearm. This was going to need some serious cleansing and antiseptic cream, along with a great big bandage, preferably with a Hello Kitty design. Hello Kitty makes everything better.

There were cuts on my legs, too, though they weren't as bad. Apparently, this is why people wear long sleeves when they go camping. Not that I was ever going camping. This nature thing was completely overrated.

The hole was slightly wider than my arm span. I groped around the walls, hoping to find some kind of handhold: a rock, a tree root, anything. But every jagged stone tumbled out with the lightest pressure, thick, black dirt crumbling around it.

I continued working my way around the perimeter, hoping to find roots to grab on to. I kept my touch light to avoid setting off an avalanche, even as I tried not to think of avalanches. Or spiders. Or worms.

And then—wait. A stretch of moss-covered wall felt unnaturally flat, and the moss itself felt just plain unnatural, like AstroTurf. I groped along the surface until my hand bumped against a protrusion. At first, I figured it was another rock, but no, it was smoother than the rocks, and straighter. Eyes adjusting to the dimness, I made out what appeared to be some kind of man-made handle. I turned it to the right and pushed.

Click.

To my surprise, a door swung open, the space beyond completely dark, the air stale and cool.

"Hello?" I called, just in case someone was in there. Like the Mad Hatter. Or Indiana Jones. I could really use Indiana Jones right about now. Sadly, he did not appear.

The cool air gave off a metallic smell. Was this some kind of storage space attached to Henry's camp? Weird that someone would put it out in the middle of a field, without any warning or notice posted nearby. A sign that said DON'T STEP HERE—YOU'LL FALL INTO A DEEP HOLE would have been extremely helpful.

Don't freak out, I commanded myself. *Henry will be here soon.*

No way was I stepping into the blackness beyond the door. I took a wobbly step backward and let the heavy door click back into place. At least the door meant that people had been here before. People who might return.

I hobbled back to the middle of the hole, tilted my head up, and yelled as loudly as I could. "HELP!"

Nothing.

"I'M IN THE HOLE!"

More nothing.

"Please?"

That one came out as a whimper. It didn't matter. Obviously, no one could hear me. No one knew where I was. Fear made me shiver.

Peter will send help.

Of course! Peter was still out there, waiting for me. When I didn't show up within the hour, he'd go for help. I couldn't have walked much more than a mile from the access road. It wouldn't take long for rescue crews to find me. All I had to do was sit down, remain semi-calm, and wait.

I settled down on the cold ground and looked up to the sky for reassurance, only to see that the light had changed; the blue had grown more intense. It had to be, what? Five o'clock? Five thirty? Soon the sun would fall and darkness would swallow the hole. And all the creepy critters that were now sleeping in the dirt around me would slither out of the walls and onto my arms and legs.

Do. Not. Panic.

I tried to focus on my breathing, like they do in yoga. Not that I had ever tried yoga, which had always struck me as only slightly less unappealing than camping. But that was too bad since right now I could use every relaxation technique available. Unfortunately, trying to focus on my breathing made me breathe too fast and too deep, which made me light-headed. This was no time to pass out.

And then, just as the sky began to fade to purple, sounds filtered down into the hole. Footsteps pounded the ground above me. Something rustled.

I scrambled to my feet, wincing as pain shot through my injured ankle. "Hello? HELLO?"

From above—silence. Had I imagined the noises? No. Someone was up there. I was certain.

"I'M IN THE HOLE!"

More silence. And then . . . whispers. Unless it was the wind? But no, those were definitely voices. People from the nature school, probably. Or maybe Peter with the rescue crew, figuring out how to get me out of there. Maybe they didn't hear me yell. Maybe the dirt walls muffled my voice too much.

I took a deep breath and let out such a scream so loud and bloodcurdling, my throat actually hurt. Then, holding my breath, I waited for a response that didn't come.

Above me, the voices grew louder. They were arguing about something. If I could hear them, why couldn't they hear me?

A face peered over the edge of the hole and looked down at me. It was a man, middle-aged, ruddy cheeked, and unsmiling, with a pale, straggly beard that failed to camouflage an unusually square jaw.

I waved my arms. My T-shirt, the pony design excepted, was

white. Well, white-ish. It was pretty dirty. Still, it would show up against the dark background. There was no way the man with the square jaw could have missed seeing me.

The face disappeared. But that was okay. *Everything was going to be okay.* They knew where I was. They would save me. They just had to figure out how get me out of here without caving in the hole. (That was not a comforting image, and I immediately tried to unthink it.)

The footsteps above grew heavier. They were carrying something—a plank, or maybe a board. A straight edge obscured my view of the sky. That made sense. They needed something to brace the mouth of the hole so it wouldn't cave in.

Except . . . why were they covering the entire opening? How could they get a ladder down to me? Or a rope? How was I supposed to get out?

Then they dropped the board over the opening of the hole, sealing me in darkness except for a few cracks of light at the very edges. I heard voices—male and angry. I screamed, but they only paused for a moment before resuming their argument.

A crack of light above grew a fraction wider. Something fell down from above, hard and cold. It grazed my arm and landed on the ground. Overhead, they slid the board back into place. A few more thumps, and they dragged something over the board, shutting out the last remaining cracks of light.

That was when the buzzing started. It came from above, a muffled yet undeniable *Zzzzz*. It sounded like a machine. Or a swarm of wasps. Or a chain saw.

I sank to the ground and hugged my knees, my entire body shaking.

This couldn't be happening—and yet it was.

No one could save me now.

Thirteen

THEY HAD THROWN down a mini flashlight, like something you'd attach to a key ring. The beam was narrow but bright. It danced around the walls in starts and jerks, like a tiny fairy who had just downed her fourth espresso.

If only they had tossed down a bottle of water, too. My thirst had gone from uncomfortable to insistent. I licked my lips and ran my tongue against the roof of my mouth, but that only left my lips chapped and my mouth parched. The ache in my ankle had subsided to a dull throb, but the scrape on my arm, now at least an hour past the time when it should have been cleaned, felt raw.

Above me, the muffled buzz continued, even as there were no more sounds from the men. I had no way of knowing whether they were still up there, waiting, or if they had left me here to die or suffocate or be attacked by killer bees or chain-saw-bearing robots or whatever that sound was.

With every tingle of my skin, I brushed away a spider or worm that was real or imagined—I couldn't even tell the difference anymore. Every once in a while, I turned on the little flashlight and did a quick sweep of my body to make sure nothing was crawling on me.

Something tickled my thigh. I told myself it was just my imagination and flicked the flashlight beam over it just to be sure—only to discover an enormous beetle making its way up to the edge of my shorts.

I screamed, brushed the bug away, and pushed myself to my feet. And then I screamed some more because maybe, maybe, maybe there was someone above me. Someone with really good hearing.

Flashlight in hand, I returned to the fake-mossy section of the wall, turned the handle, and pushed open the door. The narrow beam revealed a small vestibule, about the size of an elevator. To my surprise, there was another door straight ahead, set in the middle of a concrete wall, about a foot off the ground.

I hoisted the guitar over my shoulder and stepped into the tiny space, thinking, *At least the concrete lining means the walls won't cave in.* At least I hoped that was what it meant. The heavy door shut behind me. Panicked, I dropped Henry's guitar on the ground and turned back to the door. Tiny flashlight in one hand, I tugged on the knob, relieved when it turned and the door opened back up to the hole. Gently, I let the door close again and made my way across the space.

The far door had what looked like a metal steering wheel for a handle. I balanced the flashlight on the ground, pointing straight up. From that angle, the light was pretty useless, but no way was I going to immerse myself in total darkness.

Using both hands (and grunting from the effort), I tried turning the handle to the left. When that didn't work, I reversed directions. The wheel gave way, resisting at first and then suddenly—

Click.

The door in front of me hadn't opened. No, the sound came from behind. I grabbed the little flashlight and stumbled over Henry's guitar on my way back to the first door, the one that led to the hole. This time, the knob didn't turn. I had locked myself in.

My entire body began to shake as thoughts ran through my brain. *Don't panic, don't panic, don't panic . . . even though you are trapped inside a little tomb of a room with no food or water.*

A scream began to bubble its way up my throat.

Don't scream. . . . There is no guarantee how long the air down here will last. . . . You can't waste a single molecule.

I returned to the far door, stumbling over the guitar again, and put the flashlight on the ground, not bothering to balance it but just letting it spin on its side. Hands shaking, I jerked the round handle to the right, fully expecting the resistance I had encountered before, but it unlocked and swung toward me so fast, the force almost knocked me to the ground.

"Hello?" I called into the darkness ahead. Of course no one answered, but the sound of my own voice provided some comfort. The buzzing was louder here than it had been in the anteroom.

I flicked the little beam around the space in front of me and stepped inside. On the wall next to the door, something looked like a light switch. I flicked it up, heard a buzz even louder than the one coming from outdoors, and . . . *on*. It didn't just look like a light switch; it was a light switch. The buzzing sound came not from killer bees but from a generator. The sudden brightness hurt my eyes, but after a few blinks they adjusted.

Ahead of me lay a long, white tubular room. Built-in bunk beds provided sleeping space for eight, while a table with bench seats provided seating for four. There was a built-in desk and a compact kitchenette with a little stove, a little sink, a compact microwave oven, and a fridge that, sadly, turned out to be empty. Next to the kitchenette, a wide-screen TV took up most of a wall. I pushed a button, but nothing happened.

With its curved walls and built-in everything, the room looked like something you'd see on a submarine or a spaceship—not that I've ever seen a submarine or a spaceship, but Henry and I watched a lot of movies. For the record, I've never had any great desire to go inside a submarine or spaceship, but after being trapped inside the little elevator/coffin anteroom, the tubular room was one heck of an upgrade.

Open shelves lined every free inch of wall space. Mostly, there was food: powdered milk, powdered eggs, bags of beans, canned vegetables, tuna, chicken, and sausages. There were barrels of rice, flour, sugar, and assorted spices and seasoning packets, along with an unopened bottle of Sriracha sauce and an enormous ziplock bag filled with Taco Bell salsa packets.

I couldn't imagine what I'd do with any of that, so I was relieved when some cardboard boxes, stacked on the highest shelves, turned out to be filled with dehydrated meal pouches: lasagna and stroganoff and jambalaya and much, much more.

But what I really needed right now was water. I turned the tap on the little sink. It vibrated, gurgled, and spewed water at a surprisingly high pressure. An open shelf above held plastic cups. I took one and filled it, closed my eyes, and sniffed. I smelled nothing—which meant nothing. Maybe the water was okay to drink. And maybe it teemed with microbes or radon or arsenic.

But my body needed fluids, and unless I drained some liquid from the canned corn, it was tap water or nothing. I downed the water in a few big gulps, refilled the cup, and drank more. It tasted a little dusty, a little metallic, but at least it was cold.

My thirst quenched, I examined the rest of the provisions. There were batteries, iodine tablets, propane canisters, medicine packets, hydrogen peroxide, and bandages in varying sizes. There was glue, paper, plastic bags, twisty ties, wire, string, and burlap. There were books and matches, needles and thread, and so much more. It was like I'd stumbled into an episode of *Hoarders: Subterranean Edition*.

At the far end, beyond shelves stuffed with sheets, towels, pillows, and blankets, a narrow door opened to a spectacularly small toilet and shower room.

What was this place? Some kind of nuclear bomb shelter? I thought those had gone out of style years ago. Maybe it was a hermit house, though surely the hermit would have turned up by now.

A writing pad sat on the corner of the desk. Only now did I notice that it was covered with unfamiliar writing.

Welcome! And make yourself comfortable.
You have plenty of food, and the air is clean.
TV needs to be plugged in. No cable but lots of DVDs in lower cabinet.
Water is probably okay to drink, though you should add iodine tabs to be safe.
Enjoy your stay.

"Hello?" I called out, but of course no one answered me.

I hadn't simply fallen in a hole. Someone had been expecting me. I had been lured out here in the middle of nowhere, led to a trap, and then shut in darkness until I found my way into this underground prison.

Henry wouldn't do this to me. But someone who knew Henry did, someone who knew he could be used against me. What did that person want from me? A hundred old news clips flashed through my brain: girls who went off one day and simply disappeared—some forever, and others for what felt like forever, presumed dead while being held captive by some lunatic. At least if the tap water turned out to be contaminated enough to kill me, I could knock "long-term captivity" off my list of things to worry about.

It was so cold in this underground tomb, and I was so frightened. I retrieved the guitar from the anteroom and shut the spaceship's door behind me. I heard a click and yanked on the door—once again, I had locked myself in. I could only hope I was locking my jailers out.

I pulled a blanket from the cupboard, wrapped it around myself, and curled up on the couch, fully intending to stay awake, to watch the door, to protect myself from my captors. But within minutes, I was fast asleep.

Fourteen

WHEN I WOKE up, the scrape on my arm stung, my ankle ached, and I was still imprisoned underground. But I was alive, and that was something. The long room was much brighter than before. A quick check revealed a series of solar tubes in the ceiling—narrow reflecting pipes that ran up to the earth's surface, sneaking in tiny splashes of daylight. Maybe other tubes were letting in air from above.

Or maybe I'd use up all available oxygen and suffocate down here. That was another possibility.

My stomach growled. I pushed myself to my feet, careful not to put too much weight on my injured ankle, and limped over to the food cabinets. I climbed onto the desk chair and pulled down the cardboard box with the premade meals, going with a southwestern omelet, which I made even more southwestern by dousing it with three packets of Taco Bell fire sauce.

From the bathroom shelves I retrieved a surprisingly fluffy white towel. At home, our towels dated back to before I was born, and all softness had long since been washed out. But the fluffy towels didn't make me happy because remembering the scratchy towels at home made me think of my mother and brother and whether I'd ever see them again. Such an enormous knot of panic lodged in my chest that I began yanking things out of the closet with a new vengeance, just to get my mind off my situation.

Behind the towels, some black knit fabric turned out to be several pairs of drawstring pants and long-sleeved T-shirts. I took the smallest pair, and shoved the rest back in the closet. Then I dug around some more until I found a bar of soap and a comb.

In the tiny bathroom, I shut the door behind me. The shower was an odd contraption, with no drain, just a big metal pan to collect the water underneath. It made sense once I realized that the toilet would flush only after water had been deposited into the tank.

But that wasn't the worst of it. The smell of iron and sulfur that filled the room when I turned on the water wasn't the worst of it, either. Nor was the lousy water pressure. No, the biggest problem was that the shower had *no hot water.* Had my body been just a little less encrusted with blood and dirt, I would have turned off the tap and just changed into the black stretch clothes, but I had to clean my scrapes and get the dust and soil out of my hair.

By the time I had scrubbed every inch of myself with Ivory soap, I was shivering so hard I almost stumbled climbing out of the icy metal bucket. Cold, soapy water sloshed on the grainy concrete floor.

Once I'd dried off (the towel really was nice), I applied antibiotic ointment to the scrape on my arm and covered it with several large Band-Aids—not Hello Kitty, but they would have to do. Then I wrapped an Ace bandage around my ankle, looping the stretchy flesh-colored fabric around the bottom of my foot.

The black knit clothing was too wide and too long, but it was a relief to get out of my shorts and T-shirt. Further rooting around in the linen closet turned up a stash of black socks, which I slipped onto my icy feet. Weirdly, my black outfit made me feel not just warmer, but better, more secure, and braver. Like a ninja.

I returned to the long, white room. There was really nothing for me to do but wait, even if I didn't know what I was waiting for. And to stay down here without going completely insane meant I'd have to stay busy. I went to the shelves crammed with books and papers and pulled out a booklet.

Beekeeping in the 21st Century. Okay, that was unexpected. I pulled out another. *Herbal Remedies.* And another. *How to Survive a Zombie Apocalypse.*

Peter would love that one.

I settled on the couch with the zombie book and began to read.

Fifteen

THE DAY PASSED. And then another. And another. No one came to rescue me, but no one came to maul or mutilate me, either, so it was a wash . . . sort of. This subterranean exile couldn't go on forever. Peter would have told the authorities I was missing. Search crews would have spread out all over the forest. They would find me. It was just a matter of time.

I thought about school and all the things I was missing. An essay revision in English. A class party in Spanish. A chapter test in history, and another in math. I never imagined I could miss late nights doing geometry homework, stressed out because I was barely pulling a B and because I'd never catch up on my sleep.

My daily routine was the only thing that kept me from completely freaking out. If I didn't think more than an hour or two ahead, I could get through this. After all, I had light. I had water. I had surprisingly tasty food. (Having grown up in a family that didn't cook, my standards were pretty low.) Most important, my air showed no signs of running out, which made me think there must be some kind of ventilation system in place.

This, then, was my schedule:

When the light from the solar tubes woke me up, I got out of bed. I pulled down one of the cardboard boxes and chose my meals for the day. After eating breakfast and cleaning my dishes, I heated water on the stove, which I'd add to the shower basin. After that first morning, I'd sworn off the torture of cold showers, opting instead for warm sponge baths with the quickest possible cold rinse at the end.

After bathing, it was on to inventory. I had no idea how long I'd be down here before my rescuers came. (*When* they came, I told myself again and again and again. Not *if.*) I needed to know what food and supplies were available. Besides, taking inventory required complete concentration, which took my mind off things like suffocation, dehydration, and aliens intent on medical experiments.

By day three, the inventory was complete. There were tons of miscellaneous supplies, including scissors, hammers, screwdrivers, sewing supplies, bandages, tape, tarps, lanterns, propane tanks, and fire extinguishers. There were ten rolls of cinnamon-flavored dental floss, which seemed excessive.

As for the food, I recorded the following:

- **Premade individual meals:** 72 (and diminishing daily)
- **Rice:** 10 lbs. white, 10 lbs. brown
- **Pasta:** 9 boxes
- **Dried beans, assorted:** 20 lbs.
- **Flour:** 10 lbs.

- **Sugar, Salt:** 5 lbs. each
- **Dry yeast:** 40 packets
- **Olive oil:** 5 lbs.
- **Canola oil:** 5 lbs.
- **Oats, Cornmeal:** 5 lbs. each
- **Dehydrated eggs:** 10 lbs.
- **Dehydrated potatoes:** 10 lbs.
- **Dry milk:** 6 boxes
- **Velveeta cheese:** 4 blocks
- **Canned fruits (peaches, pears, mandarins):** 20 lbs.
- **Canned vegetables (peas, corn, green beans, broccoli):** 20 lbs.
- **Jarred fruits and/or vegetables (unidentifiable):** 14 jars
- **Canned tuna, chicken, sausages, Spam:** 40 cans total
- **Peanut butter:** 3 giant jars
- **Orange Tang:** 3 canisters
- **Homemade beef jerky (I hoped it was beef):** 6 large ziplock bags
- **Sriracha sauce:** 1 bottle
- **Taco seasoning:** 20 envelopes
- **Taco Bell salsa packets:** 83
- **Garlic salt:** 1 small jar
- **Instant coffee:** 4 large jars
- **Tea:** 71 bags
- **Honey:** 10 jars

When I ran out of real stuff to inventory, I began a fantasy list of all the stuff I wished I had down here. Highlights included Frosted Flakes, chewing gum, glitter nail polish, and a kitten.

After inventory, I spent time doing sit-ups and push-ups before moving on to lunch. Making lunch meant opening the pouch I had chosen at breakfast, mixing it with the metallic-tasting water, and nuking it for sixty seconds. It was tempting to wolf down the food while standing at the counter, but I forced myself to use dishes and sit at the table.

After cleaning my lunch dishes, I'd read for a couple of hours. It was unlikely I'd find anything more entertaining than the zombie survival book (my favorite tip: "Avoid medical schools, which attract the undead"), but I was learning all kinds of stuff about how to forage in the forest, avoid bears, and use honey as an antibiotic—though maybe not when bears were around. Did bears really eat honey? Or was that just Winnie-the-Pooh?

Since the scrape on my arm was healing nicely, if itchily, I didn't need to put the honey thing to the test. My ankle was also getting better, though it hurt first thing in the morning. On the third day, I tried adding jumping jacks to my fitness routine, but that might have made things worse.

Instead of this wilderness survival stuff, I really needed to be reading about the Renaissance for AP Euro. Also, our English teacher had recently handed out a new novel, something set in Africa. The book was sitting on the coffee table at home. It had a red cover, and I was supposed to have read the first three chapters by Monday. And then there was chemistry. That textbook was intense—not something I could skim when I got back. I was going to be so far behind.

If I got back.

I won't allow myself to think that way.

After reading came arts and crafts, my favorite part of the day—as much as you can have a daily highlight when you are trapped fifteen feet under the earth. The summer before, I had volunteered at our town day camp, where I was quickly dubbed the Glue Guru. Beads, macaroni, yarn, poster paint: bring it on. Alongside the little kids, I'd made masks, necklaces, and flowerpots that served little purpose aside from being adorable—which, if you ask me, is purpose enough.

For underground arts and crafts, I started with my black knit clothing because the pants were too long and I kept tripping on them, while the sleeves kept coming unrolled. A hem and a drawstring (made with crocheted red dental floss) turned the bottoms into harem pants. I attacked the top with scissors, widening the neck and hacking off the sleeves.

When my clothing was as good as it was going to get, I moved on to mosaics. My mother had shown me how to smash glass and pottery in a pillowcase. I set aside a plate, a bowl, and a mug for my meals. The rest of the crockery I demolished with a hammer, gluing the resulting mosaic pieces to a chair. With flour, glue, cornmeal, and Tang, I concocted a grout, which I smeared over the shards.

The glass mosaic chair was super ugly—also kind of dangerous—but it kept me occupied, so when that project was complete, I moved on to food mosaics, which gave me new appreciation for all those beans I had inventoried: so many shapes, sizes, and colors! On the door to the bathroom, I fashioned a palm tree out of brown lentils and dried peas. Rice represented tropical sand, while cannellini beans formed clouds drifting above the palm fronds. On the other door, I went in an entirely different, more abstract direction, gluing the beans in squiggles and swirls, a style I refined while covering a patch of the ceiling.

By the time I gave up on the ceiling—standing on the desk chair hurt my back, plus I was afraid I'd fall off—I'd been underground for six days. I'd given up my fantasy inventory and had tired of reading about leaves, bees, animals, and all the other above-ground things I might never see again.

I forced myself to eat, even as I recognized that the ready-made meals wouldn't last forever. Most days, I took a sponge bath, telling myself that cleanliness mattered. Reminding myself, *At least there is water.*

Two or three times a day, I stood under a solar tube and screamed at the top of my lungs, hoping a search crew would hear me and investigate. But no one came.

I watched a few action movies because those were the only DVDs available. I quickly tired of explosions and tidy endings. The heroes made everything look so easy. Nothing was that easy, ever.

Where was everybody? Why hadn't they found me?

I examined every inch of the bunker, looking for a secret doorway, a ventilation window—anything. But there was no way out of here except for the way I'd come in, and that door, decorated now with beans, wouldn't budge unless I set off an explosion with the propane tanks. As muddled as my thinking was, I knew that kind of tactic only worked in the movies.

I couldn't take this much longer. The food wouldn't last forever, especially now that so much of it was stuck to the walls.

I screamed until my throat hurt and the sound coming out of my mouth was little more than a squawk.

And then, on day seven, to my fear and relief and astonishment, a rattling sound came from the anteroom. After some scratching and banging, the door flew open.

Sixteen

THEY WERE ALIENS. Definitely. Shaped like humans but with big bug eyes and vents where their mouths should be. One of them rushed toward me, and I screamed because that is the natural reaction to an alien invasion, and besides, I had gotten really good at screaming lately.

The alien halted and whipped off his head. No, wait—it was a gas mask. And it wasn't an alien, after all. It was Henry.

Henry had saved me. Of course he had.

"It's *you*," I said.

Behind him, a male voice commanded, "Get back in the decontamination room. And put the mask on!"

In addition to Henry, there were three others, all wearing gas masks.

"She's fine," Henry said. "If she were infected, she'd be sick by now." His dark eyes glistened.

"Henry? What's going on?" My voice cracked.

"He's right," said a different voice. "Quarantine's over." The man pulled off his mask. I didn't know him, yet something was familiar.

"I fell in a hole," I babbled. "Out there. And I called for help and people came, and I thought they'd get me out, but instead they put something over the hole, and I found my way in here, and I thought I was going to die; I really thought I might die."

Henry continued to look at me, eyes shiny, but he didn't say anything. Why wasn't he saying anything?

"I came to the mountains to look for you," I said. "I thought you were here. And you are—now, I mean. But were you here before? How did you know to look for me? Are there search crews? Did you see Peter? I brought your guitar."

"Daisy . . ." Henry's expression was odd. Unreadable. Behind him, the man who had mentioned the quarantine looked vaguely angry. Or maybe that was just his natural expression because his chin, under a scruffy blond beard, was so weirdly square.

Wait.

"It was you," I said to the man with the square jaw.

"Daisy—" Henry said.

"It was him," I told Henry, suddenly feeling cold. "He trapped me in the hole. He knew I was down here, and he just covered up the hole and walked away."

"Daisy—"

"I was so frightened. I thought I was going to die."

"Daisy . . ."

And then I knew. I held Henry's dark, shiny eyes. Waited for him to explain. But he didn't, so I filled the silence. "You were there. Weren't you? When they trapped me."

The two other gas masks came off, revealing first an unfamiliar teenage boy and then the man who had scolded Henry, who had told him to stay away from me. Henry's father.

"Mr. Hawking." My voice was hoarse. Henry's tall father had always intimidated me because he rarely spoke and because he looked like a skinny, cranky Mr. Clean.

"You have put us all in danger," he said. It seemed an odd choice of words for someone who had imprisoned me underground for a week. "I hope we don't regret allowing you to come here."

"*Allowing* me?"

The guy with the square jaw strode into the cylindrical room. He was wearing army fatigues, the desert camouflage kind. "There is something stuck to the doors. And the ceiling. Are those . . . beans?"

The teenage boy—also wearing desert camo and also with a square jaw—loped across the room to the mosaic chair. "What are these white bits? Like pottery or something. Was this the . . . dishes?"

"I was just trying to protect you," Henry said, his eyes pleading.

"From who?"

He shook his head. "Not a *who*. An *it*."

Now Square Jaw was at the far door, examining the palm tree mosaic. "She glued food to the door!"

The boy with the matching chin and pants laughed. "Mama said to bring her some of those beans. Said she was gonna use them for supper."

"You are welcome to lick them off," I snapped. "I'm out of here."

I grabbed my shorts and T-shirt from the floor and slipped on my pink sneakers. Henry could carry his own damn guitar. I pushed my way past the teenage boy, half expecting him to stop me, but he just gave me a creepy half smile and let me pass.

I was halfway through the anteroom when I stopped short. It was too bright in here. Too warm. The second door, the one that led to the hole I'd initially fallen into, was closed. Instead, a rope ladder ran up the concrete wall to an escape hatch at the top. Daylight streamed down from above.

I scrambled up the rope ladder and hauled myself out onto the ground and into the hot, dry sunshine. As I pushed myself to my feet, I tried to remember where the road was so I could run toward it.

Something moved in the corner of my vision. I spun around and found myself facing a pack of children armed with slingshots and arrows.

Clearly, that was the moment to say, *Don't shoot!* But the whole situation was so bizarre, I had no words.

"Don't come any closer." A little girl held her bow steady. She was young—maybe eight, nine years old. Like the rest of the kids, she wore army pants, which she had paired with a dingy white tank top.

An older girl, about my age, slapped at the bow. "Kadence, put that down!"

I don't know much about archery, but smacking any kind of loaded weapon didn't seem like an especially good idea.

"I don't wanner to gemme sick," Kadence whined.

"She made it through quarantine," the older girl said. "She's fine."

"She don't look fine," said a screechy-voiced boy of maybe eleven. "Her hair is a funny red color and her clothes is weird."

"My clothes *are* weird," I corrected. "Subject-verb agreement"— then, glancing at the black harem pants cinched with red dental floss—"I didn't have much to work with."

There were six in all. Two girls were teenagers, and the younger kids were between maybe five and twelve, two boys, two girls. Collectively, they had a *Children of the Corn* vibe, with pale eyes and pale hair, along with that weird square chin.

Something clattered behind me. I turned to see the others climbing out of the hole. Henry was last. He hauled his guitar case and gas mask over the edge and scrambled out after them. Then he crossed over to me.

"I want to go home," I said.

Henry shook his head. "It's not safe." He put the gas mask down and dusted dirt off his jeans—not because he is especially fastidious, but because he didn't want to look at me.

"Peter and my mother must be freaking out. I need to call them. Now."

Henry straightened but still refused to look at me. "I told Peter this was a nature program, and you'd get school credit, I said that my parents had agreed to supervise you, and we'd bring you home in a couple of weeks when the program was over."

"So you . . . saw Peter? And told him I was fine?" All this time, I'd assumed Peter would be out looking for me. That whole crews would be out looking for me.

He picked up his guitar case and looped the strap over his shoulder. "Yes."

"But this isn't a nature program."

He hesitated. "No."

After three weeks away, Henry looked different. His hair was shaggier. Sunburn colored his cheeks and nose. But it was more than that. He held himself straighter, with more tension, like he could spring at any moment. And the way he wouldn't hold my eyes: That wasn't Henry, at least not the Henry I knew.

"Why did you cover the hole?" I demanded.

"I didn't. Mr. Dunkle did."

Mr. Dunkle. That would be the man with the square jaw. Which would make the children Dunkles as well. Dunklings?

"But you let him trap me," I said.

"I didn't want to! I wanted to explain what was going on and tell you to go into the bunker. But the others were afraid you might have a satellite phone and that—"

"*A satellite phone?* Are you serious, Henry? We don't even have cable!"

"I know! I told them you wouldn't have one but—"

I shook my head with confusion. "Even if I had been able to call someone, what difference would it have made whether or not I'd talked to you?"

"We didn't want anyone to know we were here."

I stared at Henry. "Who are you?"

"I'm just me. Same as I've always been."

I looked into his eyes. I'd never noticed how unreadable they were. "I don't think so."

Mr. Hawking and the man with the square jaw, Mr. Dunkle, approached us, so I changed the subject. "Will your parents really bring me home?"

Henry looked uncertain. "Eventually, maybe. I hope so."

"There won't be a home to go to," Mr. Dunkle said.

"There might be," Henry said.

"Don't count on it." He scratched his beard.

I shook my head. "I don't understand."

Mr. Hawking said, "We'll explain everything once we get back to the compound."

The children were starting to fidget. "I'm hungry," one of the little girls whined.

"You're in luck then," Mr. Dunkle answered. "'Cause your mama's cooking up a great big pot of possum stew."

I checked his face to see if he was joking, only to realize that the man had never told a joke in his life.

"Is this some kind of cult?" I asked Henry.

His father answered. "Of course not. People in cults are crazy."

Seventeen

IT WAS A sweaty half-hour walk (hike, climb, scamper, trudge) to the compound. During that time, I confirmed that the man with the square jaw was named Mr. Dunkle, and the Children of the Corn were all his. The teenage boy was named Kyle. At seventeen, he was the first-born Dunkle. The two oldest girls were Karessa ("with a *K*") and Kirsten. The remaining four children were Kevin (nicknamed Killer), Keanu, Kadence ("with a *K*"), and Kelli-Lynn.

I am guessing the Dunkle parents never invested in a baby name book.

Karessa, who was sixteen, told me that her father's name was Kurt, and her mother's name was Barb. I didn't know whether to feel sorry for Barb or to applaud her individuality.

The sun was so bright that it hurt my eyes. The forest wasn't nearly as dense as it had been in Big Bear, and the underbrush had turned a burnt yellow. Underground, the bunker had been cool; up here the air crackled with autumn heat.

I had more questions than I could count ("What is this place?" "What is the compound?" "How many of you are there?" "What is the infection everyone keeps talking about?" and on and on), but after failing to receive any answers, I gave up and reviewed the *K* names once more.

There were two more Dunkles, Karessa told me, two-year-old twins, a boy and a girl.

"Keith and Kimmy?" I guessed.

She pursed her lips. (Note to self: All those *K* names are *not funny*.) "Kentucky and Kansas."

I nodded, like, *Yeah. Of course.*

"We call them Tuck and Sassy. They're napping right now. That's why I was able to come."

I nodded again and kept walking, pushing myself to stay ahead of Henry. I could hear the guitar case thumping against his body with every step. I wouldn't look at him. I still couldn't believe he had done this to me.

And yet: I was furious and confused, but I wasn't frightened. I had spent a week underground and was now being led to an undisclosed location, but at some level I knew that no one would hurt me because Henry wouldn't let them.

"Are you having withdrawals?" Karessa asked. She wore her blond hair in two French braids pinned to the top of her head, which made her look, from the neck up, like she had stepped out of another century. From the neck down, she looked like she had stepped out of army boot camp.

"Am I . . . what?"

"Experiencing withdrawal symptoms. My daddy says that all

the kids in American high schools are addicted to methamphetamine. So I wondered if going off it would make you feel sick. Or maybe you detoxed in the bunker?"

I checked her face. She was serious. "I don't do drugs."

"Really?"

"Truly."

"It must be hard to resist all that peer pressure."

"Um . . . not really."

"But you see them a lot, right?" she pressed. "Like, in the hallways and the bathrooms and the cafeteria?"

I thought of Gwendolyn. "From what I've heard, the drill team is pretty heavily into heroin. They shoot up before every football game. But it's not so bad since the pep club held a bake sale to raise money for disposable needles."

Karessa blinked furiously.

"I'm kidding," I said.

"Oh!"

Her eyes were wide. Karessa exuded an innocence I'd never seen on a girl her age, unless you count smarmy characters on kiddie TV shows.

The walk was long, and the bugs were biting. Scrambling up a rocky hillside, I glimpsed a panorama of mountains, valleys, and trees that in another situation would have impressed me with its majesty but right now disturbed me with the vast expanse of land uninhabited except for the circling birds of prey and whatever creepy critters they preyed on.

Something pricked my arm. I slapped and came away with a bloody mosquito.

Just when I thought the wilderness would go on forever, we

came upon a chain-link fence topped with the kind of barbed wire that lent the forest a homey, maximum security prison kind of look.

I peered through the fence. "Are those beehives?"

"We go around," Mr. Dunkle commanded, jostling his way to the front of the pack.

"They are," Henry said, catching up to me. "Soon we'll be able to make our own honey."

I didn't respond but instead turned to follow Mr. Dunkle. We wound along the fence, stepping through long grass and ducking under tree branches. When the fence reached a corner, we turned and followed it some more. Through the fence I spied a yellow school bus, a shed, and a Porta-Potty—which explained the pungent odor that cut through the sweet mountain air. A spiderweb snagged my face. I yelped and stumbled into a bush, leaving prickers on my black harem pants.

When the fence rounded another corner, the vegetation thinned out. A rough dirt road disappeared in the trees. Inside the fence, a row of tall bushes blocked the view until we reached a padlocked gate, which Mr. Dunkle undid with a key attached to his belt. He swung open the double gates, and we stepped into the compound.

An enormous house loomed against the blue sky. It was made of wood and stucco and stack stone, all topped off with a red clay roof largely covered with solar panels. Giant log columns flanked the enormous front door. I don't know much about architecture, but this place seemed to mix about five different styles, and not in a good way.

The Hawkings' black Expedition, along with a couple of other large vehicles and one small car, sat on a swath of white gravel that passed for a driveway. At the edge of the lot, next to the fence, a big, beat-up RV, coated with a layer of brown dust, managed to steal some shade from the forest beyond. Otherwise, the yard was all tan dirt, interrupted here and there with weeds and piles of tires, plywood, broken plastic chairs, and assorted toys.

"Not the place you'd expect to find a McMansion," Henry said, coming up from behind. "Wait till you see the backyard. It's got a pool. And a spa. You might not want to go swimming, though."

"I looked this place up on Google Earth," I said. "Using the coordinates you gave me. All I could see was green."

"It was hidden by trees until we got here, but that meant the solar panels didn't work."

For the first time, I noticed the fat stumps scattered around the yard and alongside the house.

Henry said, "Daisy, I know you're freaked out, but I'm so glad you're here."

"I'm still not ready to talk to you."

I hurried to catch up with Karessa. At the front door, she used the brass bear door knocker to tap out a complicated rhythm. The door swung open to reveal yet another pale girl. It was so dark inside the house that it took a moment for my eyes to adjust enough to realize that she wasn't another K-Kid.

"Gwendolyn?"

She wore her yellow DRILL T-shirt, which seemed absurd under the circumstances. If I had a verb shirt right now, it would say PANIC.

"You're alive," she said, like she might say, *You cut your hair,* if she cared what I did with my hair.

"They almost killed me, but it didn't take."

Gwendolyn raised her eyebrows. She took a couple of steps forward and joined us on the front step. She'd acquired a sunburn since

I'd last seen her. "You thought *we* are the danger? You should be thanking us."

I held Gwendolyn's gaze. "Just tell me one thing. Are we on the cusp of a zombie apocalypse?"

"Ugh." She rolled her eyes in disgust. "We should have left you to perish along with the rest of them."

"Is that a yes?"

To my left, someone giggled. Kirsten, the second-oldest Dunkle girl, held her hand over her mouth, trying to contain her amusement.

I let out a long breath. "No zombie apocalypse?"

She shook her head. A smile appeared around the edges of her hands.

"That's a relief." It was, actually. It was also a relief to hear someone laughing and acting almost human.

"Amusement is not the appropriate reaction at this time!" Gwendolyn spun around and disappeared into the house, just as another female figure, this one dark haired, appeared and stepped into the daylight.

I almost didn't recognize her. "Mrs. Hawking?"

"Daisy."

Gone were her crisp, conservative work suits, replaced with khaki trousers and a matching shirt, buttoned to the neck and wrists. A red kerchief hung around her neck. She looked like a Boy Scout leader on the verge of heatstroke. Her short, sensible haircut lay flat, and her severe face was even thinner than before.

Her eyes ran up and down me. I didn't look so great myself.

She looked over my shoulder, to where her husband stood next to some tires. "No signs of infection?" she asked.

Mr. Hawking shook his head.

"You're sure?"

"We wouldn't have brought her here if there was a danger."

She narrowed her eyes at me for a moment before addressing her husband once more. "Has she been briefed?"

"Negative."

Mr. Dunkle approached. "As the chief OPSEC officer, I should be in charge of the briefing." He tilted his square chin up.

Mrs. Hawking adjusted her kerchief. "That's not necessary."

"OPSEC is always necessary."

"We realize that," Mr. Hawking said. "Better than anybody. But my wife and I have agreed to assume responsibility for Henry's . . . friend. So we will take responsibility for her intelligence and training as well."

"But—" Mr. Dunkle began.

"Headquarters," Mr. Hawking interrupted, pointing in turn at his wife, Henry, and me before striding up the steps and into the house.

Mrs. Hawking held my eye and nodded once. "Follow me."

Eighteen

THE FRONT HALL was one of those soaring two-story affairs, with a giant three-tiered fountain (running dry, sadly) and a wrought-iron chandelier that looked like it had come out of a medieval castle. Twin staircases curved around the sides of the foyer and led to opposite ends of an exposed hallway above.

Henry and I followed his parents up the right-hand stairway. Downstairs had been surprisingly cool, but the air grew hotter and heavier with every step.

Mrs. Hawking paused to pick up a plastic wrapper, muttering something under her breath. They led us along the exposed hallway to a big, doorless space that would be called a bonus room if they were normal people in a normal place. The drywall had been taped but not painted. Mismatched carpet remnants partially covered the plywood floor.

"This room is headquarters," Mr. Hawking said. "You don't come in here unless invited."

In a sane world, the bonus room would have a pool table and an Xbox, but here in Krazy Kountry, it featured a long laminate table like you'd see in a school library, and an enormous whiteboard. Pinned to the walls were maps of the forest, the state of California, the United States, and the world, dotted here and there with multicolored pushpins.

Mr. and Mrs. Hawking sat on one side of the table. Henry chose a seat on the opposite side, and I sat down next to him. The air crackled with tension and reproach. It felt like I'd been called to the principal's office for pulling a fire alarm or cheating on an exam. If I'd been expecting them to apologize for, oh, say, imprisoning me underground, I would have been disappointed.

As usual, Mrs. Hawking did most of the talking. "We are accepting your presence among us only because we had no choice. When Henry told us he had revealed our BOL and you were on your way . . ." Her nostrils flared.

"BOL?"

In the distance, there was a crack. I jumped a little, but no one else seemed to notice the noise.

"Bugout location," Henry said.

"We cannot take in every Pollyanna who appears at our gates," Mrs. Hawking continued. "After years of preparation, we have formed a community of carefully selected, like-minded individuals. If we are going to offer you shelter and protection, you will follow our rules and become a fully contributing member."

"A community? How many of you are there?" I asked.

"In addition to ourselves and the Waxweilers, there are two families we expect to arrive at any time. The Wards and the Platts.

Fine people. Dr. Platt trained at USC." She turned to her husband. "Any word from them today?"

Mr. Hawking shook his normally shiny Mr. Clean head, which was now covered on the sides and back with a salt-and-pepper stubble. He needed a shave, too.

"What about the Dunkles?" I asked.

Mrs. Hawking cleared her throat. "Their status in the community is . . . different. But they are an integral part of our society. They are here for the long term. As are you."

Fingers of panic crept up my spine. "I just want to go home."

"That's not an option," Mrs. Hawking said. "Not now."

"Of course it's an option!" When I stood up, the metal legs of my chair caught against the edge of a carpet remnant, but I managed to grab the chair just before it tipped over. "Give me a phone. Someone must get service out here because Henry sent me a text. I'll call my brother. He'll come get me."

Mr. Hawking cleared his throat and took a moment to glare at his son, whose attention was fixed on the table.

"There's no reception here," Henry said. I didn't look at him.

"We didn't want you here, Daisy; I won't lie," Mrs. Hawking said, like that was some big revelation from a woman who had once told her son in front of me that he should widen his circle of friends. "But now that you've arrived, you can't leave."

My eyes darted around the room, looking for an escape route. But even if I could get out of this house, I'd never find my way back to the road.

"Will somebody please tell me what is going on?"

The Hawkings sat in grim silence for a long moment before reaching wordless agreement. Mrs. Hawking broke the news. "We're facing a possible tee-ought-walkie."

"Probable," Mr. Hawking amended.

"A probable tee-ought-walkie." Mrs. Hawking nodded.

My head was starting to hurt. "Tee . . ."

Henry said, "Those are initials: TEOTWAWKI. Pronounced tee-ought-walkie. It stands for . . ." He glanced at me before setting his attention back to the table and lowering his voice to an embarrassed mumble. "The end of the world as we know it."

"Like . . . the song?"

He shook his head and looked at me sideways. "No. For real."

I searched for amusement in his dark eyes but came up empty. "Don't go getting all *Hunger Games* on me, Henry."

"This isn't a game," Mrs. Hawking said, her habitual scowl deepening.

These people were impossible. "*Hunger Games* isn't a game," I informed her. "It's a book. Also a movie."

"Is that right?" she said. "Well, while you and all the other Pollyannas have been reading books and watching movies, we have been getting ready for the inevitable moment when TSHTF."

When I squinted with confusion, her husband translated. "When the, er, sewage hits the fan."

All of a sudden, I understood. How did I not catch on earlier? All that toilet paper should have tipped me off. And before that, the outdoorsy stuff and the paranoia. But the thought never crossed my mind because I had once believed that Henry told me everything. And this was a big thing not to mention.

"You're preppers!"

Mrs. Hawking loosened her neckerchief and undid her top button. It was seriously hot up here. "We prefer the term 'self-reliant.'"

"You can't seriously believe the world is ending."

"When it comes to the fall of Western civilization," Mr. Hawking said, "it's always been a question of when, not if. Societies grow and thrive—and then they collapse, sometimes gradually, and sometimes in response to a cataclysmic event. Look at Rome."

He waited for my response, but all I could think was, *I've never heard him talk so much.* And also, *I'd like to see Rome someday. London and Paris, too.* But first I had to get out of here.

Mr. Hawking continued, "We were overdue for a societal collapse, especially when you consider all the possibilities for our demise." His stubbly face shone with sweat. "An undervalued currency could cause a run on banks. A massive earthquake could destroy infrastructure and overwhelm resources. Thanks to the *efficiencies* of modern transportation, a flu pandemic could sweep through the entire planet in a matter of days."

Henry's parents exchanged a look I couldn't read.

There was another crack in the distance. I gasped.

"Squirrel hunting," Henry explained.

Getting back to the subject at hand, Mrs. Hawking tapped the table. "EMP."

Mr. Hawking looked skeptical. "*Theoretically*, our enemies could use a nuclear device to set off a burst of radiation that could send out an electromagnetic pulse that would shut down the entire electrical grid."

"Asteroid," Mrs. Hawking said, as if ticking items off a list.

"An asteroid could do major damage," Mr. Hawking agreed. "As could a nuclear bomb. Or a flood. Or a heat wave. When you consider all the possibilities, it's astonishing that our society has lasted as long as it has. And yet, most people go about their merry ways, expecting things to always be the way they have always been.

The only sensible course of action was to be prepared to G-O-O-D at a moment's notice."

"Get out of Dodge," Henry explained.

"We've been preparing for several years," Mr. Hawking said. "As any sensible person would. And even now . . . the compound . . . we thought the renovation would be finished, or at least further along."

"But why leave now?" I said. "Society is messed up, sure, but it could be around for another hundred, two hundred years!"

The Hawkings shook their heads, even Henry.

"Everything was fine at home," I said.

More head shaking.

"There was no asteroid," I said. "Or earthquake or flood or . . . the electromagnetic thing. There has been no apocalypse." When they continued to look at me with doubt, I added, "I may not be as smart as your son, but I would have noticed an apocalypse."

"The world has not ended . . . *yet,*" Mrs. Hawking said. "But the enemy is among us, and the enemy is . . ." She closed her eyes and covered her mouth as if the sentence were too painful to continue.

"What?" I demanded.

"A lemur," Mr. Hawking said. At least I thought that was what he said, though when my brain tried to make sense of it, I rejected the interpretation.

"I thought you said a lemur." I waited for him to clarify.

"Well, lemurs," he said. "Plural."

I was surrounded by crazy people. There was no other explanation. I thought of the adorable little animals with the striped tails and enormous eyes. "Are these . . . exploding lemurs?"

"Of course not!" Mrs. Hawking snapped.

"It's not the actual lemurs we fear." Mr. Hawking really, really needed a shave.

"I'm a little afraid of the lemurs," Henry muttered.

Mrs. Hawking said, "The danger lies not in the lemurs them-selves, but in the disease they carry."

"*What* disease?"

Henry's voice cracked. "Madagascar plague."

Nineteen

HENRY'S PARENTS HEADED out to perform their Very Important Compound Tasks and left us alone in the bonus room without even telling us to leave the door open. Because, conveniently, there was no door.

I stayed in my hard chair while Henry wandered over to the pushpin map of the world. "You've heard of the Madagascar plague, right?"

"Of course. It's the disease that turns you into an animated talking animal."

His look turned stern. He didn't say anything.

I tried to remember news articles I had read, headlines I had seen. The disease sounded vaguely familiar. "Is that the one where people vomit blood or the one where they can't breathe?"

He ran his fingers over a cluster of pushpins. "Both. A bunch of cases first showed up last year in Madagascar. People thought it was bubonic plague because they've had outbreaks of that as well and the symptoms are similar, but it turns out to be something entirely new."

"It sounds horrible. And I feel awful for the people who are getting sick in . . . wherever Madagascar is. Australia?"

Henry raised his eyebrows. I took that as a no.

"It's not my fault the American education system stinks at geography. But, Henry, there's no deadly epidemic out there. You're hiding out for nothing."

He stopped to look at me. "Nobody was out sick from school?"

I thought of all the empty desks at school. "Sure. Lots of people. There was this flu-ish thing going around—nothing deadly, just a nasty virus. After Gwendolyn disappeared, I went over to this girl Bethany's house because she'd been out of school, and I wanted to see if she had gone away, too. But she was just home with a really bad cold."

Henry nodded. "That's part of the reason why people don't know how serious this is."

"You're going to tell me a toxic lemur was to blame for Bethany Bratt's runny nose. And that her runny nose was more than just a runny nose."

"No." He shook his head. "Right before the plague hit, there was an outbreak of another virus—not technically a flu, but it came with a fever, body aches, cough . . . all the usual symptoms. People were flooding doctors' offices and the ERs. That's a big part of why the first plague patients weren't quarantined. Everyone just assumed they had the other thing. Did you hear about anyone at school getting seriously ill?" he asked.

No students jumped into my mind, but then I remembered

history class. "Mr. Vasquez was out for a few days. Someone said he was in the hospital, but I don't even know if that's true. But he wasn't *dying*. Nobody was. Speaking of Mr. Vasquez, we learned about bubonic plague in history class. You would have, too, if you weren't holed up in the mountains. In the Middle Ages, a disease could wipe out a huge part of the population, but that was before antibiotics and sanitation. Stuff like that doesn't happen anymore, at least not in America."

Henry sighed. "It's too hot up here. Let's go out to the woods."

Henry led me through the foyer and into an enormous, unfinished kitchen. From there, a short hallway took us into an exercise room filled with stationary bikes, a stair stepper, and a rowing machine.

I tapped the handlebar of a stationary bike. "Doesn't everyone get enough of a workout being outdoors? You know, with all that squirrel hunting and people trapping?"

"These power our generator, along with the solar panels. Mr. Dunkle was supposed to put in a windmill, but he hasn't done it yet." He considered. "There are a lot of things Mr. Dunkle hasn't done yet."

He opened a door, and the backyard took my breath away. No, I'm serious. The stench flooded my sinuses. I clapped a hand over my nose.

Henry spread his arms. "Welcome to the farm. I don't know who's supposed to be cleaning out the chicken coop, but they're slacking off. The goats don't exactly help, either."

The ground was partially covered with pavers; otherwise it was all concrete dust, dirt, and animal poop. Everywhere I looked, there were pails and tools and rubber boots and garbage. It made my own backyard look downright tidy.

As promised, there was a pool. Henry never said it had water in it. Instead, it was a great big white hole, empty except for a skateboard.

"We're going to use the pool for aquaponics," Henry said. "Supposedly."

I hesitated. "Is that like water aerobics?"

He raised his eyebrows. "It's when you raise fish and plants together in a shared aqua environment so they feed off each other's waste products."

I rolled my eyes. "I totally knew that."

A couple of yards away from the pool, a separate spa, slightly raised and rimmed with fake boulders, did have water, which was good news for the geese swimming (and presumably pooping) in it, as well as for the little goats dipping their heads down for a toxic drink. In addition to the geese and goats (I counted five), there was one depressed-looking sheep, a bunch of chickens, and a giant rabbit hutch.

Keeping my hand over my nose (and watching my step), I went over to the hutch. Two brown bunnies stared at me with their dark marble eyes, perfectly still except for their twitching noses, while more baby bunnies than I could count hopped and squirmed around them.

One of the Dunkle boys came up next to me. It was the one they called Killer, looking the part in green army fatigues. "You like rabbit?" he asked. His voice hadn't changed yet, but a tiny break gave a preview of things to come.

"Yeah, they're cute."

"No, I mean to eat."

"Wait. You mean you're raising these to . . ."

"Perfect food source." He poked at the mesh with a dirty index finger. "We feed 'em leftover vegetables or bug-eaten plants from the garden, they keep having babies. Coupla months, the bigger babies will start having their own babies. Soon there'll be so many, we're gonna have to build another coop. Be eatin' rabbit every day."

Beyond the animals was the dirty yellow school bus I had seen through the fence. "Field trip to hell," I muttered, joining Henry near the edge of the empty pool.

"Who owns this place?" I asked.

"The four families in the consortium. We got it cheap a few years ago when the guy building it ran out of money. The adults liked that it was so far from civilization. They called it the bugout location from the beginning, but we all knew it was just supposed to be a vacation retreat. We were waiting till the construction was done to furnish it. Oh well."

I lowered my voice. "If the Dunkles aren't part of the consortium, what are they doing here?"

Across the yard, one of the little blond girls slipped on a pair of oversized rubber boots and clomped over to the goats.

Henry said, "My parents and some of the others met Mr. Dunkle at a prepper convention about a year and a half ago. He was in the Special Forces once, which my dad thought was cool. But mostly the families hired him because he's done a lot of construction work. At least he said he had. He and his family are allowed to live here in exchange for renovating the property. But they've been here a year already, and . . ." He shrugged.

I thought of the paper I'd seen in his parents' office. "This consortium—is it the same as the Shooting Star Society?"

He stared at me. "How do you know about that?"

"Um . . ." He wouldn't mind that I'd used the security code to get into his house, but breaking into his parents' office might be crossing a line.

He shook his head. "Never mind. It's probably better if I don't know. The Shooting Star Society doesn't exist."

"But the sun-catcher in your window . . . at Gwendolyn's house, too."

"One of the Platt kids made those for everyone a couple of Christmases ago, gave them to everyone in the consortium. And I think it was just because they were so tacky that no one wanted to hang them, but someone suggested we save them to use as a secret signal in the event of a bugout."

"But the address in Big Bear . . ."

He stared at me. "You went through my parents' files?"

"Not all of them."

He ran a hand through his dark hair. "And I told my parents they were being paranoid, believing that anyone would ever take the time to go through their papers. They put the shooting star thing on a bunch of papers to mislead anyone who tried to track us down. The address is for an empty lot."

"Yeah, I know."

A smile spread across his face. "You tried pretty hard to find me, huh?"

I refused to smile back. I was still mad.

He said, "My parents own that piece of land. We used to go up to Big Bear a lot, and they were going to build a cabin. But

Mr. Waxweiler convinced them that Big Bear was a bad place to bug out—too close to LA. Mostly, I think, he just wanted them to go in on this property because he couldn't afford it on his own, and Mrs. Waxweiler would only agree to buy a bugout location if it looked like a fancy retreat."

"But how did all the building stuff even get here?" I thought about the scrambling we'd had to do to get here from the bunker.

"A fire road runs in front of the house—connects to the state highway. Goes pretty close to the bunker, too, but it's shorter to cut through the woods."

On the other side of the yard, chicken wire enclosed a broad patch set aside for farming—which may be a generous term for a whole bunch of random plants crammed together in a few raised beds, but whatever. Another of the little blond girls (I couldn't remember her name, but I think it began with a *K*) crouched at the edge of the garden, pulling weeds.

We tiptoed around animal poop to the very back of the fenced enclosure, where two raised white boxes emitted an almost electrical buzz. Guess I'd been right about those beehives.

I remembered the pamphlet I had read while trapped—no, imprisoned—underground. "Did you know that honey never goes bad?"

He nodded.

"And that honey has antibiotic properties?"

Another nod.

"It's annoying that you always know everything."

At the far corner of the fence, Henry spun a combination lock around until it popped. He pushed open the gate, and we stepped into the wilderness. White-barked trees reached for the sky, their delicate leaves shimmering in the hot breeze. I took a deep breath:

only good smells out here beyond the compound. Above us birds tweeted lovely songs while squirrels leapt among the branches.

Squirrels.

"Are they done hunting yet? Because I don't want to get shot."

"Hunting only happens on the other side of the property. We're good. Besides, Killer never misses a chance to shoot something, so if he's back at the house, it means fun time is over."

I wasn't angry at Henry anymore—just baffled that he had fallen for his parents' bizarre tale. After all, he was the one who had always said they were paranoid. But maybe it's easier to tell the difference between sane and batty when you are living in normal society and not holed up in an unfinished McMansion with a tribe of blond conspiracy theorists.

Ahead, gurgling sounds filtered through the dense autumn air. We rounded a prickly bush and took a few careful steps down a hillside, to a clear, shallow stream rimmed with bright green plants.

I dipped my hand into the chilly water. "Is it safe to drink?"

Henry shrugged. "Probably. But we don't take chances. We have a water filtration system back at the compound so advanced that Mr. Waxweiler says it can make urine taste like bottled water."

"Ew."

"I know."

"Good bottled water? Or supermarket brand?"

Henry laughed. It was so good to hear that sound it made me feel like I was with my best friend again.

"I haven't tested it," he said. "And I don't plan to."

I crouched down and splashed my face before settling on the bank and leaning back on my hands. "Henry. About this end-of-the-world stuff."

His face turned grim. "It's true."

I backed up. "How long has your family been preparing for disaster?"

He shrugged. "My parents? Like, forever. All those camping trips we took were really bugout test runs. We'd pack our bugout bags and time our escape and then compare all the stuff we brought along. I thought it was stupid, but sometimes I got to miss school, so that was cool."

"But why take off for the wilderness when you have so much survival stuff at home? I mean—ten years' worth of toilet paper?"

"It's always best to get away from population centers in a crisis, but my parents stocked up on supplies in case we had to shelter in place. Like if there was an earthquake and the roads were impassable. And that's only two years' worth of toilet paper, by the way. So—I take it you searched my whole house."

I nodded. "I didn't know what else to do. I found the note you left me in your room."

"What note?"

"The one that said 'Save me.'"

"Oh. That." He squatted next to the stream, cupped his hands, and splashed his face and hair. Henry's dark hair was on the unruly side when I'd last seen him. Now it was almost long enough to tuck behind his ears.

"It was for me, right?"

He nodded. "I thought my parents were out of their minds when they told me we were bugging out for real. I didn't want to go. At the pond I was going to ask you to hide me. But I chickened out. I knew how ridiculous the whole thing sounded." He shrugged. "When I got home, I started to write you that note, but I couldn't even figure out what to say beyond 'Save me.' Then I came to the conclusion that after a week or so, my parents would realize it was a false alarm and we'd come back."

"It's been more than a week," I said.

He hesitated. "It wasn't till I got up here that I realized this thing really could wipe out civilization—or kill a lot of people, at the very least. That's when I sent you the coordinates. I wanted to save you. Help you escape before things turn bad."

He sat down next to me on the bank, pulled off his sneakers and socks, and dipped his pale, narrow feet into the water. Immediately, the hems of his jeans turned dark. He either didn't notice or didn't care. Remembering his swim in the murky pond, I guessed the latter.

He said, "Madagascar is an island off of the southeast coast of Africa. It's where lemurs come from."

"Yes, I saw the movie. With you, as I recall."

"Yeah, well, real lemurs can't talk, but they're still pretty cute, which means some people want them as pets. They are also primates, like humans, which means they can get us sick more easily than other animals. It's illegal to export them, but of course people smuggle them out. There's a network in Eastern Europe. They pretend to be breeders, but all their animals were actually poached from the island."

"And some of the lemurs had the plague."

He nodded. "Last month, six lemurs were brought into Texas, and at least two of them were infected."

He held my eyes. Clearly, this was my moment to express shock and fear and to thank him for saving me from the dangers posed by two lemurs in Texas.

"This is fascinating," I said. "And it would make a great movie.

But here's the thing: There is no Madagascar plague epidemic. No one is dying. And there was no good reason to lure me up here and imprison me underground."

"I didn't want to put you into quarantine," he said.

I crossed my arms over my chest. "You let them."

"It was the only way they'd let you come. It was the only way I could save you."

I shook my head. "Everything you're saying—I know you believe it. But it's crazy, Henry."

He spun around on the rock and slipped his socks and shoes back on over his wet feet. "I need to show you something."

Twenty

HENRY'S ROOM WAS upstairs, beyond the bonus room. It was surprisingly small for a house this size, plus, like most of the house, it was unfinished: The floors were plywood, and the one smallish window had yet to be trimmed.

Instead of a real bed, a single mattress had been shoved into the corner. No baseball-themed comforter here, just a bottom sheet and a few rumpled beige blankets. A cardboard carton, turned upside down, served as a night table. There was no reading lamp, no desk, no chair, no rug. At least his guitar was here now. Since he didn't have a stand, he left the instrument in its case and propped it up in the corner.

The walls were plain except for a photograph of us tacked above his bed. It was from the summer. We had taken a box of orange

Popsicles to the pond, but most of them melted before we got around to eating them. That seemed like a long time ago.

"Did you decorate the room yourself?" I forced a note of cheer into my voice. "You have a real eye for design."

"There's a room next door the same size as this," he told me. "It's for one of the other families, the Wards, but you can stay there till they arrive. There's a couch—looks pretty comfortable."

"Are you sure the Wards are coming? Why aren't they here yet?"

He shrugged. "My dad sent them a message before we left. No one's been able to make contact with them or the Platts for a couple of weeks, but this is where they'll come. Unless they're sick already."

I felt the need to state the obvious. "Or . . . maybe they haven't shown up because there was no reason to leave." I sat down on Henry's mattress. It was so much harder than his bed at home, and the dust tickled my nose.

"You don't believe me about the plague."

I considered. "I believe that this Madagascar thing exists. I just don't believe it's a serious threat."

He stood over me for a moment before speaking. "Wait here."

He went into the room next door and returned with a couple of sheets of paper. The first one he showed me was a statement of some kind. At the top, it said *Forever Friends Pet Insurance: Benefit Statement.*

"Your mom's company?"

He nodded.

Underneath the heading were names of a pet owner, Catherine Williams, and her insured animal, a male cat named Jeronimo. The payable benefits list included a whole lot of drug names, medical procedures, and codes.

I looked up from the paper. "So?"

Henry sat on the mattress next to me and pointed to a notation: *Yersinia malagasi*. "See the diagnosis? That's the bacteria that causes the Mad Plague—that's what the press is calling it. The cat was never anywhere near a lemur. They think the disease was transmitted by a flea."

"Is the cat okay?"

Henry shook his head.

"Poor kitty."

"The owner died, too. They tried all kinds of antibiotics, but nothing worked." He handed me the second sheet of paper. "This is a memo from the president of my mom's company."

CONFIDENTIAL INFORMATION MEMORANDUM

TO: All Claims Managers

FROM: Richard Baracov

RE: *Yersinia malagasi*

We are all understandably shaken by the news of a human death resulting from bacterial infection with *Yersinia malagasi* (*YM*), which medical professionals are assuming was transmitted by her companion feline. Unfortunately, this case was not isolated. There have been reports of five other pet infections in the past week, two of which have been transmitted to humans. Please note that there have been no human-to-human contact cases confirmed.

We remain confident that an effective treatment will be identified shortly and urge your discretion regarding the case. Please remember that you have all signed privacy agreements in regards to our clients and that any contact with the press is prohibited.

I handed back the paper.

"This is real, Daisy. We are on the verge of a pandemic."

"I never understood the difference between a pandemic and an epidemic."

"A pandemic is bigger. More people get sick. More die."

"Three people doesn't sound like a pandemic. Or even an epidemic."

He shook his head. "That was just the beginning. The day after that memo was written, that woman's boyfriend got sick. He was dead within days. It was all over the Internet. Didn't you see it?"

I shook my head.

"That was back when the CDC was insisting the Mad Plague wasn't very contagious. But in most of the human cases, the bacteria has infected the lungs. Once that happens, it goes airborne. You can catch it in a classroom, on an airplane, in a store—anywhere. The disease can travel between humans, between animals and humans, or through fleas. There are antibiotics to treat the bubonic plague, but if there is anything that cures the Madagascar plague, no one has found it yet.

"In the week you've been underground, there have been over a hundred human cases reported in eleven states. Isolation wards are maxed out. Some health workers are refusing to go to work. It has passed a tipping point. There's no way to contain this thing."

"Everything was fine," I said, trying to convince myself.

"I know this is scary, but look, the odds of this actually being tee-ought-walkie are slim."

"The end of the world as we know it." My voice was flat.

He forced a smile. "Would it help if I played the song on my guitar?"

"Not really."

"A lot more people are going to get infected," he conceded. "But it will all blow over in a couple of months. Either there will be a cure or there won't, but epidemics pass, even pandemics pass, and life goes on."

I swallowed hard. "Unless you're dead."

"Yeah. There's that."

"If what you're saying is true, I can't just hang out here while Peter and my mother are in danger."

"Peter never leaves the house. He'll be fine. And your mother's office is small—that leaves less opportunity for infection."

"My mother just got back from a cruise." I started to shake. "With thousands of people."

"But no pets," Henry said. "At this stage, that's a pretty safe place to be."

Footsteps sounded in the corridor. A child's voice called out, "Lunch!"

Henry sprang up. "I'll figure out a way to get a message out to them. It may take a few days, but we'll find a way to keep them safe. I promise. Come on. Let's eat."

Twenty-One

"I'M NOT EATING possum stew," I told Henry, following him into the enormous kitchen.

"It's not really possum stew. They just call it that."

"What is it then?"

He shrugged. "Lamb, maybe?"

Remembering the depressed-looking sheep in the backyard, I shuddered.

The air was so cool that my sweat made me shiver. "Solar panels run the air-conditioning," Henry explained. "But it only works downstairs."

We approached the giant stove, and that was when I got my first look at Mrs. Dunkle. I was expecting meek and mild, maybe even sweet. Instead, I found myself under the glare of a wiry, sour-faced woman in army fatigues and a filthy, cherry-patterned apron. She grabbed my arm—hard—and thrust a ladle in my hand.

"Ow!"

Instead of apologizing, she said, "Where in Sam Hill have you been? You were supposed to be on duty an hour ago!"

"Who's Sam Hill?" I asked, baffled, the ladle dangling from my hand.

"It's just an expression," Henry said. "So she doesn't have to say *hell*."

"Work assignments are over there." Mrs. Dunkle pointed across the room, where several whiteboards, mounted on unfinished drywall, held a colorful web of names and duties, such as LUNCH PREP. And LOOKOUT. And SEWAGE REMOVAL.

I was speechless. (It happens.)

"Serve!" Mrs. Dunkle yelled.

For a moment, I thought she was going to shove me. The line between her eyebrows was so deep one could only assume she had been frowning nonstop since childhood, perhaps since first recognizing the injustice of not having been given a name that began with the letter *K*. She wasn't especially large—I had a good two inches on her—but she exuded a toxic energy that felt dangerous.

Behind me, in a semi-orderly line, the little Dunklings waited with mismatched plastic bowls in their unwashed hands. They shoved one another but managed to avoid their mother's gaze.

The first kid in line—blond, square chin, first name began with a *K*—handed me his bowl. I slopped some stew inside. Hunks of meat swam in a greasy broth speckled with something greenish and something orangish. It smelled gamey.

"Not. So. Much." Mrs. Dunkle hit the counter with her fist. "You see how many people gotta eat?"

After indulging in a brief fantasy that involved the giant stew pot and this awful woman's head, I took a few calming breaths and reminded myself that I'd be out of here soon. I filled the next Dunkling's bowl with half a ladle's worth.

"Well, you can give her more than *that*. Oh, just let me do it." Mrs. Dunkle snatched the ladle out of my hand.

An image of my mother flashed in my head, and I gulped back a sob. If only I could know she was okay.

We ate lunch in an oversize room at the very front of the house, with views out to the decrepit RV, the dirt yard, assorted garbage, and the chain-link fence that separated us from the forest. Unlike most of the house, this room was finished, with slate floors, wood-paneled walls, and an enormous stone fireplace that practically begged to have a moose head mounted above it.

The furniture, however, was just as bad as in the rest of the house. The "table" was a long series of plywood sheets balanced on wooden sawhorses. The chairs were the stackable white plastic kind that people in the real world only use outside.

Karessa, the oldest Dunkle girl, entered the dining room with a sleepy-looking blond twin balanced on each hip. It was hard to believe the twins were the same age since the sweet-faced little girl (who seemed to have escaped that square chin) was so tiny and delicate, far smaller than her scowling, chunky brother. With full cheeks and his father's jaw, his head was shaped like a block.

I love kids. Have I mentioned that I love kids? And they usually love me, too. So when Karessa deposited the boy on the plastic chair next to me—"This is Kentucky. Say hello to Daisy, Tuck!"—I widened my eyes and gave him a big, bright smile as if to say, *Let's be friends!*

In response, he grabbed a spare spoon off the table and hurled it at my head. The motion caused his chair to topple over backward, which caused him to scream, which caused Mrs. Dunkle to say, "Now look what you done!"

And then things got worse.

Once Tuck stopped crying, and there was a moment of blessed quiet, Mrs. Dunkle ruined the moment by saying, "Where's she gonna sleep?" There were a lot of people at the table who could qualify as a random *she*, but I had a feeling she meant me.

"Girls' dorm." Mrs. Hawking spoke without looking up. She was squinting at her stew with something like fear.

"Outta blankets," Mrs. Dunkle said.

"We have extras," Mrs. Hawking said.

Henry looked around, baffled. "There's a couch in the room next to mine. I thought Daisy was going to sleep there till the Wards came."

"Your father and I never agreed to that, Henry."

"But no one's even using it," he protested.

"It is not *appropriate*," his mother said, "for *your friend* to stay overnight in such close quarters."

"Girls' dorm not good enough for your friend?" Mrs. Dunkle asked. It was the first time I had heard her sound even a little bit happy. Henry hadn't shown me anything dormlike earlier, but this was a big house. It could be anywhere.

"The girls' dorm is fine for me."

"It's not." Henry looked alarmed.

"Of course it is," his mother said.

Defeated, Henry hunched over his bowl and speared a chunk of gristly meat.

I said, "Is that . . ."

"What?" Henry asked.

"The sheep from the backyard?"

Henry shook his head. "No, we're keeping her for her wool. This is from Costco."

"Phew."

"What does it matter? It's a dead sheep either way. At least if it came from the backyard, you'd know it'd had a nice life."

"In that stinky backyard? I don't think so." As soon as it was out of my mouth, I realized that Henry's parents were listening to our conversation. Of course they were. These were people who installed video cameras in their kitchen.

Eager to change the subject, I asked, "Where's Gwendolyn? And the rest of her family?" As many people as there were in the room, several seats remained open at the plywood table.

The Dunkle boy with the screechy voice said, "Them's too good to eat with us."

"The Waxweilers are, um . . ." Henry faltered.

His mother answered for him. "The Waxweilers have expressed some concerns about food safety. As have we." She turned her attention to Mrs. Dunkle. "Barb, I trust you rinsed the garden vegetables in the bleach solution we discussed."

Mrs. Dunkle chewed one . . . two . . . three times. "Of course, Mrs. Hawking."

Mr. Hawking put down his spoon and crossed his arms over his chest. Despite his stubble, he really did look like Mr. Clean. To Mr. Dunkle he said, "Kurt, as we've discussed before, the unsanitary state of the backyard troubles us. We'd like you to prioritize a cleanup effort."

"What are the Waxweilers having for lunch?" I asked Henry.

"MREs—meals ready to eat, like you had in the bunker."

My mouth watered at the memory of the stroganoff and lasagna, both tastily reconstituted with a splash of iodine-sterilized water.

Henry said, "The Waxweilers brought enough MREs for six months."

"Enough to last *them* six months," Mrs. Dunkle snarled.

"Self-sufficiency is our number one priority," Mrs. Hawking announced. "Our hope, of course, is to return to our old lives. But if this truly is tee-ought-walkie, we need to be prepared to live off the land. Grow our own food, make our own clothes, provide our own energy."

"But this meat is from Costco, right?" Henry asked.

"I certainly hope so," his mother muttered.

Then, as if she knew we were talking about her, Mrs. Waxweiler appeared in the doorway. Her blond bubble hair was now flat, but she still wore flowered capris, which were a nice break from all that camo and khaki.

She wasn't there for the greasy stew; that much was clear. Instead, she made her way straight to me just as Tuck slid off his plastic chair and crawled under the table.

Mrs. Waxweiler slid into the vacant chair and popped on her fake smile. "Daisy! Thank goodness you made it through quarantine! You need to tell me what is going on at school."

Fake or not, the smile filled me with relief. Mrs. Waxweiler cared about me! And she cared about the world outside of here— the people beyond the compound. After the nasty reception I had gotten from the Hawkings and Dunkles, her concern brought a lump to my throat.

"There were a lot of people out sick," I said. "But I don't think it was anything serious. More like a nasty cold."

"No, no, no." She waved her hand in the air. "We've been getting updates about the plague. I'm tired of hearing about it. No—I need to know about your schoolwork. Homework, too. And tests. Gwendolyn said you take most of the same classes."

On the other side of the table, one of the middle Dunkle boys screamed and kicked Tuck, who had just bitten his leg. Tuck wailed. His mother ignored him.

I blinked at Mrs. Waxweiler, disoriented. I hadn't thought much about schoolwork since being trapped underground, when having enough air to breathe took priority over my overdue English essay. But if Mrs. Waxweiler thought schoolwork still mattered, things couldn't be as bad as Henry had said.

"So you think this is just temporary," I said, my anxiety easing for the first time since Henry had disappeared. "You think we'll be going back to school."

She sighed and ran a hand through her flat hair. "It's a long shot that things will go back to the way they were. Twenty percent, maybe? Twenty-five? But those odds are still higher than the chances of admission to an Ivy League school. The way I see it, the high schools will close down no matter what, even if it's just for a couple of months. Everyone is going to fall behind. But if my children make a big academic push while we're up here, they're going to be way ahead of the game when we get back."

"Ain't gonna be nothing left to go back to," Mr. Dunkle called from down the table. He was chewing with his mouth open and smiling, elbows on the table, fork pointed our way.

Mrs. Dunkle nodded her agreement. "Population was gettin' too big anyway. Too much traffic. Prices too high. All those foreigners comin' in—no room left for Americans."

Ignoring Mr. Dunkle, Mrs. Waxweiler stood up and tapped the table. "Come visit us this afternoon, Daisy? Our suite is upstairs, last door on the left."

Too shocked to say anything, I simply nodded.

Twenty-Two

I WASN'T ON the LUNCH CLEANUP list, but I helped clear the table anyway because my mother raised me to be helpful in the kitchen. (Ha! Kidding. My mother raised me to make microwave popcorn.)

The whiteboard had me down for GARDNING for the afternoon, along with Kadence and someone named Martin. Hey, that wasn't so bad. I like plants! I even planted an herb garden in my backyard last spring. It was really satisfying until I discovered that no one in my family ate herbs, probably because they are not a natural companion to Hot Pockets.

Anyway, I was so relieved to have been passed over for CHICKENS + RABITS CLEAN OUT COOP + HUTCH that I almost didn't care what I did. According to one whiteboard, when I was done in the garden, I'd help with dinner prep, and after that I was free.

Henry, on the other hand, was supposed to spend the afternoon hunting, then he had patrol duty from nine o'clock until midnight. I had a little chunk of time between lunch and my gardening shift, so Henry took me upstairs to get my bedding.

"You're really going hunting?" I asked.

In the room set aside for the Ward family, he opened a big cardboard box and pulled out a pillow, sheet, and blanket. "Not sure. I've got some pressure in my face, right behind the eyes. Might be coming down with a sinus infection."

"You shouldn't push it then."

"Wouldn't want to hold the others back." Linens in his arms, he led me downstairs and to the back door. He paused before going outside. "I can work on my parents. You shouldn't have to sleep in the dorm."

"It's not that big a deal."

"It kind of is."

―――――――

The girls' dorm was housed—for lack of a better word—in the school bus, right next to the chickens and goats and geese. At the moment, the sheep seemed to be hiding. Unless it really had been killed for the stew? No, no—I was going with hiding.

I climbed the steps into the bus. An acrid smell cut through the dense heat and made me gag. The bus was empty except for one of the younger Dunkle girls, who was spraying a window with an unmarked bottle.

"Hi," she said.

"Hi." I shielded my nose with an edge of the blanket and took little sips of air. "Which one are you?"

"Kelli-Lynn. I'm seven." With a dirty-looking rag, she wiped the window a few times and moved on to the next, holding up the bottle for a big, stinky spritz.

The bus was rigged much like the underground bunker had been, with four sets of bunk beds along the walls and overstuffed shelves everywhere else. At least the bus was aboveground.

"This is where you all sleep?" I asked.

"The boys get to stay in the RV with my parents." Kelli-Lynn crawled on a bottom bunk and sprayed a window. "It's not fair."

Kelli-Lynn wore her pale hair in two tight French braids. Long pants and a *Toy Story* sweatshirt were probably intended to protect her from bug bites and poison oak, but right now, heatstroke seemed like a more immediate danger. The little girl's face was bright red and sweaty.

The windows were cracked open, but it didn't help much. The hot, acrid air stung my nose. "What's that stuff that smells like vinegar?"

"Vinegar." She moved on to the next window, spritzed, and rubbed. Then she tilted her square chin at the upper bunk, one of only two not buried in clothes. "You'll want to sleep up there. 'Cause otherwise you're stuck next to Kadence, and she cries in her sleep."

When Kelli-Lynn finished with that window, I hauled myself to the edge of the upper bunk and proceeded to make up the remarkably thin mattress. Sweat trickled down my forehead.

"Where do you sleep?" I asked.

"There." She pointed to a bottom bunk covered in a Dora the Explorer quilt.

"Does Gwendolyn sleep out here?"

Kelli-Lynn snorted. "Gwendolyn sleeps in the big house. She got a room bigger'n this whole bus."

I looked around. "This bus isn't that big."

Kelli-Lynn shrugged. "Better'n the last one." Before I could process that, she added, "Gwendolyn has her own bathroom, too."

Bathroom. Wait. I looked at the front of the bus. I looked at the back of the bus. Nothing.

"Where is our bathroom?" I asked.

"We're supposed to use the Porta-Potty, but sometimes they'll let you use the one in the big house, near the kitchen. Or if it's the middle of the night, just use a jar."

First Mad Plague . . . now sleep criers and pee jars. This was a lot to take in.

"Where did you live before here?" I asked, thinking, *Idaho? Montana? The moon?* But no.

"Anaheim."

"Anaheim?"

"That's where Disneyland is," she said.

"I know. I live nearby."

Kelli-Lynn sat down on a bottom bunk. "We went to Disneyland once. I got to meet Minnie and Mickey and Goofy, and then I got my picture taken with Belle. Daddy said we couldn't buy the photo 'cause it cost too much money, but at least I got to meet Belle. And then Killer went on Space Mountain, and that made him throw up, so we had to leave."

Kelli-Lynn turned to the closest window, sprayed, and rubbed extra hard.

———

Back in the yard, assaulted by the midday heat and animal stench, I realized that gardening was not a pleasant duty after all. Also, that there were worse smells than vinegar.

Kadence, the little girl who had earlier threatened to impale me with an arrow, crouched by the vegetable beds, rubber boots pulled over her camouflage pants. "I like your hair," she said, which was a big step up from *Don't come any closer.*

I pulled my ponytail around to the front and gave my cherry-red ends an affectionate tug. "Thanks."

"Could you do that to mine?"

I imagined dipping her flaxen braids into steaming hot Kool-Aid. Grape, maybe. And then I pictured her mother's face when she saw the purple hair. Actually, I pictured her mother's hands around my neck.

"Probably not a good idea."

There were four raised vegetable beds. I could see several kinds of squash, basil, corn, tomatoes, peppers, and a bunch of different greens. The garden was organic, by which I mean there were a bunch of bugs around the tomatoes. There were bees, too, doing their work before heading back to their hives.

"So, are we . . . picking vegetables? Or weeding?" I asked. Wow, it smelled bad.

"Fertilizing." Kadence held a shovel that was much too big for her to manage.

My stomach dropped. "With . . . ?"

"Poop."

"From . . . ?"

"Goats." She pointed to the animal pen. "I got stuck with this job because I talked back to Mama. What did you do?"

"I was born. I think that's what I did wrong." I knelt down next to her, trying not to think too much about what I was doing. Or smelling.

"Who's Martin?" I asked. "Isn't he supposed to be here?"

She snorted. "Martin don't do nothin' he don't wanna do."

"But who is he?"

"Gwendolyn's brother. He's in the house. In his own room. Mama says he's spoiled."

I couldn't believe I was living in a world where not sleeping in a bus counted as spoiled. I tried to remember what day it was. Sunday? Monday?

"So tomorrow you have home school?" I asked.

"Nah, we don't do schoolwork, not since we moved up here. Mama and Dad say book learning won't do us no good when the world ends. There's more important things we gotta know."

"Like . . . how to fertilize with goat poop?"

Kadence dug at the earth. "I shouldn'ta talked back to Mama."

Twenty-Three

THE NEXT THREE hours were unpleasant. That's all I'm prepared to say about "organic fertilizer." Well, okay, the last hour, spent weeding and picking tomatoes (Kadence had to show me how to do it properly because I am stupider than an eight-year-old) might have been pleasant if only it weren't so daggone hot out there.

Kadence also taught me to say *daggone*.

Afterward, I had time for a short shower in the downstairs bathroom that had been set aside for the Dunkles' use. I would have made it a long shower, but I was fifth in the line and the hot water ran out after maybe three minutes. Still, after my sponge baths in the underground bunker, I was grateful to have hot water to run out—and clean clothes, to boot. Thanks to Mrs. Waxweiler, who did laundry for the entire compound, I got to change back into my own T-shirt and cutoff shorts. The air-conditioning in the house was up so high that I was actually cold.

Upstairs, it was warmer. Like, slow-roast warmer. The last door on the left was closed. I knocked, half hoping no one would answer, but in an instant I was face-to-face with Mrs. Waxweiler.

"Daisy—good! We were just talking about you. Come in."

What Mrs. Waxweiler had called a suite was really just a huge, L-shaped bedroom. A door at the far end of the room presumably led to a bathroom. In one branch of the L, a flowered comforter covered a big blow-up mattress. Astonishingly, Mrs. Waxweiler had accessorized it with throw pillows. In the other, closer branch of the L, Gwendolyn sat at a long folding table, hunched over our AP Euro textbook.

I took a few steps into the room, but there was nowhere to sit except on the bed, so I just stood there.

Mrs. Waxweiler asked, "What did you get on the last AP Euro test? Not the Middle Ages one—Gwennie is studying for that right now—but the one before it."

"I don't remember," I lied. Actually, I'd gotten a 78. It was a really hard test! Even Henry got a question wrong! But there was no way I was going to admit that to Mrs. Waxweiler.

"Gwennie said that most of the class failed."

"I didn't fail," I said.

"Gwennie got a sixty-nine. That's a D!"

At that, Gwendolyn looked up, scowling. "D-plus. And it's weighted, which makes it a C-plus, practically a B-minus."

"Mr. Vasquez gives a lot of chances for extra credit," I assured Mrs. Waxweiler, even as I couldn't believe we were having this conversation. When I'd left town, Mr. Vasquez had been hospitalized.

Gwendolyn's history grade was probably not his biggest concern right now.

"The test after that, the one Gwennie missed. Do you remember what was on it?"

"There were a lot of questions about the plague," I said.

She let out a grim laugh. "That should be easy, then."

———

In the kitchen, Kirsten stood at the black granite counter, a huge mound of potatoes in front of her. When she saw my shirt, her eyes lit up. "You like My Little Pony?" At fourteen, Kirsten was the second-oldest Dunkle girl, but though she was slighter than Karessa, she seemed older—probably because she wore earrings and makeup and because her hair, falling in loose waves around her shoulders, seemed more suited to modern-day high school than, say, a covered wagon train.

I examined the rainbow horse on my shirt. "It's meant to be ironic. But, well—yeah. Actually, I kind of do. So does Henry, though he'll never admit it."

"We've got some of the DVDs here."

"You mean, there's a television?"

"Oh yeah. Runs off a stair stepper. The other two families get first dibs since it's their house, but sometimes we all get to sit down for a show after dinner." She handed me a peeler. "Here you go."

"Thanks." I took a potato from the pile and ran the peeler over it. Nothing happened.

Kirsten finished up her potato, chucked it into a big bowl, and started on a second. I tried again with my peeler, pushing a little harder this time. Still nothing.

"I think my peeler's broken."

Brow furrowed, she put down her (identical) peeler and took

mine. And then she proceeded to peel a potato without any trouble.

"Huh," I said.

She handed the peeler back to me. "Maybe you were doing it in the wrong direction?"

"Maybe." I tried again. And failed again.

"Yeah, you're holding it backward." She demonstrated the correct method.

"Got it."

"Haven't you ever peeled a potato before?" she asked.

"Of course." I tried to look nonchalant, but I'm a terrible faker. "No. Never. I don't think we even own a peeler."

By the time we'd worked through the pile, my peeling skills had improved considerably. But when Mrs. Dunkle came into the room and put me in charge of making mashed potatoes, I had to admit that I didn't know how.

Mrs. Dunkle rolled her eyes. "Well, first you boil them. You can do that, can't you?"

"Sure," I said. Because any idiot can boil water, and I've been making ramen noodles since I was small.

But it turns out that potatoes are different, because when I filled a pot halfway with water and stuck it on the stove, Mrs. Dunkle said, "Is there something wrong with you in the head?"

When I didn't answer (because I couldn't speak without crying), she put another big pot on the stove and dumped in the potatoes. She covered them with some of the water from the first pot; the rest of the water she saved for later use.

"When it starts to boil, turn the heat down," she said.

"Okay." My voice quavered.

"Then cook 'em for a half an hour."

"Okay."

"Then mash 'em with milk and butter and salt and pepper."

Kirsten piped in, "She has to drain the water before she adds the other stuff."

"I'm assuming she'd figure that out."

I shot Kirsten a look of profound gratitude. I would have dumped the milk and butter right into the boiling water. Absolutely.

"When you drain the potatoes, save the water so we can use it again. We reuse all our water, even from the toilets."

I didn't ask what the recycled toilet water was used for. Some things are best left unknown.

———

By the time dinner was ready, I had not only learned how to make mashed potatoes, but I also knew how to treat a scald (immediately run the burned hand under cold water). I had mastered (sort of) the art of peeling carrots, which is much like peeling potatoes, though you have to cut off the top and bottom when you're done. Who knew? Finally, I'd gotten out of chopping onions, probably forever, because nobody wants human blood in their meat loaf.

When everything was ready, Mrs. Dunkle handed me a plate heaped with meat loaf, mashed potatoes, carrots, and peas.

"Take these up to his highness."

I was confused. As usual. "Your husband?"

She looked at me the way she generally did, which is to say, like a moron. "No, Martin."

I was about to say that I didn't know where Martin's room was, but the house, while vast, only had two floors. How hard could it be to find him?

Pretty hard.

"Martin? Hello?" I wandered down the hall, calling, but there was no answer.

Then I wandered down the hall again, knocking on each door in turn. Still no answer. There was no way I was going to take the plate back down to Mrs. Dunkle. I made my way down the hall one last time, knocking on each door loudly and then opening it up a crack.

"Hello . . . ? Anybody here?"

I opened the door to Henry's room (I'd forgotten where it was), and then found his parents' room, which was just as tidy as their space back home, if more sparsely furnished. Next came Gwendolyn's room. She had decorated the walls with photos of herself with her drill squad, along with posters of butterflies and puppies. I would never have pegged Gwendolyn as a butterflies-and-puppies kind of girl, but people can surprise you.

At last, I knocked on a door and got an answer. A tall, lanky guy sat on the rough floor, with papers, pens, highlighters, and books spread out around him. I'd seen him at school before. Gwendolyn's brother, of course. His hair was darker than hers, his face longer, but they had the same suspicious look in their eyes.

He frowned for a minute before pushing a button on his iPod and pulling buds out of his ears. "Who're you?"

"Daisy Cruz. Henry's friend? I've got your dinner." I looked around for someplace to put the plate and finally settled for a patch of floor without any papers on it. "I thought your family only ate MREs."

He snorted. "My parents and the Hawkings had a *leadership conference* about an hour ago. They never just talk. They have conferences. Whatever. The Hawkings made a big thing about how we all have to stick together as a community and all that bull, and my parents agreed to join them for the evening meal, at least for now. But one more hit of food poisoning, and it's back to the MREs for good. Until they run out. And then, who knows."

I nodded, not knowing what to say.

His expression suddenly softened. "I've seen you before. Are you Pete Clay's sister?"

"Yeah. You know Peter?"

"We played basketball together last year. Wait—is Peter here?"

I shook my head and swallowed hard. "He drove me up here and then left. I didn't know. . . . If I'd known . . ."

He ran a hand through his hair. "I hate—" And then he stopped and changed course. "SATs are this Saturday."

"You're taking the SATs?"

"Of course not. I mean, I took them already, last spring, but I bombed, so I spent the whole summer taking a prep course. And now I'm still studying for them because my mother keeps telling me I should, and besides—what else am I supposed to do? My whole life I've been getting ready for my future. Do well in high school. Get into a good college. Get a good job. Work hard and everything will fall into place. Like we can control our destiny. Like we can control anything."

He picked up a thick book: *Ace the SAT!* He opened it, squinted at a question, and scrawled something. He pushed so hard that his pencil snapped. He dropped the book on the floor.

"They'll be offered again," I said. "In January, maybe?"

He shrugged. "Unless everything's changed."

I bit my lip. I didn't want to think about that possibility.

He said, "I just want things to be the way they were."

"Me, too."

He met my eyes. "The Dunkles act like this is *fun*. They've been preparing for doomsday forever, so now they get to feel all smug that they were right. They can't wait for the Golden Horde to arrive so they can pick them off."

"The Golden Horde?"

"That's what they call the people who will flee the cities when things get really bad."

"Like my brother and mother," I said.

Martin said, "We're supposed to protect our resources from them. To turn them away, or worse. What I don't get is—what's the point of surviving if you turn into that kind of person? Isn't it better to die than to give up your soul?"

Footsteps sounded in the hall, and Kirsten appeared in the doorway. "Mama said . . . never mind what she said. We need you to help us serve."

"Thanks for bringing me dinner," Martin said. "Come visit me sometime. You know, when you want to have a few laughs."

That made me crack a smile. "I'll do that."

———

When I finally managed to sit down to dinner, the hunters in the group were just finishing up their daily dead squirrel reports. Not surprisingly, Killer led the pack with four hits, which meant he'd get an extra helping of meat loaf. Little Kelli-Lynn, age seven, was right behind with three dead squirrels. And to think that when I was seven, I wasted my afternoons on things like double-digit subtraction.

Gwendolyn's mother waited until I had mouth my full of (runny) mashed potatoes before she said, "Daisy, have I ever met your parents? I've attended so many booster club and PTA meetings over the years, I lose track."

I washed down the potatoes with lukewarm tap water. "Probably not. My mom works in Norwalk, plus she teaches art classes at night. So she doesn't have much time to volunteer."

"And your father?"

"He lives in North Carolina. He's not very . . . I don't see him much. But we keep in touch."

To my father, keeping in touch mostly meant posting pictures of cats with captions on my Facebook page. When I was younger, he'd fly out to California every July for a visit, but it was always awkward, and I'd feel kind of relieved when he left. He and his new wife had a baby a couple of years ago, though, so it's been hard for him to get away.

Still. I've always known that he cares about me. He's kept up on his child support payments, at any rate, which is how we have managed to maintain our luxurious lifestyle.

"That's too bad," Mr. Waxweiler said in his disturbingly high voice. "About the divorce, I mean."

I kept my face neutral. "It's not that big a deal. There was no big drama or anything. They split up when I was three, so as far I can remember, it's always just been my mom, my brother, and me."

"That's tough on your brother, though," Mr. Waxweiler pressed. "Having his dad on the other side of the country. A boy needs a role model."

Before the censor in my brain could tell my mouth to stay closed, I blurted out, "Oh no—Peter's got a different father. We're not even sure who he is."

Everyone stared at me.

"What I mean is . . . it's not like my mother . . . my mother has an idea who it might be. She's just not a hundred percent sure.

She was young and irresponsible back then—she's not like that anymore." I forced a laugh. "Someday we are going to invite all the guys who might be Peter's father to a Greek island for a sing-along, and we'll sort it out once and for all!"

Jaws (many of them square) dropped. Nobody ever gets my jokes.

"It's a reference to *Mama Mia!*" Henry explained. (I'd made him watch the movie.) "You know—the Abba musical."

Still nobody laughed.

"What'd you say your last name was?" Mr. Dunkle peered at me from the far end of the table.

"I didn't. But it's Cruz."

"What are you? Mexican?"

"Uh . . . on my dad's side, yeah."

Mr. Dunkle narrowed his eyes at me. "Oughta go back to his own country."

I blinked at him. Did he really just say that? Sensing tension, the blond Dunklings were uncharacteristically still around the table.

I said, "My father was born in San Diego."

Mr. Dunkle pointed at me with his grimy fork. "Right over the border. That's what they do. Sneak over here and take our jobs. Oughta send 'em all back."

"My father is an engineer." I couldn't believe I was having this conversation.

"Fancy job. Probably took it from an American."

I began to shake. "My brother—you know, the illegitimate one?" My voice was rising. "He has blue eyes. Also, he sunburns really easily. So we're pretty sure he's all white."

"Stop it!" Mr. Hawking slammed his cup on the table. (It being plastic, the effect wasn't as dramatic as it could have been.)

I jumped a little, thinking he was talking to me. Instead he stood up and glared at the square-jawed man at the other end of the table. "You will join me in headquarters. Now."

Nobody moved. Then Mr. Dunkle forked a piece of meat loaf into his mouth and chewed. Slowly. Finally, he spoke. "Sure thing, boss. Soon's I finish my supper."

As one, the Dunklings returned to eating.

A hot ball of tension settled in the pit of my stomach. I couldn't eat. I pictured Peter's sleepy blue eyes, his unshaven face. I remembered the way my mom had looked in her flowing dress on the day she left for the cruise. I thought of the photos my father had texted of the half sister I had never even met.

My family wasn't perfect, but it was mine.

Twenty-Four

IT WAS MY first night sleeping—or trying to sleep—in the Bus to Nowhere. Though the outside temperature had dropped, the air inside the bus was stifling. Heat rises, of course, and there was only about a foot and a half between my sweaty face and the curved metal roof. It was around ten o'clock, maybe a little later. With no clock or working phone, all I could do was guess. It was way too early to sleep, even if I'd been comfortable.

For the past hour or so, I'd lain sprawled on my thin, lumpy mattress listening to one Dunkle girl hum, one snore, and two others whisper.

When the tapping sounds came, I assumed they were from the wind or a goat or maybe the sheep. (Here I was being optimistic. I hadn't seen the sheep since trying to eat that greasy stew.) But when taps turned to smacks, Kirsten, below me, whispered, "Henry's outside. He wants to talk to you."

I sat up so fast I whacked my head on the ceiling and said a bad word.

Across from me, Kadence said, "That's a bad word."

"Of course it is. That's the whole point."

Henry moved along the side of the bus like a thief, barely casting a shadow in the moonlight. "Come to the lookout with me." He took off toward the back fence without waiting for a response.

We made our way out the back gate and followed the fence around the perimeter. It was okay if anyone saw Henry; he was scheduled for lookout duty. But I was a different story. I held my hands out to protect against spiderwebs, but they laced my face anyway.

Once we got to the front of the compound, we followed a rough, weedy road through some trees, around a bend, down one hill, and up another. Shrill birdsong made me think of the smoke alarm that used to go off every time something burned in our oven at home. Eventually, we removed the batteries.

At last, Henry and I turned a corner and came to a little clearing. A brown wooden shed perched on rickety stilts. It looked like a kids' playhouse or a prison tower.

Henry scrambled up the ladder. I followed. The structure was sturdier than it looked.

"Are you the only one on duty?" I asked when we reached the top.

"Kyle's supposed to be here, but he'd rather smoke in the woods. I'd rather be alone anyway."

"But you're not alone. You're with me."

"I'd rather be alone with you than alone with myself."

I was glad of the dark because he couldn't see me smile.

A narrow platform, like scaffolding, ran around the structure. We ducked through a low door into a dark, musty space slightly larger than it looked from the outside. The wood walls were unfinished, the floor covered in the kind of outdoor carpet that is supposed to look like grass but just looks like spiky green plastic.

"Nice tree house," I said.

"I thought you'd like it."

Furniture consisted of two beat-up armchairs and a chunky wood side table. Henry's guitar leaned against a corner.

"What are you looking out for, exactly? Expecting an invasion?"

He shrugged. "I'm out here most nights, and all I've seen so far are a couple of bears."

"*Seriously?*" And I'd thought lemurs were the only animals I had to worry about.

"A few coyotes, too. Maybe a mountain lion, though I couldn't be sure. This property is surrounded by national forest land, but almost no one drives out this far."

One of the armchairs had been pulled up to the big window, which was just a big, open cutout. Henry nudged the second chair next to the first. I sat down and gazed at the tapestry of the night sky.

"The stars are so bright out here."

This mountain sky looked nothing like the murky purple I was used to at home. The stars twinkled and pulsed like something alive. Behind them, black velvet spread deep and dark and endless—beautiful but also frightening. The sky was so big, and I was so small. I'd never felt my insignificance quite so profoundly.

"Do you remember that time?" I said, knowing we were thinking the same thing.

"Yeah," he said.

One night last summer, we spread a blanket on the overgrown grass in my backyard, then we lay down and stared at the sky, determined to spot shooting stars, each of us stockpiling secret wishes. But the sky was too bright, the stars too dim. We counted eight airplanes and then went inside.

"Are there more stars in the sky or grains of sand on the beaches?" I mused.

"Dunno. When we get back to the house, I'll Google it."

I smiled in the darkness.

We were quiet for a few moments, and then Henry said, "If you had to spend the rest of your life in a space station or an undersea colony, which would you choose?"

"Neither. I'd go home."

Right now, it was nice out here, I had to admit. The air had cooled, and the smells of pine and eucalyptus drifted through the air. Beyond us, night birds trilled their sad songs, while crickets played their violins.

I broke the silence. "I'm still mad at you."

"I know."

We stared at the stars and listened to the birds.

"Undersea colony," I said.

"Me, too."

"I keep thinking about that project we did freshman year in geography, you remember?"

"Of course I remember. That's when we met."

He picked up his guitar and ran his fingers gently over the strings. The notes danced around us like ghost sounds. "Thanks for bringing my guitar. My parents wouldn't let me. Said we only had room for *essentials*."

"But for you, music is essential."

He played a few more notes. "You're the only one who understands that about me. Actually, you're the only one who understands me at all." He slipped his hand in his front pocket and pulled out a plastic guitar pick. "I brought a bunch of these along. I don't even know why."

"Because you knew I'd come for you. And bring your guitar."

He smiled—the first real smile I'd seen out of him since I'd gotten here. This was Henry. This was my friend.

"What are you waiting for?" I asked. "Play."

He shifted in his chair and got into position, his right arm bent over the body of the guitar, his narrow left fingers poised. And then he closed his eyes, took a deep breath, and began to play. It was a new song, something I'd never heard before. It was sadder than the songs he usually played, but also richer.

When the final notes drifted out into the darkness, I said, "That was beautiful. Who wrote it?"

"I did."

"When?"

"Over the last couple of weeks. In my head. I'd close my eyes and pretend I was playing my guitar. And I'd think of you."

"Henry . . ."

"Your mom and Peter. I know. I'll figure something out."

A beam of light darted through the window. Henry said, "Don't worry, it's just Gwendolyn. She's on patrol."

"But I thought the patrol people walked around the perimeter of the fence."

"They do. Until they get bored."

The walls shuddered as Gwendolyn climbed the ladder. When she saw me she said, "Oh."

"Good to see you, too."

She shoved her hands in her pockets and leaned against a wall, which could probably give her splinters, but whatever.

"So, what happened at school after I left?"

I thought about it. "A few people were out sick—I thought it was just the flu, but nobody was panicking or anything."

"No, I mean what was *happening*. Did we win against Buena Park?"

"Win . . . what?"

"Football." She gave me a *duh* look.

"Oh—right! Um . . . I have no idea."

She looked exasperated. Or maybe just disappointed.

I said, "I talked to a couple of your drill teammates when you disappeared."

She perked up. "Which ones?"

"Some girl named Bethany Bratt? She's in my math class. A couple others, too, but I don't know their names."

She nodded. "Did they say anything about replacing me? Or tryouts?" It seemed like a weird thing to be worrying about under the circumstances.

"No. Why would they replace you?"

"If a drill team member has more than two unexcused absences, she is off the squad. No exceptions." Her voice cracked.

"The end of the world seems like it should be a decent exception."

"This is not the end of the world!"

"Then why are we here?"

Gwendolyn leaned against the wall. "Removing ourselves from society is the only absolute way to prevent infection. My parents say we have to wait here until people are done dying or until someone discovers a cure, whichever comes first."

"Until people are done dying," I repeated, suddenly feeling nauseous.

"My dad keeps talking about our money and what's going to happen to our house. And my mom says we should look on *the bright side*, that with a smaller population, we'll have more opportunities." Gwendolyn's voice turned shrill. "But what if this is a false alarm and we go back and everything's the same? I won't have my spot on the drill squad anymore! And I'll have failed all my classes, and nobody will like me because I ran away."

Gwendolyn began to sob. "I miss my dog," she wailed.

"Her parents took it to the pound," Henry explained. "Because dogs carry fleas, and fleas carry the Mad Plague."

"I would have used Frontline on him," she whimpered. "Every month. That would have gotten rid of any fleas. He could have gone on patrol with me. He was part golden retriever, part beagle, part something else—they never knew what. His name was Mabrey."

I helped Gwendolyn over to my chair, where she curled up into a ball. "I left my friends without warning them. I could have saved them, but I didn't. If they die, it will be all my fault."

I said, "It might help if Henry played a song."

She nodded, and Henry began to play, his sad melody wrapping around us like a silky blanket.

Twenty-Five

"YOU GIRLS GET a move on! Sun's almost up, and we gotta put up all those tomatoes!"

Now there's a string of words, coming from a screeching Mrs. Dunkle, that I never expected to start my day. Any day. But then, I never expected to live in a school bus, either. Life is full of surprises.

I sat up and whacked my forehead against the metal roof. "Ow!"

"Watch your head!" Kirsten chirped from below.

I peered over the side of my bunk. "Put the tomatoes up *where*?"

"Huh?" She looked up from buttoning her shirt. It was solid olive today, a big step up from the camo. Well, a step up, anyway. "Oh! *Putting up* means canning. We're canning tomatoes today. Don't worry. It's easy."

She unscrewed a jar of glitter powder and whisked some over her cheekbones. "Want some?"

"Sure." I stuck my pinkie in the pot and dabbed a spot on each cheek. When putting up tomatoes, a girl needs to look her best.

———————

A few words about my experience canning tomatoes: boiling water, slippery fingers, broken glass. Within an hour, Mrs. Dunkle excused me from my duties, which I thought was a good thing until she told me to go clean the bathrooms. All the bathrooms. With bleach.

Did you know that straight bleach can actually burn a hole in your clothes? Neither did I! I didn't know you were supposed to dilute the bleach with water, either. By the second bathroom (there were five), my prized My Little Pony shirt was looking seriously unmagical.

The bathrooms were equally unmagical, or at least unfinished. None were painted, two lacked faucets, and one had a sign taped to the toilet that said DON'T USE THIS.

"It's not that big a hole," Karessa said, checking my T-shirt. She had discovered me in the bathroom off the kitchen, fighting back tears. For once, she didn't have a small child attached to her body. Since the twins were napping, she got to can tomatoes instead. Sometimes you just get lucky.

"But it's a hole." I poked at it with my fingernail. "I have two shirts, and the one I like *has a hole.*" I'd found the T-shirt at Buffalo Exchange one Saturday when I was shopping with my mother, who was a big believer in recycled fashion. Used or not, the shirt was one of my favorites, even back when I owned more than two shirts.

Karessa leaned down to inspect the damage. "All's you need to patch it is a little piece of white fabric."

I shook my head. "I can't sew."

"Really?"

"Really." Bonus points to me for not adding, *And I can't churn butter or work a loom, either.*

She straightened up and shrugged as if to say, *Not a big deal.* "I can fix the shirt for you. Just give it to me in the bus tonight."

"Seriously? Wow. Thanks."

Now I was doubly glad for resisting my sarcastic impulse. From what I'd seen, Karessa was a genuinely nice person. As the oldest girl, she was like a second mother to the little Dunkle kids—you know, the nice mother. Karessa worked hard, she never complained, and she did exactly as she was told. So, either she was a genuinely nice person or she was a genuinely nice robot. In the bus tonight, I would listen for mechanical sounds or maybe beeping.

———

After lunch, Henry's parents asked (told) me to join them upstairs in headquarters. Once again, we sat in molded plastic seats at the long laminate table. Once again, I felt like I'd been called into the principal's office.

At the last minute, Mr. Dunkle burst into the room and claimed the head of the table. Irritation flickered over Mr. Hawking's face, but he forced himself to nod at the other man. Mr. Hawking had apparently located a razor, though not a good one. Dark red nicks covered his smooth cheeks and shiny head.

"We need to find a place and a purpose for you in the community," Mrs. Hawking announced.

"What community?"

"This community. Here. The compound."

"Oh."

"According to Mrs. Dunkle, your kitchen skills are . . . lacking." Her eyes flickered to my hands, which had amassed an impressive collection of burns, one of which was starting to turn yellow.

"Whaddaya expect?" Mr. Dunkle said. "Dad gone, mom working all day, nothing but convenience foods in the freezer."

Mrs. Hawking's face tightened. She worked longer hours than my mother, and her pantry had always been way better stocked with snacks than mine.

Ignoring Mr. Dunkle, she continued, "And the job you did on the bathrooms . . . did you really not know that you're supposed to rinse off the bleach?"

My face burned. "Um . . . at home we just use those premoistened wipes to clean. And a Swiffer."

She nodded. "We don't use premoistened wipes here. Bleach, vinegar, rags—that's all you need. Much cheaper, much more versatile."

In my family, we saved money on cleaning products by not cleaning very often. But then, the Hawkings used a cleaning service. They weren't exactly bleach experts, either.

"In any event," Mr. Hawking said, "there must be some way you can make yourself useful. Do you have any experience with, say, carpentry?"

"You mean like, building stuff?"

"Yes."

I shook my head. "No."

"How about sewing?"

"No."

"Knitting?"

"Definitely no."

"Gardening?"

Mrs. Hawking answered that one for me. "Kadence said she kept pulling out the seedlings along with the weeds."

I gritted my teeth. First Kadence threatens to impale me with an arrow, and now this. Just when I thought we were becoming pals. She was the most treacherous eight-year-old I had ever met.

"Have you ever hunted?" Mr. Hawking asked. "Or fished?"

I shook my head.

"Beekeeping?" He looked doubtful.

"I read a book about it!" Points for not adding, *when I was imprisoned underground.* "But . . . not really."

"What about gutting deer? Or tanning hides?" Mr. Hawking said.

"You're kidding, right?"

Mrs. Hawking sighed—twice. The first time it was quiet and involuntary, the second loud enough to let me know that she found me completely useless. In case I hadn't noticed. "There must be *something* you can do."

"I can draw. And . . . I'm pretty good at algebra." There must be other stuff, but that was all I could come up with.

Mr. Dunkle leaned forward. "You know what good those skills will do in the new world? Zero."

The Hawkings exchanged a look.

"I volunteered at an art camp last summer," I said. "So maybe I could work with the kids. Teach them some stuff about art or maybe help them catch up on their schoolwork."

Mr. Dunkle perked up at that one. "Babysitting!"

"Not exactly. What I had in mind was—"

"That might free up Karessa a bit." He was nodding. "Give her more of a chance to help out her mother. This one"—he pointed at me—"could take over changing the diapers and giving the little kids their baths."

I said, "I meant helping out with the older kids. I've done some babysitting in my neighborhood, but they're all out of diapers. And at camp we weren't allowed to touch anyone. Like, at all. So I've never—"

"Fine," Mrs. Hawking said. "From now on, Daisy's in charge of the twins."

Mr. Hawking scowled at Mr. Dunkle and cleared his throat, which was clearly intended as a statement of some kind. When the bearded blond man didn't react, Mr. Hawking said, "You can go tell your wife."

After Mr. Dunkle left, I stood up, my brain swirling. Sassy, the girl twin, was adorable, but how was I going to control her demonic little brother?

Mr. Hawking did that throat-clearing thing again, directed at me this time. As I am not fluent in Ahem, I was semigrateful when his wife translated. "Daisy. Please sit."

Mrs. Hawking had always had a severe look about her, with that narrow face and perpetually pursed mouth. Now her cheeks were even more sunken, and there were circles under her eyes. She had taken to wearing bobby pins in an effort to control her hair.

I braced myself for yet another speech about my general uselessness. Instead, this:

"My great-grandparents came to America from Italy."

"Right." I knew that already.

"They arrived with no money, no English, and few connections.

Their lives were hard, and their children's lives were hard, and their children's children's."

Here I lost track of the generations. All I knew about Henry's mother was that both parents died when she was young, and she wound up living with a distant aunt. Henry said this was why she was so focused on worst-case scenarios: Because when she was a kid, anything that could go wrong did go wrong.

Mrs. Hawking blinked several times, trying to find the right words. "What we want you to know, Daisy, is that our reservations about you have nothing to do with your ethnicity. We do not condone any kind of prejudice, and we have raised our son to judge people by who they are and not where they came from."

"Isn't it better not to judge anyone at all?" I said.

Mr. Hawking cleared his throat.

"You should go find the twins," Mrs. Hawking said.

Twenty-Six

IF ONLY I'D stayed best friends with Jennifer Park, I wouldn't even be here.

Jennifer Park and I met on the first day of first grade. By October, we'd discovered that we both loved Polly Pockets, which was enough to cement a bond that continued through junior high school—even when Jennifer informed me that Polly Pockets were no longer cool and that we should focus our attention on Bath & Body Works scented lotions instead. The summer after eighth grade, we were busy planning our first day of high school—what to wear and what to smell like—when Jennifer's father destroyed our cherry-blossom-scented future by getting a job in New York.

It was worse for Jennifer (as she reminded me repeatedly). Our junior high fed into several different high schools, but at least I'd know a few people in ninth grade. (Whether or not I wanted to know them was a different story.) But Jennifer, stuck on the other side of the country, would be all alone.

Henry was in several of my freshman classes, but I didn't notice him at first because I pretty much kept my eyes on my notebook or my cuticles or the ground. About a month into the year, our AP Human Geography teacher assigned a group project, and Henry and I were put together, along with two other students. The assignment was called The Last Place on Earth. We were to imagine that modern society had been wiped out by rising water levels and a string of violent storms and that a small group was left to create a new civilization in one of several locations. The point was to think about how a place influences the culture that springs up around it. Anyway, I was hoping for Australian Undersea Colony, but our group got Nevada Waterfront instead.

"We need to meet at my house," a girl named Danica said. "Because I've got tennis every day after school and my church group on Wednesdays and cello on Thursdays and . . ." Bottom line: Danica was a busy and important person, and we needed to work around her busy and important schedule. Two whole weeks went by before Danica committed to a time and date, but when I showed up at her house, her mother told me I must be mistaken: Danica was at an informational session for students planning to spend their summer building houses in Costa Rica.

I showed Danica's mother the text message confirming the meeting, and she said that Danica must have sent another text after that. Which she didn't, but whatever. (I did have a brand-new text from Jennifer Park in New York: I made cheer!!!!!!!!!!!!)

I was about to call Peter to come back and get me when a black Expedition pulled up in front of Danica's house and a slight, dark-haired guy with intense black eyes got out of the passenger seat.

"She's not here," I told him.

"Let me guess. Church? Tennis? ASB? Cello? Mandarin? Mixed martial arts? Soup kitchen? Greyhound rescue? Any of those?"

"Something better." I found myself smiling.

The driver's door opened, and a severe-looking woman in a black pantsuit walked around the car. I gave her a cordial smile. She did not smile back.

Henry looked up, still thinking. "Danica's planning her senate run. Or donating a kidney. Or curing Ebola."

I mimed hitting something with a hammer.

"She's building something?"

I nodded.

"Furniture?"

I shook my head.

"A house?"

I swirled my hand to indicate he was on the right track but needed to take it further.

"Multiple houses?"

I nodded.

He frowned with concentration. And then: "In one of those tropical places so that it's like a vacation but it looks good on a college application?"

"Yes!" We high-fived. We laughed. And then I immediately felt embarrassed because I do not normally high-five strangers. Or anyone. Plus, his mother was there, and she still wasn't smiling.

"Meeting's canceled," Henry explained.

"We should just go ahead without her," I said. "This thing is due on Friday. We can go to my house."

Another car pulled up, and we told the fourth member, a guy, our new plan.

"Your parents will be there?" Henry's mother asked me.

"My mom should be home, yeah."

She offered to drive the other two of us, so we all piled into the big black vehicle. An awkward silence filled the car. When we pulled up in front of my house—blue paint peeling, white trim dirty, wooden roof warped, grass overgrown—it occurred to me that maybe I should have waited for someone else to volunteer a house.

"I'll call you when I'm done," Henry told his mother. But she got out of the car and followed us up the cracked walkway. "She likes to meet people's parents before I go over to their houses," Henry explained, blushing slightly. At once, I felt more embarrassed for him than I did for myself.

When I pushed open the front door, his mother gawked at the loose knob. "The house was *unlocked*?"

"My mother and brother are home."

The nostrils on her pointy nose flared.

My mother and Peter were in the kitchen—a nice homey scene, except my mom was sorting broken glass and my brother wasn't wearing pants. His boxers were patterned with pink flamingos, which made it even worse. But it didn't matter what these people thought, I decided on the spot. We were group partners, nothing more. After Friday, we'd probably never speak to one another again.

"Um, Mom, this is, um . . ." I had no idea what Henry's last name was.

"I'm Henry's mother." So I still didn't know what his last name was. "I like to meet the parents of my son's friends." Her eyes swept the kitchen. (Figuratively, of course. The kitchen hadn't been swept literally in weeks. Maybe months.)

My mother held out her hand and beamed. "Elise."

Mrs. Hawking (I know her name now, of course) stared at the hand but didn't move. It was beyond awkward. Finally, she said, "I believe you have a glass shard stuck to your palm."

It went downhill from there. Mrs. Hawking asked about hazardous household products (as if Henry were a toddler who might guzzle Drano), smoke and carbon monoxide alarms, neighborhood predators, and guns.

"Of course I don't have a gun!" my mother said, giving the responsible answer at last.

"When stored and handled properly, firearms can be a crucial component to a home security plan," Mrs. Hawking responded.

I really thought she was going to make Henry leave, and I was going to be stuck doing the entire project with just the fourth group member, who barely spoke and whose name I can't even remember, but finally Henry's mother told him she would be back in an hour. She left my house without touching anything.

I thought there was no way we would be able to finish the project in an hour, but fully formed ideas about starting a new civilization poured out of Henry's head at a rate that, in retrospect, I should have found suspicious. He talked about how living in a desert climate near the ocean would affect irrigation, harvest rituals, family structures, housing styles, art, music, folklore, nutrition, and more. Much, much more. I scribbled down notes. The fourth group member lounged on the couch and asked about snacks. (It was the first time he had said anything at all.) I suggested he check our freezer for burritos, and he disappeared into the kitchen.

Henry took a break from talking about siestas in oceanfront Nevada. ("Thanks to the ocean, average temperatures would be significantly cooler than they are now, of course, but the UV rays at that latitude would still be hazardous, especially if you take into account a damaged ozone layer, a population of primarily European ancestry, and the disruption of sunblock manufacturing. So, it would make sense for the population to go home for several hours in the middle of each day, which would in turn affect meal, social, and mating rituals.")

"My mother is overprotective," he said as soon as we were alone.

I looked up from taking notes. "She didn't like me very much."

He shook his head. "It's nothing personal. She doesn't like anyone."

He smiled. I smiled back.

"I'm an only child," he said.

I nodded.

"Don't take it personally," he said.

"Okay."

Later, he told me how both of his parents survived childhoods stained by abandonment, illness, alcoholism, and even suicide. Both worked hard at careers they disliked so they would never, ever be poor again. Both believed that the only person you can rely on is yourself—which may be why their relationship seemed more like a business partnership than a marriage. But most of all, both would do anything to keep their son happy, healthy, and safe.

And so they let me come over to their house, and they let Henry come over to mine, because our friendship made him happy (even though they wished he'd branch out). And because I brought him his homework when his delicate health made school attendance risky. But mostly because as tough as they were on themselves and the rest of the world, neither one could say no to Henry.

That was the one thing we had in common.

Twenty-Seven

IT WAS THE dead of night when Kirsten kicked the bottom of my bunk, rousing me from a really good dream about eating Korean tacos at the mall. Which could never happen in real life, because there is no Korean taco stand at the mall!

"Huh?"

"It's Henry. Outside." Kirsten was out of her bed, pulling on a sweatshirt.

At dinner, Henry had whispered something about late-night lookout duty, but engaging in hand-to-hand combat with Tuck during bath time had drained me. I'd collapsed into a deep, grimy sleep as soon as my head hit my crappy flat pillow.

I sat up too quickly and whacked my head on the metal roof. "Ow!"

"Watch your head," Kirsten said.

"Gee, thanks." I slid off the bunk.

"I'm coming with you." Footsteps light, Kirsten made her way to the front of the bus and opened the door with just the slightest creak. And then she was out.

When Henry saw her he whispered, "What are you doing here? Are you going to tell your parents on us?"

"Yeah, right." She thrust her hands into her green cargo pants and strode toward the gate. Her pale hair rippled in the moonlight.

With no clouds drifting in front of the half-moon, the night was brighter than before, but the sounds and shadows on our walk through the forest still creeped me out. Was that a bear I heard? A mountain lion? I wanted to take Henry's hand for comfort, but that would be weird. Instead, I kept as close to him as I could.

My black harem pants snagged on a bush; I yanked at them. The bush rustled.

Ahead of me, Henry halted. "You okay?"

I freed the fabric, taking a few prickers along with it. "I'm good." I shivered in the cool night air; too bad I'd cut the sleeves off the black knit shirt.

At last, the lookout tower came into sight. Lights twinkled from the window.

"Wait here." Henry motioned for Kirsten to hold back, then he hauled himself up the ladder and through the door. After a moment, he appeared on the deck and gestured for us to follow him.

Kyle and Gwendolyn sat in the armchairs, looking out the window. Their eyes were glazed as if they were watching YouTube and not the night sky. A whiff of cigarette smoke hung in the air.

"This is like a party," Kirsten said.

Her brother snorted. "Wild times on the compound."

"We were just talking," Gwendolyn said to no one in particular.

"Was anyone else on patrol duty with you?" Henry asked Kyle.

"Martin was supposed to be here," Kyle said. "But *so weird*, he didn't show up." He laughed.

"Shut *up*," Gwendolyn said.

"Just messin' with you. Not your fault your brother is too good to work." Kyle leaned over and gave Gwendolyn's arm a playful smack. In doing so, his foot shot out to one side, knocking over a bottle previously hidden from view.

"Oops." Kyle picked up the bottle. "Good thing it's empty."

Gwendolyn giggled.

"What was in there?" Henry asked.

"Moooooooonshine." Kyle stretched his arms up to the ceiling.

"I don't think so." Henry bent over to retrieve the bottle. He checked the label. "Napa Valley port. My parents were saving this for a special occasion."

Kyle grinned. "Can't think of anything specialer than the end of civilization."

Henry placed the bottle back on the floor. "They're going to be pissed if they find out you took it. But whatever. I don't care."

"Who's gonna tell 'em?"

Henry shrugged. "Not me."

"Not me," Kirsten echoed.

Kyle set his cool gaze on me. "Emo girl?"

I tugged at the cherry-red ends of my hair. "I am *not* emo. I'm just . . . me. And I'm not going to tattle, not that anyone would listen to me, anyway."

Kirsten picked up the bottle. "It's kind of pretty. Too bad we can't use it for a vase or something."

"Kyle's gonna bury it." Gwendolyn was slurring her words.

"Eventually," he said.

Gwendolyn turned in her chair. "You gotta get ridda it now! No one can know I've been drinking!"

"Drinking *and* smoking," Kyle said. "Big night for our little Gwennie."

"You promised you wouldn't tell!" she said. "Smoking's even worse than drinking because my dad keeps talking about fire danger and—"

"Relax," he said. "I'm not gonna tell. And all the evidence will be gone by morning. But . . . hey. It sure is a pretty bottle. Why not have a little more fun with it?"

Kyle placed the bottle on the fake grass carpet and flicked his wrist. The bottle spun for one and a half wobbly rounds. Kyle grinned.

Spin the bottle. Oh my God. No way was I kissing Kyle. But Kyle couldn't kiss his sister, and if he wanted to make out with Gwendolyn, he would have done it earlier.

But I was in luck. Kyle had another game in mind.

"Truth or dare. Who's in?"

"I'm in!" Kirsten plopped down on the floor and crossed her legs, waiting.

I caught Henry's eye. He lifted one shoulder as if to say, *What do you want to do?*

In response, I lifted a shoulder, too, as if to say, *I'm in if you're in.*

"Sure, why not," Henry said.

We pushed the armchairs against the wall, and the five of us sat in a tight circle on the fake grass carpet. Kyle retrieved a magazine to place under the bottle. I checked the title: *American Warrior.* Naturally.

Kyle spun first. It landed on Gwendolyn.

"Truth or dare?"

Her eyes darted left and right. "Truth," she said, finally.

Kyle tapped a finger on his cheek, considering the possibilities. "What is the worst thing you've ever done?"

Gwendolyn bit her lip. She looked scared, which was ridiculous. What could she have possibly done? Messed up a turn on her drill routine?

"I cheated on a test," she said at last.

"You need to be more specific."

"Math. It was math."

"Still more specific."

Her lip trembled. "It was our algebra final. Last year. This girl I knew, she was a senior, and she was helping the teacher out—grading papers and stuff. She got ahold of the test, the answer key, too. And she copied it for, like, six of us."

"That test was graded on a curve!" I burst out. Gwendolyn and I had been in the same algebra class. I got a B-minus on the final, which had dropped my semester grade from an A-minus to a B-plus.

"I had a C going in!" Gwendolyn wailed. "I needed a good grade on the final! I needed an A!" She was working hard to keep from slurring her words.

I said, "That's no excuse."

She opened her mouth, started to say something, and then stopped, took a deep breath, and nodded her head. A tear slid down her cheek.

"Um, a bit of perspective?" Kyle said. "Grades don't matter no more. Spin, Gwennie."

She did. It landed on Henry.

"Truth."

"Um . . ." She wiped her face. "Have you ever kissed anyone?"

"Lame," Kyle said.

"Fine. You ever made out with anybody?"

"Still lame," Kyle said.

I thought, *Of course Henry has never kissed anyone. He would have told me.*

"Yes," Henry said.

I swiveled my head to look at him, but he just hugged his knees and stared at the ground.

"Specifics," Kyle said.

"Her name was . . ." He paused. "Hannah."

"Hannah Branson?" Gwendolyn said.

He nodded.

"At Winter Formal?" My voice sounded tenser than I intended.

"Well, yeah, then and . . ." His voice trailed off.

"And when?"

"There were a couple . . . a few other times. I went to her house to study once, and there was this time in the hall after school. . . ." He hugged his knees tighter.

I couldn't believe this. "So—three times?"

"Maybe a couple more than that," he mumbled.

"Oh."

I don't care, I told myself, even though my stomach burned with . . . what? Jealousy? Disappointment? Henry and I were never a couple. He was free to go out with whomever he chose, even if it was someone shallow and nasty like Hannah freaking Branson.

Kyle said, "Did you just make out, or—"

"We just made out."

Kyle sighed with disappointment. "Fascinating. Spin, Henry."

Henry flicked his wrist, and the bottle made a wobbly half turn, landing on Kyle.

"Decisions, decisions," Kyle said. "Your dare would be lame. Let's go with truth."

Henry rolled his eyes. He just wanted to get this over with. "Okay, what's the worst thing you've ever done?"

"You need to be more specific."

"You weren't more specific when you asked Gwendolyn the same question."

"That's because I knew she wouldn'ta done anything really bad."

"Fine. Then what's the worst . . . crime you've ever committed?"

"You're that sure I've broken the law."

"Yes."

Kyle grinned. "You're right. Not a lotta times, but . . . oh, what to choose, what to choose?" He looked at the ceiling and bobbed his head from one side to the other, thinking. "I gotta go with the time I burned down a house."

"Seriously?" Gwendolyn said. That sobered her up. Sort of.

"It didn't burn all the way to the ground," Kyle said. " 'Cause the firefighters got there in time. But it had to be knocked down after that." He spun the bottle with a flourish. It landed on Henry again.

"We're not done yet," Henry said. "Where was the house?"

"Temecula?" Kirsten piped in, a touch of fear in her voice.

"Yup."

"But you said—"

"It was an accident," Kyle said. "I'm not *an arsonist* or anything. But this friend of mine—we weren't really friends, he was kind of a dirtbag—this guy I knew, his family had a cabin, but they were out of town, so I kind of . . . let myself in. And I was messing around and, yeah. It caught on fire."

"What were you messing around with?" Henry asked.

"Gasoline and rags." Kyle threw his head back and laughed. "Kidding! Jeez—if you could see your faces! It was an electrical fire. I put a piece of bread in the toaster—well, it was more like a roll. I kind of had to force it in. Then I went into the other room to watch TV. They had this sweet setup, big-screen TV, surround sound—that's the only reason I went over in the first place. I start watching HBO, and I forget about the toast. It caught on fire and . . . whaddaya want me to do? Call the fire department and say I'd broken into this house?"

"The police came to talk to us," Kirsten muttered.

"And then we moved," Kyle said. "The next day. Temecula was getting old, anyway. Not that Anaheim was any better. So, my man Henry—truth or dare, what'll it be?"

"Dare." Henry glared across the circle.

Kyle grinned. "Go back to the compound and set fire to the house."

Henry continued to glare.

"Kidding! Jeez. I can't believe we are the last people on earth, and I am stuck with you people."

"We are not the last people on earth," Gwendolyn said.

"Not yet." Kyle grinned. "Henry. I'll make this easy on you. Now that we know you're such a make-out artist, let's see you in action."

I swallowed hard. I didn't want Henry to kiss me, not here, anyway. If only I had let him kiss me that time at the pond. If only . . .

"Kiss Gwendolyn," Kyle commanded. "For a full minute. After that we'll get bored."

My mouth dropped open. I waited for Henry to protest.

Gwendolyn sighed and crawled on all fours into the middle of the circle. "Less juss get this over with."

Henry froze for a moment and then he was all action, lunging into the center of the circle and taking Gwendolyn in his arms. I couldn't believe what I was seeing. For a moment I forgot to breathe. I scrambled to my feet and stumbled out of the room, onto the platform. The moon was so bright, it was almost like daylight. I dropped to my knees and put my feet on the ladder.

"Daisy, wait." Henry appeared at the door.

I scrambled down the ladder, jumping past the last few rungs and stumbling on the prickly ground before bounding toward the forest, away from the compound, away from Henry. It didn't matter where I was going as long as I wasn't here.

"Daisy, stop!" He was behind me.

I picked up my pace for a moment, but then I was in a stand of trees, and it was dark, and I couldn't find a path. I held my arms out in front of me, picking around branches, crunching through dead underbrush, hoping I didn't walk into something awful.

"You'll get lost!" he said.

"So?"

"You could starve to death."

"I will not starve to death," I said with conviction. "I would die of dehydration first. You should know that, Henry. You're supposed to be so smart."

A branch scraped my cheek. I pushed on.

"I didn't want to kiss her!" he called out.

"Who? Gwendolyn? Or Hannah?"

"Gwendolyn. It was just—it felt like a challenge. Like I had no choice. Kyle never would have let it go."

"Since when do you care what other people think?"

"Since I've been trapped in this horrible place, where I can't get away from anybody. The only thing that's kept me going is you. It was just a kiss!"

"Just."

"You've probably been kissed lots of times before."

I crossed my arms over my chest. "I would have told you. I tell you everything."

"You mean you've never . . ."

"Let's just go back." I almost said *go home*. Because that was what I wanted to do. What I had to do.

Henry took a few steps toward me, paused, and then took a few steps more until he was an arm's length away. "Do you want me to kiss you?"

"What?"

"Maybe now's not the best time."

I had nothing to say to that. Instead, I walked around him, back into the small clearing where the lookout tower stood. He followed me, but when I finally spoke, I didn't face him.

"I'm leaving, Henry. Not tonight, because you're right, I'd get lost. But tomorrow, when it's light, I'm out of here."

"Please, don't."

"My mother and brother are out there. Even if your parents have blown everything out of proportion, which I'm assuming they have, I can't just stay here. If there's anything I can do for my mother and my brother, I'm going to do it."

"We can help them," Henry said. "From here. We'll get a message to them."

"You said that yesterday, but you haven't done anything. Besides, what good will that do?" My voice rose. "They can't just shut themselves up in the house. My mother has to go to work. They'll have to buy groceries." I stopped speaking because I was afraid I would cry.

Henry came over, and I let him take me in his arms. I hugged him back and let my tears drip down his neck.

His breath was warm against my ear. "Martin leaves the compound about once a week. He drives just close enough to civilization to check on news reports. I used his phone to text you."

"But what good will it do to send them a message? They can't come here. So what am I supposed to say—that this horrible disease is spreading and good luck to them?"

"No. I've thought about it. They can go to my house and wait this thing out. Peter's been in there already, right? Will he remember the security codes?"

"Probably not."

Henry said, "We can text them. The house has food and water, an air-filtration system, a bunch of medical supplies. They can live there for at least a month, probably two, without leaving."

I took a step back and looked at his face. Those sharp eyes set a little too close together, the straight eyebrows, the mouth that turned at the very corners.

"I don't trust you anymore," I said.

"I know. And I don't blame you. But this is the only chance, Daisy. If you go back . . . you could die. You could all die."

I nodded. Henry was right. I had no other choice.

Twenty-Eight

DAYS PASSED. HENRY worked in the garden or tended the bees while I took care of Tuck and Sassy. And by *took care of*, I mean was abused by, at least in the case of Tuck, who screamed, "GO AWAY!" every time he saw me and never passed up an opportunity to kick my shins or smack my face with his fat, sticky palm.

Gwendolyn and Martin spent their days upstairs, studying for tests they would probably never take. Their father drove off in his big pickup truck one morning. When he returned, he headed upstairs with the Hawkings. Later, I snuck into the bonus room. They'd given up on pushpins. Instead, there were numbers scrawled across the continents: 97,992 in North America, 27,133 in Europe, 175,114 in Asia.

Did those numbers represent animals? People? Illnesses? Deaths?

Were they actual cases or projections? The tension in the house had grown so thick, I didn't dare ask anyone.

That night, Mr. Waxweiler announced in his high voice, "The Platts and Wards won't be joining us. At least not soon. Perhaps not ever."

"Are they sheltering in place?" Gwendolyn asked.

"Yes."

"As we should have done," Mrs. Waxweiler said, sounding bitter.

Her husband ignored her. "There is an illness in the Platt family. Their youngest, Sebastian. Dr. Platt is ministering to him at home. No other family members have shown signs of infection."

"Yet," Mrs. Waxweiler muttered.

Later, when I was walking to the bus, I heard them in the side yard, arguing. "You promised there would be a doctor here!" Mrs. Waxweiler said. "We could be home right now, eating food from our stockpile, watching the news. . . ."

"Until they stop broadcasting," Mr. Waxweiler countered. "Or the power grid goes down. Eventually our food would run out. Or it would be stolen. We've got a week, maybe two, before civilization collapses. After that, there's no getting out of the cities. It'll be a war zone down there."

"But the cell phone towers are still working."

"Today they are. Tomorrow, who knows?"

Henry and I sat next to each other at meals, but I wouldn't look at him except to implore, *When?* If he made me wait much longer to get word to my mother and Peter, I would sneak off in the middle of the night. Sooner or later I'd hit a bigger road. I'd never find my way back to the spot where Peter had dropped me off, but at some point the dirt road in front of the compound had to join up to something bigger. Someone would drive by and help me.

Or, you know, leave my mutilated body on the side of the road. One of those.

In response to my question, Henry would give me a pleading, helpless look, and I'd go back to jabbing at whatever nonmeat items were on my plate. My clothes were getting so droopy, I needed a piece of string to hold up my shorts.

Nights, Henry had lookout duty, but he didn't ask me to join him. I would have said no. I think he knew that.

At last, on the evening after Mr. Waxweiler's announcement, Henry slipped me a note: *Meet at Martin's car—daybreak.*

———

Martin's car stood out as the only small vehicle in the compound. No duct tape or old bumper stickers marred the bright blue, two-door sedan. Inside, though, it was just as filthy as Peter's junky car. Crumbs and dust coated gray velour upholstery, while the floor lay buried under gas receipts, Subway wrappers, a Best Buy catalog, and two empty Starbucks cups, one marked *Martin*, the other *Sienna*.

It was still dark when we pulled out of the driveway. Martin kept the headlights off until we made it out of the compound gates. We drove slowly down the rough lane, Martin's shocks protesting. At last we turned onto the unpaved road that would take us out of the forest.

Martin plugged his iPod into the stereo. Soon, the car was filled with a hip-hop song that played so constantly last year, I thought I would never want to hear it again. Now it sounded like normal life. Like sanity. Like home.

After maybe five minutes, we passed the little clearing where I had left Peter. It seemed so long ago. We continued on and on, bouncing and swaying as the car twisted and turned through the mountains and along perilous cliffs. We saw no signs of humanity. Henry had been right. If I had fled the compound on foot, I really could have died.

At last, the road smoothed out. Then the trees thinned and the vista opened. The sun was just coming up. The pink sky lighting up the mountains was so beautiful, it made the scene look unreal.

When the road forked, Martin took a right. Soon, Lake Casitas shimmered in the early-morning light. Martin pulled over to the side of the road and turned off the engine. The music stopped.

"This is the magic spot. We should get reception here." It was the first thing anyone had said since we'd left the compound. Martin pulled a cheap phone from his pocket and pushed the power button. Outside, the sky gave way to shades of lavender and blue.

"Your parents let you keep your phone?" I asked from the back. Henry was in the front passenger seat, which made it easier to avoid eye contact.

"No way," Martin said. "My father canceled our plan. Because, you know, he didn't want the government using our GPS against us. Because we're so important that they'd want to track us down. Ugh. This thing is so slow." He shook the phone, as if that would make it load faster.

"Is that why your phone was disconnected, too?" I asked Henry.

"Yeah." He tried to make eye contact, but I turned my attention back to Martin.

"Your parents must have a phone. How else would they get their information?"

"My dad's got one, but it's not on a plan, and he only turns it on when he's at least twenty miles from the compound." Martin shook his head with disgust. "He loves all the fake military crap. The drills and the maps and the camo. My mom just went along with all the survivalist stuff because she figured it was just a hobby for my dad. Like fishing or golf."

"But it looks like maybe the preppers were right," I said.

Martin kept pushing at the buttons. "You can be right and still be crazy. You can be right and still forget what matters."

"I'm sorry about your dog," I said.

At first I didn't think he heard me. But then he let out a long, sad sigh. "Mabrey was such a good little guy. And he wasn't sick. There was no reason . . . no reason at all."

"Where'd you get that phone?" I asked.

"Target. Three months ago." Martin glanced back at me, a half smile on his face. "My mom said I was spending too much time texting and talking to my girlfriend. Talk about surveillance. She was supposedly worried that it might affect my grades, but it was obvious she just didn't like Sienna. I bought this phone so she couldn't track my calls."

"Sienna . . . is she on cheer?"

"Yeah."

Martin's girlfriend was a year ahead of me, but she was one of those people always surrounded by a pack of friends, her name constantly being shouted in the hallways. She had hair bleached a little too light for her olive skin, enormous brown eyes, and a loud laugh.

Martin said, "A signal—finally!"

"Can I call my mom now?" As soon as I said it, I realized just how afraid I was of making the call. Because what if she didn't pick up? What would that mean?

"Doubt the signal will be strong enough for a call. But you'll be able to get a text through. Let me see what Sienna says first."

He pressed the little buttons on the phone and frowned. "Nice," he said, voice tight with sarcasm.

"What?" Henry asked.

"It's an old text, but Sienna said she forgives me for bailing on Homecoming because it's been canceled anyway. Does she really . . . *oh my God!*"

"What?"

"Oh no. *No.*"

"What?"

Martin looked up from the phone, eyes wide with horror. "You know a guy named Rudy Barretta? Your grade, honors kid?"

"Yeah. We were lab partners freshman year."

"He's dead." His words hung in the air.

Moments passed before any of us could speak. Rudy Barretta, dead? It was unthinkable. I'd just seen him a couple of weeks ago. He once asked me to a dance. Rudy Barretta could not be dead! The numbers and pushpins on the maps had been frightening, but this name, this face, made the whole thing real.

"Anyone else?" Henry asked at last.

Martin blinked at the phone. "Sienna sent me a bunch of texts. I've only read the first two." Hands trembling, he poked at the buttons.

"Mrs. Jessup has it, too. You know the English teacher? She's— let me check Sienna's next text. . . . *Crap.*" He let the phone fall in his lap and stared first at Henry and then at me as if we could say something to make it all better. "Gone."

"So it's really happening?" I said. "In school? At home?"

Martin read through all of Sienna's texts, reporting as he went.

One freshman and two sophomores at our school were dead; eight others were in the hospital. All local schools were closed until further notice.

Rudy Barretta's only sister, a freshman at Cal State Fullerton— gone. There would be no funeral. No one would come. Too dangerous.

Hospitals overwhelmed. Restaurants closed. Mall open for now but probably not much longer. No bottled water in the stores. No Purell. A run on first-aid kits, canned foods, ice.

"Why ice?" I asked.

"In case the power goes out."

"Why would the power go out?"

Henry explained, "If things get bad enough, people will refuse to go to work. The grid would go down because there'd be no one there to keep things running. From there, it's just a hop, skip, and jump to complete economic collapse."

"So . . . it really is the end of the world?"

Martin shook his head. "No."

"Not yet," Henry said.

"I need to talk to my mother." My voice was shrill.

"Doubt the call will go through, but you can try." Martin handed his phone back to me.

Hands shaking, I thumbed in my mother's number, but Martin was right. Reception was sketchy, and it didn't connect. I switched to texting mode, adding Peter to the message before realizing that I didn't have the vaguest idea what I was supposed to say to them.

Hi, I began. And then I deleted it.

I miss you, I tried next. No.

Sorry . . . but that made it sound like I had chosen to leave them. I would never desert my family on purpose.

At last I went with this: I am safe and pray you are too. Henry's house has everything you need. Go there and don't leave. I will come home as soon as I can. I love you. Daisy

I added the security system codes and then hit the send button. And then I sent them another message: Please text back so I know you are okay.

After I passed the phone back, Martin hunched over it for a long time, sending a long text to Sienna.

"She texted back!" he said.

"My mom?" Hope washed over me like a fever.

"No—Sienna. Thank God, she's okay."

Henry turned to face me. At last I met his eyes. In that moment, I understood why his parents had run away. I couldn't bear losing Peter and my mother. I'd do anything to save them.

"Sienna's got a sore throat. She's freaking out." Martin put his hand over his mouth and closed his eyes.

I looked out the window. The sun had fully risen over the mountains. It was going to be a beautiful day.

At last, Martin turned the engine back on and plugged his iPod back into the radio. Hip-hop filled the car, but this time it didn't make me feel normal. Nothing could.

Out on the road, Martin continued in the direction we had been heading, around the far side of Lake Casitas, away from the forest. Down. "I need to talk to her," he said. "We'll get better reception farther down the mountain."

Soon, we passed a few low houses, and Martin pulled into a dinky gas station. After passing bills to an attendant who opened the door just a crack, Martin filled his car tank. Then he retrieved two plastic red gas cans out of the trunk and filled them as well.

Henry said, "Mr. Waxweiler said a lot of places have run out of gas. We're lucky to get some."

"Yeah. I'm feeling really lucky right now."

"They're going to be okay." Henry offered his hand, but I refused to take it.

"You don't know that." My voice was hoarse. "All you know is that you're going to be okay, and your family is safe. But my family, the rest of the world . . ."

Martin got back in the car and pulled his cell phone from his pocket.

"Did my mother text back? Or my brother?"

"No. Sorry."

He started up the car and pulled back out to the road, heading down, down—toward civilization and the sea.

Twenty-Nine

WE CONTINUED DOWN the winding road, toward the ocean. Toward freeways and stores and schools. Toward people.

A pickup truck passed us. "That's the first car we've seen in a while," I said.

Martin said, "Just wait. When everybody decides it's time to G-O-O-D, this road will be jammed."

"I forget what that stands for."

"Get out of Dodge."

I gazed out at the empty road. "What good would it do to take off for the mountains if you don't have any place to go once you get there?"

"It could get dangerous in town," Martin said. "Lootings, shootings. Plus, people will want to get away from the epidemic. They'll figure they've got less chance of getting sick in a place with no people, even if that means sleeping in tents and trying to survive off the land."

"Did you ask Sienna to come with you?" I asked.

"I asked her," Martin said. "My parents almost killed me, but I couldn't just leave without saying anything."

"She said no?"

"She was mostly worried about what everyone was going to say when I disappeared like that. She didn't believe things could get this bad. But then, neither did I. I didn't blame her for not leaving town. If it had been up to me, I would have stayed, too."

At the bottom of the mountain, we saw signs for the 101 freeway. Martin drove past the ramps. We rounded a bend, and the ocean spread out below us, deep blue and sparkling. We continued along the frontage road.

I opened my window. Salty air with a touch of fog brushed my face. The road wasn't crowded, but there were other people out, all going about their daily business in delivery trucks and SUVs and little sedans.

Just as I had almost convinced myself that things weren't too bad, I saw a hand-painted sign in front of a gas station that said NO GAS. Next to it was a convenience store, also with a sign: NO CASH. NO BOTTLED WATER. NO PROPANE. CLOSED UNTIL FURTHER NOTICE. STAY SAFE!

Martin turned into a quiet residential area of tiny bungalows. He pulled over and got out of the car to phone Sienna. Mad Plague could be transmitted through droplets in the air, but the street was deserted except for a few stray dogs.

That was odd. Occasionally a dog got out of its yard and ran loose in the streets, but never had I seen more than one loose dog out alone.

"People are afraid of fleas," Henry said. "So they're setting their animals loose."

"What about shelters?"

"They're probably full. Or closed."

I twisted around in time to see a little terrier paw at some garbage cans. It took all my strength not to leap out of the car and rescue the little guy. But what good would that do? Mr. and Mrs. Waxweiler abandoned their own dog. If I tried to bring a stray into the compound, it would be banished—or worse. My mother never let us a have a dog because she said it wasn't fair to leave it alone all day. But if we'd gotten one, she never would have deserted it, that much I knew.

Across the street, a woman walked by, hauling grocery bags. That seemed encouraging: Stores were open; people were out. Plus, she wasn't near enough to Martin to pose a threat.

Then I noticed that that the woman was wearing a surgical mask. I rolled up my window.

Martin got back in the car. "Sienna doesn't have a fever. And she thinks maybe the sore throat is because she's been crying so much. Everyone in her family is fine so far, but they've been quarantined because one of her mother's coworkers is sick."

For the first time, I noticed a yellow sheet of paper taped to the front door of the nearest bungalow. The house across the street had one as well.

"When does the quarantine end?"

"If no one shows any symptoms after a week, they can leave the house. Not that they'll want to."

"Can I call my mother?"

The phone rang four times and went to voice mail. I tried Peter:

no answer. Then I tried my mother one more time before giving up. I gave the phone back to Martin.

"Sorry."

I nodded. If I tried to speak, I'd probably cry.

"As long as we're down here, let's go for a ride," Martin said.

We got on the 101 freeway and drove up the coast, the Pacific Ocean on our left, the Santa Ynez Mountains on our right. Soon, the city of Santa Barbara, with its white stucco buildings, red roofs, and palm trees, rose above us like a misplaced Mediterranean dream. It looked like the kind of place where everybody was happy all the time, where nothing could ever go wrong.

Martin took an exit into the city, and we drove through quiet streets lined with pretty pastel houses landscaped with roses and bougainvillea, birds-of-paradise, and palms. About every fifth house had a yellow quarantine notice on the front door.

When we spied an H street sign, Martin followed it to a hospital. We couldn't get close to the building because so many cars were double-parked on the street. In the parking lot, tents had been set up to treat the overflow of patients. And still there wasn't enough room for the stricken: A long line snaked around the rows of cars. Medical workers in hazmat suits wound their way around the crowd with water and blankets, clipboards and blood pressure cuffs.

"They didn't run away," I said.

"Who?"

"The hospital workers."

Henry shook his head. "They'll wish they had."

"Not necessarily," Martin said. "At least they won't have to live with the guilt."

Before I knew it, I was crying. And I hate to cry. Henry leaned over the front seat to rub my shoulder. "It's okay. Everything is going to be okay."

I shook my head: Nothing would ever be okay again. I took deep breaths until I managed to control myself, because really, I had no right to feel bad when all these people were suffering and I was safe. My mother and Peter would go to Henry's house. They would get through this. We all would. Anything else was unthinkable.

Soon, we were back on the 101. I thought I saw seals in the waves, but no: They were surfers, still going about the business of living, refusing to give in to panic and fear.

At a town called Summerland, Martin took the exit. Right off the highway, an empty parking lot overlooked a deserted beach. Steep wooden steps led to coarse sand below. It was breezy down there. The air felt so pure—cool and clean. The roar of crashing waves soothed me. Miles out, oil rigs stood against the horizon like alien spaceships. I remembered Peter joking about alien abductions. An alien abduction was starting to sound like a good thing.

I pulled off my sneakers and walked to the water's edge. Icy water slid up over my feet and then sloshed back into the sea. Parallel to the shore, a dolphin arced above the surface and dove back down in a single, fluid motion. Another followed, and another. Dolphins traveled in pods. If one member of the pod got ill, would the others desert it?

Henry came up beside me. We stood there silently, squinting at the brilliant water, letting the waves run over our feet and soak the bottom of his jeans. He rolled up his sleeves. There were no dogs on the beach, no risk of flea bites.

I said, "Are you going to run into the water like you did at the pond?"

Out where the dolphins had been, a pelican soared a few feet above the water, looking for fish, seeing nothing.

"I will if you will," he said.

I shook my head. "There's no point."

In front of us, the ocean breathed in and out, maintaining the rhythm it had established long before humanity even existed. The ocean would always be here, even when we were not. That was something.

Henry reached out his hand. I took it and held on for dear life.

Thirty

THEY WERE WAITING for us when we got back. The Waxweiler and
Hawking parents stood guard on the front steps, between the ridiculous columns. Martin took his time parking the bright blue car in
its usual spot next to the front of the house. He even let the song on
his iPod finish before turning off the ignition.

Henry got out first and moved his seat forward so I could
squeeze out of the backseat. The three of us walked to the house
together, stopping a few paces before the steps.

Mrs. Waxweiler spoke first, her voice quavering with anxiety
and going up at the end, as if she were asking a question. "You need
to tell us when you are going to take off like that, Martin?"

Head down, Martin stomped up the steps. He was navigating
his way around the adults when his father grabbed his arm. Martin
was tall, but his father was huge.

"Wait a minute, young man!" Mr. Waxweiler said. "You owe us an explanation."

Martin tilted his chin up and narrowed his eyes. "I went to get gas. Before all the pumps run out."

"You were gone for hours."

"We had to go into town," Martin lied. "Everything else was closed."

Fear replaced panic on Mr. Waxweiler's wide face. "Did you . . ."

"I left the money outside the attendant's station. Like you taught me. And I used a paper towel to pick up the pump." He had done neither of those things.

"Did you talk to anyone?" Mr. Waxweiler asked.

"No."

"Did you see anything?"

"We just got the gas and came back. I'll be in my room."

Mr. and Mrs. Waxweiler hesitated for a moment, and then they followed their son inside, leaving a dangerous stillness in their wake.

Hands clenched at his sides, Mr. Hawking glared at Henry, while his wife trained her evil eyes on me.

"You. Can't. Do. That," Mr. Hawking said. "*Ever.*"

"Was this Daisy's idea?" Mrs. Hawking asked. "Because we have only allowed her to remain here because she assured us that—"

"Why do you blame everything on Daisy?" Henry said.

"People are dying!" I said. "Don't you understand that?" These people didn't scare me anymore.

"Of course I understand!" Mrs. Hawking's face contorted. "You think you're the only one who has family out there? My cousin and her kids . . . I begged them to come with us, but . . ." She shook her head.

"Are they okay?" Henry asked.

"I don't know," she whispered.

"We must focus on the present!" Mr. Hawking boomed. "On the tasks at hand. That is the only way we will get through this. And we *will* get through it, make no mistake. Henry, you were assigned to beekeeping duty this morning. You're late."

He turned and walked into the house. His wife, her eyes shiny from tears she refused to spill, gave me a final murderous look before following him.

"You should have left me on the beach," I told Henry.

"I'll never leave you."

Thirty-One

"MOVE OUT! MOVE out! Move out! Move out!"

It was the middle of the murky, moonless night, and a man was yelling. I sat up and whacked my head on the roof.

"Ow!"

"Watch your head," Kirsten said.

"What's going on?"

"Bugout drill." She had twisty pink curlers in her hair. She pulled a sweatshirt over her pajamas, careful not to mess up her handiwork.

"But haven't we already bugged out? Isn't this compound the bugout location?"

"Yeah, but we need to practice in case we ever have to BO from the BOL."

My eyelids were heavy, and sheer exhaustion was pinning me to the thin mattress. "Would anyone notice if I just didn't show up?"

Kirsten reached under her bunk and pulled out a green backpack. "Oh, they'd notice. Believe me."

I was the last one off the bus. The kids, illuminated by a cluster of LED lanterns, stood in line right in front of the putrid animal spa.

Mr. Waxweiler loomed over the kids, stopwatch in hand. When I took my place at the end of the line, next to one of the little kids, he pressed the watch and said, "Seven minutes. Too slow!"

"Daisy held us up," said Kadence, who seemed to grow more weaselly every day.

Mr. Waxweiler strode down the line. "We are each of us, in the community, only as strong as our weakest member."

Wow, in just a couple of weeks, I had gone from being an interloper to the weakest link. That was what I called progress.

I leaned forward and checked the others. I was not the last to show up, after all. Martin had stayed in bed, and his parents were pretending not to notice. Martin was my new role model.

"BOB inspection. Gwennie, you take the lead."

Mr. Dunkle emerged from the shadows. "It's Kyle's turn to be squad leader."

Gwendolyn's father held himself up even taller. "Kyle will lead the next evacuation drill; Gwennie's in charge of inspections. We talked about this."

"You talked. I didn't agree."

Without answering, Mr. Waxweiler turned his back to the other man and faced his daughter. "Begin, Gwennie."

Mr. Dunkle squeezed his hands into fists. Meanwhile, Gwendolyn took two steps forward, turned in perfect drill formation, and strode to the end of the line—otherwise known as me.

"Where's your BOB?" she demanded.

"I don't have a Bob."

"Bug. Out. Bag."

"I know what it stands for. But I don't have one."

Gwendolyn was mad at us for leaving her behind when we'd gone down the mountain. Now, she frowned. I thought she would yell. Instead, she said, "Weakest link!" and moved on to seven-year-old Kelli-Lynn, who was wearing Cinderella jammies with pink hiking boots.

"Kelli-Lynn!"

"Yes sir! Ma'am!"

"Squad leader."

"Yes, squaw leader!"

"Open your BOB!"

"Yes, squaw leader!"

Kelli-Lynn squatted down and unzipped her Spider-Man backpack, probably a hand-me-down from one of her brothers. Or maybe it had been her choice. For a kid who had been exposed to very little television, she showed a showed a remarkable affinity for kiddie pop culture.

Kelli-Lynn lined up her survival items on the dusty ground. There were three ready-to-eat meals, a Hello Kitty aluminum water bottle, a plastic bag filled with iodine tablets. There was a thin *Frozen* blanket, a big black trash bag that could be used as a tarp, tent, or poncho. Or even a trash bag. There were ziplock bags, twine, aluminum foil, a tiny screwdriver, bandages, antibiotic cream, some tape, and thumbtacks.

The contents of Kelli-Lynn's bugout bag bore a remarkable resemblance to our kitchen junk drawer at home.

"Okay—assessment," Gwendolyn barked. "Henry?"

"Um . . . looks good to me." He was in the middle of the line, wearing drawstring pants and a white T-shirt. His hair stuck up at funny angles, and he was blinking with fatigue.

He looks cute, I thought involuntarily. Right away another part of my brain jumped in with, *This is no time to start thinking that way*. And then I turned my attention back on the BOB checks because the argument in my head was almost as annoying as Gwendolyn.

"Keanu!" she barked. "What is missing from Kelli-Lynn's BOB bag?"

"Fire starter!" Keanu squealed. Keanu had one of those nails-on-chalkboard voices that would have been annoying coming from an eleven-year-old girl in glitter jeans, but from a boy of the same age in camo fatigues, it was downright unsettling.

"Yes!" Gwendolyn said.

"And a knife!" Keanu screeched.

"Yes again!"

"But she's seven," I said, because somebody had to.

"I'll be eight in April." Kelli-Lynn clutched her *Frozen* blankie for emphasis.

"Which means that right now you're seven." I get points for not adding, *And in ten years you'll be seventeen, and in twenty-five years you'll be thirty-two. And then you can be trusted with sharp objects and pyrotechnics, but right now you should stick to fairy wands.*

Gwendolyn spun around to face Kelli-Lynn's father, clasping her hands behind her as a sign of respect or maybe as a way to keep her hands warm. "Mr. Dunkle, has Kelli-Lynn received fire and knife safety training?"

"Yeah. Course. All my kids is trained from when they're little."

Gwendolyn spun again to face the formation. Gwendolyn needed to get back to her drill squad, almost as much as she needed her dog.

At the thought of all the abandoned dogs we had seen, sadness pierced through my exhaustion. When I didn't think about what was happening outside this weird little village, it felt like we were playing a game. Soldiers or scouts or something. But this was real. Very, very real.

Gwendolyn advised little Kelli-Lynn to fill her Spider-Man bag with matches and a Swiss army knife. Then she took inventory of Killer's bag—all good except she told him he was "maybe a little heavy on the weapons." Because, really, does a thirteen-year-old need a hunting knife, a Swiss army knife, *and* a bow and arrow?

Mr. Dunkle chuckled. "What he really wants in his BOB is an AK-47."

It was more of the same for the next couple of bugout bags. Henry's BOB, presumably packed before he left home, included a photo of us on the Hermosa Beach pier. He didn't say anything about the picture, just put it on the dirt between his power bars and matches.

Gwendolyn nodded at Henry's stash, and he stuffed everything back inside. The inspections were almost complete. Maybe I'd get some sleep, after all.

And then Gwendolyn reached Kirsten. Kirsten was old enough and smart enough to have all the basics: the MREs, the water-filtration system, first-aid kit, soap, blanket, matches, knife, etc.

But the fun came when she pulled out the last items from her raggedy black backpack and placed them on the dirt:

- Fuchsia nail polish
- Polish remover pads
- Scented moisturizer
- Plumping lip gloss
- Eyelash thickener
- Mascara

"There." She stood up and dusted her hands off.

"Can you tell me . . ." Gwendolyn was at a loss for words. I thought the day would never come. "What is the purpose of . . . those things?"

Kirsten cocked her head to one side. "The nail polish? It's for painting my nails, and the remover is for taking it off when it gets chipped. My eyelashes are really thin, which is why I need the thickener, and then once that dries—"

"I understand what these things *are*," Gwendolyn interrupted. "But the BOB is for items essential to survival."

Mr. Dunkle erupted. "Don't you go telling my girl what she can and can't pack! She's been learning wilderness survival skills since she was born. Not like you, with your weekend camping trips and your fancy school!"

If our school was fancy, I'd hate to see a plain one.

Mr. Waxweiler came to his daughter's defense. "Gwendolyn has been carefully trained in outdoor survival skills as well as leadership techniques."

"Oh yeah? You drop my kids and your kids in the middle of nowhere, with no food, no water supplies, no *nothing*, then you leave them there a few days, a week, and see who comes out alive!"

We could only hope he meant this as a hypothetical situation.

Mr. Dunkle pointed to the house. "You got your boy up there in his nice comfy room, can't be bothered to do his part for the community, can't even be bothered to get out of bed, and—"

"Gwendolyn, continue." Mr. Waxweiler, standing even taller than usual, faced his daughter. She looked uncomfortable. No, she looked scared. But to her credit, she carried on, her voice quavering only a little.

"Keanu? Can you show us what's in your bag?"

Before Keanu could comply, Mr. Dunkle threw something on the ground—I think it was a water bottle—and shouted, "This is bull crap!" He stormed off, pausing only to turn around and say to his children, "Back to bed."

The Dunklings scattered, leaving Gwendolyn and Henry looking uncertain and Mr. Waxweiler like his head might pop off his neck.

"He lied about being in the Special Forces," Mr. Waxweiler said, his jaw tight, his voice even higher than usual. "Should've known. Should've checked. A guy like that . . ." He shook his head.

"You mean Mr. Dunkle?" Gwendolyn asked.

Her father nodded.

"But . . . he was in the army, right?"

"Not sure." He took a deep breath, held it, and let out a rush of air. "Guess it doesn't matter. Not anymore."

"Are we going to be okay?" Gwendolyn's voice cracked.

Her father strode over to her and took her in his arms. Immediately she dissolved into sobs.

"I'll protect you," he murmured. "I promise you that. No matter what happens, I won't let anything or anyone hurt you."

I wondered what my father, far away in North Carolina, was

doing to protect his second family. I wondered if he was worried about me. I tried to imagine him here, on the compound, but it was useless. It had been years since his last visit. I couldn't even picture his face.

I felt tears coming. I squeezed my eyes shut. Again, I tried to conjure up my father's face. Again, I failed.

Warm arms encircled me—not in my imagination, but right here. I put my arms around Henry's neck and let the tears fall.

Thirty-Two

I DON'T EVEN know if I fully made it back to sleep before the next interruption.

"Move out! Move out! Move out!"

The shouts didn't startle me as much as the first time, but once again I sat up too quickly and, "Ow!"

"Watch your head," Kirsten chirped from below.

I might have laughed, but I was too tired and too annoyed. Also, it really hurt. I rubbed my forehead, grabbed my pink sneakers, and slid off the bunk, careful to keep my head out of the range of the bus roof.

It was still dark outside. No orderly lineup this time: Instead, the boy Dunkles, all wearing their usual camouflage, stood in a clump right outside the bus, their bugout bags scattered on the ground. One by one, the girls joined the crowd.

Mr. and Mrs. Dunkle were there, along with the twins. When Tuck saw me, he screamed and buried his face in his mother's shoulder. It made me feel special.

Once the bus was empty, Kyle took a few steps away from the crowd and shouted, "Evacuation drill! Count off!"

In no particular order, his siblings began counting off:

"One!"

"Two!"

At three, everything fell apart. Keanu and Kelli-Lynn, at opposite sides of the clump, tried to claim the number at the exact same moment, which sparked an argument about family favoritism and something that happened on a camping trip back when they lived in Temecula. Their mother told Keanu to stop being a troublemaker and Kelli-Lynn to stop being a whiner and Kyle to get his finger out of his nose and take control of his troops.

Kyle was not actually picking his nose; it was just an expression.

So then Kyle made everyone get in an actual line and start the count-off all over again.

I thought, *I could be sleeping right now.*

"One!"

"Two!"

"Three!"

And so on until they reached me (I was seven), and I said, "Where's Henry?"

"Count off!"

"Seven-where's-Henry? And Gwendolyn? And their parents?"

Mr. Dunkle said, "They're coming later. Now the rest of you, count off!"

"Eight!"

"Nine!"

And so on up to eleven, which included everyone except Kyle.

"All accounted for!" Kyle said, even though we'd already established that several people were missing.

Mrs. Dunkle came over to me with a big backpack thing. "Put this on."

Tuck was still attached to her neck, looking like he was trying to burrow back into her body via her windpipe.

For a moment I thought that Mrs. Dunkle had assembled a bugout bag for me. *She likes me after, all!* And then I realized that the backpack thing was a baby carrier.

There was no point protesting. Tuck would howl enough for the two of us. I slipped the contraption onto my back and fiddled with the straps, moving as slowly as possible to postpone the inevitable.

The instant the pack was secure, Mrs. Dunkle peeled the screaming, heaving he-devil from her body and shoved him into the carrier. I almost toppled backward, he was so heavy. The way he kicked my ribs and screamed in my ear, I thought things couldn't get worse. And then he grabbed a handful of my hair and yanked. Hard.

Karessa wandered over, sweet Sassy strapped to her back. Sassy smiled and waved at me. I smiled and waved back. (See? I'm not that bad with kids.) And then Tuck yanked my hair again.

"Ow!"

He whacked my head.

Karessa said, "Kentucky gets cranky when he's tired, but he'll fall asleep when we start hiking."

"Where are we going?"

"Into the wilderness." That didn't exactly narrow things down.

"But why?"

"This is an evacuation drill. We do them every couple months. Keeps us ready for the next time we have to G-O-O-D."

"Get out of Dodge?" I said, checking.

"Right!" She gave me a smile that said *Congratulations! Now you're one of us!*

What I really wanted was to GBTD—get *back* to Dodge. Though I'd settle for GBTS—get back to sleep.

The sky was changing colors, shades of gray seeping into the blackness. The Dunkle family was snaking around the empty pool and the vegetable garden to the very back of the yard and through the gate. I turned around to check the house. It was dark.

Tuck yanked my hair. "Guh!" he said.

And so I went.

Thirty-Three

TUCK FELL ASLEEP just before the sun came up. I don't know how long we had been hiking. It felt like an hour, but it was probably less than that. Or maybe it was more—I'd lost all sense of time in the mountains. With no cell phone, no computer, no alarm, or classroom bells, one moment stretched into the next in an endless stretch of despair divided only by meals and darkness.

With Kyle in the lead, we came to a hillside covered with brush. It wasn't that steep, but Tuck's weight made me feel like I was drowning. The heat hadn't even set in, but already sweat streamed down my face. At a boulder, I paused to catch my breath.

A couple of Dunklings scampered around. When Karessa reached the boulder, she paused to readjust her straps. Sassy held up her arms to give me a two-handed wave.

I lacked the strength to wave back. I tried to smile, but even that was too much of an effort. My breathing came in labored gasps. If we didn't reach our destination soon, they'd have to leave me behind. At this point, I didn't even mind being left for dead as long as someone removed Tuck before he started kicking me in the head. That was not a final memory I would cherish.

Karessa didn't even look winded. When she saw what a sweaty mess I was, she bit her lip with concern. "I need to ask. Are you pregnant?"

I struggled for breath. "Am I . . . what?"

"With child. You look a little . . . ill. My dad says that all the teenagers in American high schools engage in premarital sex."

I blinked in astonishment (and also to keep a big drop of sweat out of my eyes). "I'm not . . . I don't engage in . . . no."

Her mouth made an O. Then: "It must be hard to resist all that peer pressure."

"You have no idea."

We caught up with the others, climbed over some rocks, and went down a small slope to find Kyle sitting on his pack in front of a cave, shirt off, sunning himself.

Beyond the mouth of the cave, there was nothing but blackness. And probably bats. And tarantulas. And maybe mummies. The only sort-of cave I'd ever encountered was in the Indiana Jones ride at Disneyland, and even that freaked me out.

Kirsten lifted Sassy out of Karessa's pack and placed her on a blanket with some plastic spoons. She immediately began singing.

My back and shoulders ached. I had to get Tuck on the ground as quickly as possible, but I didn't know how to manage it without waking him. Fortunately, Kirsten and Karessa, who had been practicing the maneuver since they'd graduated from riding in the packs themselves, managed to unstrap me and lower the carrier without disturbing their youngest brother. A metal stand at the bottom of the carrier popped open, allowing them to balance the whole child-and-contraption unit on the ground like a decorative plant.

I collapsed near Tuck. Immediately, an ant crawled on my leg, but I was too tired to flick it off.

Mr. Dunkle chucked his enormous army pack on the ground and went over to stand above Kyle. He crossed his arms over his chest. "Lead 'em off, son."

With a barely perceptible eye roll, Kyle pushed himself to his feet and dusted his hands on his camo pants. He seemed in no hurry to lead us off in whatever he was supposed to be leading us off in.

He said, "Okay, yeah, so. We've evacuated. What's the first thing we need to—"

"Find water!" Keanu screeched before Kyle even finished speaking, like he was on a game show and there was a prize for being the first to answer.

"No," Kyle said. "Kelli-Lynn?"

Kelli-Lynn paused from trying to catch a butterfly. "Get shelter." She went back to bug hunting.

"We already *have* shelter," Keanu protested in that awful voice. "The *cave.* So next comes *water.*"

"You wanna sleep in that cave the way it is now?" Kyle asked.

Keanu tilted his chin up. "Sure."

"Why don't you go in there, then. Tell me how it looks."

Keanu stomped off into the darkness.

"Wait," I said. "We're not really going to stay out here overnight?"

Where was Henry?

Kirsten raised her eyebrows. Everyone else ignored me.

Keanu emerged from the cave.

"Well?" Kyle asked.

Keanu crossed his arms over his skinny chest. "Looks fine to me."

"You sleep on the wet ground, then," Kyle said. "Rest of us is gonna need some ground cover."

"It ain't wet!" Keanu said.

"Yeah?" Kyle said. "You just wait till it's the middle of the night. You see if it's dry enough. And warm enough."

"No, seriously," I said to Kirsten. "We are going back to the compound before dark, right?" After all, I had a perfectly nice bus waiting for me. And a smelly, scratchy blanket. And a mattress that felt like it had been stuffed with lint balls from the dryer. I missed them!

"Could be out here for days," she said.

"Days?"

"Last evacuation drill lasted almost a week. And it was raining. This is what we do instead of taking vacations or going to the mall or doing whatever it is normal families do."

I was too upset about the prospect of being stuck out here to fully appreciate that Kirsten had been the first to acknowledge that her family was not normal.

Once Kyle and Keanu finished sparring and Keanu stomped off to the cave, we determined the group's plan of action:

1. Establish shelter.
2. Find water.
3. Build a fire.
4. Find food.

We established shelter by hauling our crap into the cave and laying tarps down. It took maybe forty-five seconds. Keanu was right to sulk. Next on the agenda was finding water, but since I was the day-cave director (har, har), I got to stay back with Kirsten to watch Sassy and Tuck, who thankfully remained unconscious.

When the others were gone, Kirsten and I settled ourselves against the rock wall, the sun on our faces. Birdsong and eucalyptus filled the air.

"So what's school like?" Kirsten asked.

"You mean, is everyone pregnant and on drugs? Because Karessa asked me that, and—no."

She smiled. "Karessa would ask that. I just meant . . . what's it like? Going to parties and football games and all that stuff."

I shrugged. "I don't get invited to a lot of parties. Which is okay. That's not really my thing unless they're, like, board game parties, but the only person besides me who is dorky enough to play board games is Henry, and the two of us don't make a party. Except, in some ways I guess we do. It feels like a party when I'm with him. Used to, anyway."

"Are you in love with Henry?"

"No!" I wasn't, was I?

"I think he's in love with you."

I shook my head. Henry couldn't be in love with me. That would ruin everything. Not that there was much left to ruin.

Fortunately, Kirsten was more interested in life in the outside world than she was in Henry. "Do you go to football games? Are you a cheerleader?"

"Ha! No. I'm not a cheerleader. I went to a couple of games my freshman year." I was about to say that I found them kind of boring so I left early, but there was something so eager and hopeful about her face. I didn't want to disappoint.

"Was it fun?" she asked.

"Oh, sure," I said. "People wear the school colors, and the band plays fight songs, and everyone cheers along. And if your team wins, you jump up and down and feel proud like you had something to do with it because it's *your team*, but if they lose it's not the end of the world, you know?"

Note to self: Stop using phrases like "the end of the world."

She sighed. "I wish I could have gone to a high school."

"It's not that great," I said. And then I thought about Kirsten's little world and thought: *Yes, it is.* "Have you ever gone to a regular school?"

"For a little while. In elementary school. We were living in Arizona, and me and Karessa were still too young to take care of the babies. I don't remember much, just that I had my own locker for my jacket and that we made paper turkeys for Thanksgiving. But then we moved to Nevada, and the kids were really rough because most of them came from single-parent families. Ever since then we've been homeschooled."

I waited for Kirsten to realize that, oh yeah, I was the child of a single parent . . . but she didn't. So instead I asked, "Have you moved a lot?"

"Like every year or two."

"Seriously?"

"We either follow the work or run from the trouble. That's what my dad says. I like your hair."

"What? Oh." I examined the cherry-red ends. They were a lot lighter than before. "Too bad there's no Kool-Aid out here. We could do yours. Of course, your parents would throw a fit."

She snorted. "Doubt they'd even notice."

"It seems like they're pretty strict."

She shrugged. "We have to do what they tell us to do. Clean and cook and take care of the little ones and whatever. But besides that, we can do pretty much anything. Course, there isn't much trouble to get into out here."

"Argh!" Something stung my ankle. I flicked away a tiny red ant. I was just about to settle back against the warm rock when Tuck stirred; my outburst had woken him up.

His eyes flickered open. He looked around, and then he saw me. So of course he screamed.

"Party's over," Kirsten said, pushing herself off the ground.

Thirty-Four

WE SLEPT IN the cave. Well, other people slept. I just lay there shivering, wondering what Henry was doing right now and trying to decide whether I hated Mr. Dunkle even more than I hated his wife.

"Where's your BOB at?" Mr. Dunkle had asked when everyone was settling down for the night and I requested a blanket.

"I don't have one."

"Guess you won't be making that mistake again." He shimmied into his puffy sleeping bag.

"I couldn't have carried a Bob up here anyway because I had *your child* on my back," I called after him.

He ignored me, so I added, "And you shouldn't end a sentence with a preposition!" It probably didn't help my cause, but it made me feel better.

The Hawking and Waxweiler families weren't coming tonight,

Mr. Dunkle had told me at dinner. (And by *dinner* I mean tearing open the meals ready to eat, if you had them in your bugout bag. Which, of course, I didn't.)

Between bites of stroganoff, Mr. Dunkle let me know what he thought of his employers: "Too soft for real survival training like this. Know what I call them kind? REI preppers. Because they think the best way to prepare is by shopping. And by paying people who know what they're doing. Me and my kids, we're the real deal. When TSHTF for real, who's gonna be left standing? Not them suburbanites."

"Why am I here, then?" I asked. "You could have left me back at the compound."

He sneered. "Think I wanted you to come? Mr. and Mrs. Hawking, they pretty much begged me to take you away."

Mrs. Hawking had always been clear about her disdain for me. Still, that hurt.

"Are they going to meet us here tomorrow?" I asked.

He shrugged. "Dunno. Maybe."

Now, in the cave, which was dark except for one small lantern, Kirsten shared her ground tarp, and Karessa lent me a couple of pieces of clothing to drape over myself for warmth. But it wasn't enough. I was exhausted, but I was too cold and uncomfortable to sleep. I wanted to cry but that would only stuff up my nose, and I didn't have a tissue.

I want to go home, the voice in my head pleaded. I closed my eyes and tried to picture my bedroom. Instead, a long-buried memory bubbled to the surface.

When I was in the third grade, this girl in my class, Kimberly Kelton, had a big sleepover. I didn't want to go, but my mother said it would be good for me make some friends besides Jennifer Park, who was in a different class that year. (I had lots of friends. It just happened that most of them were imaginary.) So we went to Target, where we bought a bubble machine for Kimberly and a pink sleeping bag for me.

At the party, I discovered that the bubble machine required batteries and that everyone in third grade knows that pink is no longer cool. At least I hadn't brought along the stuffed kitty that I normally slept with.

But it wasn't so bad. After bowling, we came back to the house to gorge on a sheet cake decorated with Kimberly's edible photograph. There was a piñata and a game that hooked up to the television and taught you how to dance. I didn't talk much to the other girls, but I had fun anyway.

At midnight, Kimberly's mom, Mrs. Kelton, told us to brush our teeth, put on our pajamas, and spread out our sleeping bags. And still, it wasn't too bad. Everyone was nice, and I liked the gossip and ghost stories. But after a while, the whispers quieted down. One by one, the other girls fell asleep.

Except me. The floor was so hard. I couldn't get comfortable. The girl next to me snored. I wanted to go home. No, I *needed* to go home.

At last, I got up and crept through the house. Mrs. Kelton had left a lot of lights on in case anyone had to go to the bathroom. The clock on the kitchen wall said 2:20 a.m. There was a phone on the counter.

My mother answered on the third ring.

"Mom?" My voice quavered.

"Daisy? Are you okay?"

"No."

"You want me to come get you?"

"Yes."

Ten minutes later, her headlights shone outside the house. She was still in her pajamas, and her hair, normally held back in a braid, fell over her shoulders. My favorite stuffed kitty sat in the passenger seat, waiting for me.

"I'm sorry I woke you up," I said, blinking back a tear.

"I'll always come if you need me. You know that." She hugged me and kissed the top of my head. Then she took me home and put me to bed, where I stayed warm and cozy till early the next afternoon.

If only I could call my mother now. She would come get me, if only she knew where I was.

"I need you, Mom," I whispered, in the darkness of the cave.

Thirty-Five

SOMEHOW, I MANAGED to sleep, if fitfully. The sun, streaming through the mouth of the cave, woke me. My entire body hurt, and I was so thirsty.

Next to me on the tarp, Kirsten was still out cold. I got up as quietly as I could to avoid waking her and crept out into the early-morning sunlight. In the clearing just outside the cave, Kyle was stacking wood for a fire.

"Need help?" I asked.

"Could use some more water to boil. Stream's that way." He pointed.

Plastic jugs in hand, I traipsed into the brush. Immediately, I heard a gurgling sound. All around me, the forest pulsed with life: Bugs hummed, animals scampered, birds chirped in a chaotic chorus. It smelled so good out here, so clean.

At the brook's deepest spot—which wasn't that deep—I held the jugs under the surface. The icy water stung my hands. When the jugs were full, I capped them off and made my way back to camp.

Kyle poked at a tiny fire ringed with stones. For a guy who had slept on a rock floor, he looked pretty well rested. He'd changed his clothes, too. Instead of head-to-toe camouflage, he wore a black T-shirt and green cargo pants.

"I didn't think fires were allowed at this time of year."

He laughed. "We don't exactly follow the rules, case you hadn't noticed. Anyways, we're on rock here, and there's no wind. We'll put it out after breakfast, light a new one later."

I held my palms up toward the flame. "The heat feels good."

"Cave was pretty cold last night." He poked some more. The flame licked a dry log and spread. "My dad can be a dirtbag sometimes."

I didn't know what to say to that, so I remained quiet.

"Says it's for our own good," Kyle continued. "Learning life lessons. One time we was out in the wilderness, just me and him, and I left my purification tablets at home. Forgot my fire starter, too, so I couldn't even boil water. He had the tablets—matches, too—but he wouldn't let me use them."

"Did you just not drink anything?" I asked.

"Can't go without water. You'll die. There was a lake nearby. Ice cold. Looked good, tasted like heaven."

"And?"

He threw his stick into the fire and sat down on the stone ground. "Got the runs so bad I wound up in the emergency room." He shrugged. "But I never forgot my tablets again, plus now I know how to start a fire with just sticks and stones, if I have to.

Anyways. I'll make you a blanket with leaves and bark. You'll be warm tonight."

"Thanks."

The fire was really going now. Kyle poured the water into a big metal pot and balanced it on some stones in the middle.

"Think there's any chance the others might come today?" I asked.

Kyle shrugged. "Doubt they want to leave their big fancy house."

"Do you blame them?"

"It's not about blame. Well, sometimes it is. But those people, they're soft. Weak. They couldn't survive without us, but they don't understand that. All's they got is money, but when TSHTF, money don't mean nothing. You rich people don't get it."

I sat on the ground and hugged my knees. "Don't lump me in with them. My family's poor."

"You got a house, though, right?"

"Yeah." Our house had been my grandmother's. My mother grew up there. When my parents divorced, my mom, Peter, and I moved in with Gram, and when she died a couple of years later, we inherited the property.

Kyle peered into the pot. "If you got a house, then you ain't poor."

I almost protested. After all, we never had enough money for the stuff we wanted or even needed. My clothes were mostly second-hand. We didn't take real vacations or eat out anywhere that didn't serve food on paper plates. If the world didn't end, I didn't know how I was going to pay for college. My father had said he'd chip in, and my guidance counselor had promised to help with scholarship applications, but I'd probably have to start at the community college. Later I'd transfer to whatever school offered me the most money.

But still. We did not pick up and move every year or two. We had never lived in a school bus. I was getting a good education, I never went cold or hungry, and I saw the dentist twice a year.

Kyle was right. We were not poor.

"Water's boiling," Kyle said. "You want coffee?"

"Coffee would be amazing."

"It's just instant."

"Instant's great. Actually, anything liquid is great. I'm so thirsty I could die."

"Wouldn't want that," Kyle said.

———

Soon afterward, the others came filtering out of the cave. Karessa made a huge pot of oatmeal. At home, I'd only eat oatmeal if it was flavored—apple spice or maple walnut—but I was so hungry that I wolfed down the unsweetened glop, grateful to Kirsten for letting me use her bowl and spoon. When I'd scraped the last bit into my mouth, I peered into the pot to see if there was anything left, but it was all gone.

Along with Kirsten and Kelli-Lynn, I was assigned cleanup. I was so relieved to get out of babysitting that I would have cheerfully scrubbed the cave floors. Okay, maybe not cheerfully.

We gathered up the mounds of sticky spoons and bowls and carried them to the stream. "Do we have dish liquid?" I asked.

Kirsten laughed. "Course not. Haven't you ever been camping?"

I would have thought my query to her the day before—"Where are we supposed to go to the bathroom?"—would have cleared that up. (I am not ready to talk about her answer or my ensuing experience, by the way.)

"I have never been camping until now," I said. "And if I ever had gone camping, I would have chosen someplace with toilets and showers. And maybe a convenience store nearby."

"That's cheating." Kirsten scooped some sandy soil from the bottom of the brook and showed me how to scour the bowls.

"Why suffer if you don't have to?" I crouched down next to her and dipped a bowl into the stream.

She shrugged. "Being out here with nature, that's not suffering. You get to be a part of something bigger than you. If there's too much man-made stuff around, you might as well be back in town."

Down the bank, Kelli-Lynn pulled off her shoes, rolled up her camo pants, and waded into the water.

"Watch out you don't get leeches," Kirsten said. (And just when I was beginning to seriously consider her majestic nature argument.)

"I thought you liked towns," I said. My hands were numb from the cold water, but I was having a terrible time getting some of the oatmeal clumps off.

"I like nice towns. And malls." She scoured some more, thinking. "I really, really like malls, to be honest. But most of the towns we've lived in, they're not that nice. It wouldn't be so bad if they just disappeared."

I shuddered. "Even if people get sick, even if they die . . . the towns themselves won't disappear."

"Looters gonna loot!" Kelli-Lynn proclaimed with glee, splashing cold mountain water with her pale feet.

"The stores will all shut down," Kirsten explained. "So people will get desperate and break the store windows and steal stuff. And the power grid will go down, and the gas lines will break. But there won't be any more firefighters—either they'll be dead or they'll have left—so there will be no one to put out the fire. And that will be the end of the towns and cities."

She lost me somewhere between the power grid and the fires, but I decided not to dwell on her lapses in logic. Instead: "Doesn't this upset you?"

Her pale hair shone in the early sunlight. "No. Because we've got each other, and Daddy taught us how to be safe and how to protect ourselves from the Golden Horde."

"What is the Golden Horde, again?"

"The people that will try to take our stuff!" Kelli-Lynn chimed.

I didn't point out the obvious—that the Dunkles had precious little stuff to take.

Kirsten said, "The Golden Horde are all the people who aren't ready for when TSHTF. When it happens, they'll all flee the cities and head for the country, just trying to survive."

"But they'll all die because they don't have skills!" Kelli-Lynn added with a little—no, a lot of—pleasure. The words were jarring coming from such a sweet kid. But I guess if your parents make themselves your whole world, you'll believe anything they tell you—even if they tell you that other people don't matter.

Kelli-Lynn climbed out of the stream on the far side and wandered over to a bush. She returned with a palmful of purple berries. "What're these? I forget."

Kirsten peered at them. "Don't eat them. They won't kill you, but they'll give you a tummy ache. They're good for dying clothes, but not for eating."

"My mother is out there," I said. "And my brother."

"Isn't he just your half brother?" Kirsten asked.

"He is *my brother*," I said. "It doesn't matter who our fathers are; it just matters what we are to each other. And he's kind of—he can be a jerk sometimes. Well, not a jerk, really, just lazy. But he's my brother, and I love him." My voice cracked.

I took a breath to calm myself and continued. "My father is out there, too, not that we're close, but I still care about him. And all my teachers and my neighbors and my school friends and . . . people I don't know. Just because I've never met them doesn't mean I don't care what happens to them. They're not a bunch of ants that you stomp on."

"Daddy says family first, family second, family third!" Kelli-Lynn chirped.

Kirsten quickly scoured and rinsed the remaining bowls. "We better get back."

———

So much for getting out of babysitting. I was setting the clean(ish) bowls and spoons down on the cave floor when Mrs. Dunkle tried to thrust Tuck into my arms without bothering to notice that my hands were already full. That made me drop the bowls and spoons, which made them clatter. Which made Tuck cry.

"Now look what you've done," Mrs. Dunkle said, passing off her son successfully this time. (It was much easier now that I wasn't holding anything.)

Tuck kicked and punched me, which I took as a request to be put down. So I dropped him (not on purpose, I swear), which set off a whole new round of hysterics, and . . . well, you get the picture.

Mrs. Dunkle also left Sassy behind, but she was napping, at least for now. Everyone else took off into the woods. There were the hunters, the gatherers, the wood and stone collectors. And maybe some other categories. With Tuck screaming in my ear (and at my feet after I dropped him), it was hard to follow the conversation.

Tuck didn't stop screaming until everyone had left—at which point, looking panicked, he took off into the woods to find them.

"No, Tuck!" That kid was going to think his name was No-Tuck.

I caught up with him, but only after he had tripped over a rock and banged his chin on the hard ground. That set off a new round of tears, but to my surprise, when I picked him up, he didn't kick me. Instead, he wrapped his arms around my neck and sobbed, leaving blood and snot on my mended My Little Pony shirt. But I didn't mind at all because Tuck's feelings were all that mattered.

(Totally kidding. Unless you counted the black knit thing from the bunker, that was my *only shirt*. Of course I minded!)

Eventually, I managed to calm him down by singing an old My Chemical Romance song, which I am guessing he had never heard before. Also, I made various animal noises and danced a little. Let's just say I was thankful that being off the grid meant my performance could never end up on YouTube.

"Tirsty," he said at last, with a sniffle.

He was thirsty. Right. Good. I'd just grab him a Capri Sun or an orange juice from the fridge. Or maybe a nice bottle of Dasani.

"We'll get you some water," I said, without any idea how I was going to accomplish such a thing. The water Kyle had boiled for coffee was long gone. There were tablets and filtration pitchers somewhere, but I wouldn't dare go through anyone's stuff.

"Cuppy," he said.

"You have water in your sippy cuppy? In the . . . cave-y?"

He nodded.

That was way too easy.

I put him down. He took my hand, and we strolled into the cave. His apocalypse-approved sippy cup was right next to his sleeping bag, and miracle of miracles, it still had water left from the night before. He plopped onto the sleeping bag and held the cup with both hands, a satisfied baby *mmm* sound accompanying each swallow.

I sat down on Sassy's empty sleeping bag, took a deep breath, and exhaled with relief. Maybe this morning wouldn't be so awful, after all. The one good thing about babysitting was that it took all my attention. I couldn't worry about my mother and brother when I was so focused on keeping Tuck out of trouble. And Sassy, too, of course.

Oh my God.

I sprang up. "Sassy? Sassy!"

Tuck took a break from drinking. "Sah-zee." He went back to his water and his contented little swallowing sounds.

"Tuck! We have to go. We have to find Sassy."

He held tight to his water. No way was I messing with the cup.

"Stand up, Tuck, c'mon. We gotta go!"

"Mrrm." He scowled over his cup.

I reached down, grabbed him under the arms, and hauled him over my shoulder. He screamed with fury and whacked me over the head with his sippy cup. So much for our beautiful friendship.

I rushed out of the cave, Tuck tight in my arms, my terror giving me strength to resist the urge to drop him even though he was kicking me in some organ that shouldn't be kicked. Kidney? Liver? Spleen? Who knows? Anyway, it hurt.

"SASSY!" My voice drifted out through the seemingly endless forest. I took a few steps in the direction of the creek and then stopped. There was no reason to think she would go that way. She didn't know where the creek was. She could have headed anywhere at all.

"SASSY!" I hurried around the side of the rock wall, in the direction from which we had arrived the day before. Maybe she would try to head back to the compound? I yelled a couple more times, and when she didn't answer, I rounded the other side of the cave and yelled again.

My mind was buzzing and my arms ached from hauling Tuck. I had to alert the others. We had to start searching. I adjusted my grip on Tuck and took a few steps in the direction I had seen the gatherers heading when Kyle appeared through the leaves. Sassy was on his back, her arms around his neck.

"Gid-yap!" she said.

"Lose something?" Kyle asked.

Relief flooded through me so fast, I thought I would collapse.

"I thought . . . I thought . . ." I burst into tears.

"Mama loses her all the time, don't she, Sassy?" Kyle said.

"Gid-yap!"

"I'm not your dang horse."

"Gid-yap!"

I followed them back to the clearing. "Does your mother ever lose her in the wilderness?"

"Not real often, no." He laughed. "She'd be PO'd if she knew what happened."

"I don't even care. I'm just glad Sassy is okay." I set Tuck on the ground and rubbed my aching arms.

Sassy, unscathed by the incident, bobbed from side to side and patted her bottom. "Stinky."

"Okay. I'll change you. Somehow."

"What happened to Tuck's chin?" Kyle asked.

"What? Oh. That." I'd been so panicked about having misplaced one child that I forgot about the other's injury. It looked pretty bad actually: open and raw. "Are there bandages around somewhere? Maybe some Neosporin?"

"Got something better." Kyle loped off into the cave and came back with a jar.

"Honey?"

He unscrewed the lid of the jar and smeared a big glop on Tuck's chin.

"Shouldn't you clean out the cut first?" I asked.

"Yeah, probably. Guess I'll leave that to the person in charge of child care. Catch ya later." He turned and loped back into the woods. And just when I was starting to think maybe he wasn't such a huge jerk, after all.

The twins and I managed to make it through the morning without any more crises and surprisingly few tears—though I almost cried when just after I finished changing Sassy's diaper without wipes or running water, Tuck announced that he, too, had made a big stinky in his pants.

When the sun was high and bright, the others began returning, carrying stream-cleaned clothes, wild greens, berries, and game.

By *game*, I mean dead animals. Dead cute animals: three bunnies and a dove.

"Don't suppose they taught you how to skin a rabbit in French class," Mr. Dunkle said.

Since I was too traumatized to tell him I took Spanish, not French, I said, "If Karessa can watch the kids, I'll help Kirsten with the salad." I grabbed a jug and headed to the brook with

Kirsten. Once the water boiled and cooled, we could use it to wash wild greens. (One more thing I missed from the outside world: bagged lettuce.)

Kyle was near the brook, yanking up some vegetation.

"That's not edible," Kirsten said.

"No sewage, Miss Smarty-Pants." (This is what happens when you don't allow kids access to their peers. They say stuff like "no sewage.") "Daisy needs a blanket, but she don't know how to make one."

Kirsten squinted at me. "Seriously?" She wasn't even being snotty. She just couldn't imagine a world in which a family holiday meant something other than killing small mammals, sleeping in caves, and making blankets out of weeds.

Part of me wanted to list off all the things I *did* know how to do: use a self-checkout machine at the CVS, design a PowerPoint presentation, send a text message without looking at my hands. But Kirsten was the closest thing to a friend I had among the Dunkles, and besides, if things really did . . . hit the fan, my skills for living in a civilized world weren't going to do me any good.

But I couldn't let myself think about that. No, it was far better to just pretend we were camping.

Kyle yanked a few more handfuls of long grass and headed back to the campsite.

Kirsten pointed to the bush across the trickling water. "Think those berries would work on my hair?"

"Probably."

We finished filling the jugs and made our way back to the flat area outside the cave, where a fire was blazing with far greater intensity than I'd seen before.

"Dad musta used lighter fluid," Kirsten observed.

"That doesn't sound very natural," I said.

Kristen shrugged. "I think it's from Home Depot."

We put our water in several pots to boil. I tried not to look at the rabbits, red and naked, which lay, paws up, on a bed of leaves. Next to the carcasses, Kadence merrily plucked the dead dove's feathers.

My stomach growled, and I was filled with disgust at my carnivorous instincts.

In the end I ate salad, which sounds better than "bitter weeds with flecks of dirt," which is what it really was. (We should have boiled more water for washing.) There were some dark berries, too, but only enough for, like, three per person, so I didn't take any because I am generous, and also because I was afraid I might die.

"You like fish?" Kyle asked, sitting down beside me to gnaw on what I guessed was a grilled rabbit leg. A leg that mere hours before had been hopping.

"Only if it's not fishy," I said, thinking, *and if it's battered and fried and served with ketchup and french fries.*

"Fish that goes straight from the stream to the fire—that ain't never fishy. I'll catch you some later."

"Okay." I picked up a bushy weed from the slab of bark I was using as a plate. With a few miserable chews, it was down my throat.

"Fish sounds awesome."

Thirty-Six

MISPLACING ONE CHILD and having another injured while under my care wasn't enough to get me fired as head babysitter. Fortunately, Tuck slept away most of the afternoon, while Sassy and I made dolls out of the sticks and grass left over after Kyle had made me a blanket that wouldn't be featured in a Martha Stewart collection anytime soon but that beat freezing in the night.

There was no fish for dinner, but Kyle assured me he would try again tomorrow. His attention was starting to make me uncomfortable, but I did appreciate the blanket. And compared to the stew that Karessa and her mother were putting together for dinner— onion grass and weeds boiled with what looked like some kind of weasel—fish sounded amazing.

"You need to eat," Mrs. Dunkle said when I told her I wasn't hungry.

"I'm fine," I said, though my stomach cried out for sustenance.

"You get weak from hunger, you don't do us no good," she added, just in case I thought her concern reflected any warm and fuzzy feelings for me.

"I'll have a small bowl," I conceded. I was that hungry. But when I dipped a spoon into the watery mess, I pulled up a delicate piece of bone, and I just couldn't do it. I spilled the contents into Tuck's bowl, being careful to pick out the bones, and he downed it all in a few noisy gulps.

After dinner was cleanup time, then soon after that it got dark, and we all went into the cave to go to sleep, even though it was still early.

"Do you think we'll go back to the compound tomorrow?" I whispered to Kirsten.

"Dunno. My dad never tells us the plans."

"Do you think the Hawkings and the Waxweilers might come?"

"Doubt it," she said.

Resigned, I wiggled under my bark-grass-leaf blanket, which was surprisingly warm if not exactly soft. Unfortunately, I have a slight grass allergy.

"*Choo!*" I sneezed.

"G'bless you," Kirsten and Karessa said at once.

"Quiet over there!" Mrs. Dunkle scolded.

I squeezed my nose and held back a second sneeze. I was so tired, but I never went to bed this early, plus the ground under the tarp was cold and hard. Also, I kept thinking about my mother and brother and also Henry. He'd said he'd always protect me, and I'd believed him. What a fool.

My stomach growled. Man, I was hungry. If only I could eat a bowl of cereal . . . or a banana . . . or an In-N-Out burger. But no:

The burger had once been a cow, and in the past two days, I'd grown repulsed by the idea of eating mammals, even the less cute ones.

My stomach growled again. It was going to be a long night.

I'd been lying there maybe an hour when Kirsten tapped on my blanket. There was a little light in the cave; I could just make out her silhouette. She pointed to the outside and motioned for me to follow her. She wiggled out of her sleeping bag and tiptoed around the sleeping forms.

It was chilly outside, but Kyle had the fire going. I sat next to Kirsten; Karessa was on the other side, next to Kyle. Above us, the stars glittered against blue velvet. The moon was nearly full and very bright.

"Here." Karessa reached over Kirsten to hand me a plastic bag filled with crunchy stuff.

"Trail mix?" It seemed too good to be true.

"Our dad has at least five pounds of it in his Bob. He won't miss a little bit."

I yanked open the bag, and some of the mix spilled on the ground.

"Don't leave any out here," Kirsten said. "Bears."

"Yeah, I know." I stuffed a huge handful of nuts and dried fruit into my mouth, gagging a little.

"No need to hurry," Kyle said. "No one's gonna take it from you." He handed me a cup of water.

"Has this been sterilized?" As thirsty as I was, his story about the emergency room made me nervous.

"I wouldn't give it to you if it wasn't."

I gulped the water and took another handful of trail mix, getting some chunks of chocolate this time around. I took care to chew more slowly.

By the time the bag was empty, I felt more like myself again, less shaky and not so much on the verge of tears. "Thanks for getting that for me," I told Karessa.

"It was Kyle. I'm not brave enough to go in Daddy's pack." She laughed.

"Thanks, Kyle," I said.

"Can't let you go hungry. You're part of the family now. Family first, family second, family third."

Since I didn't know what to say aside from *You're starting to creep me out*, I just kind of half smiled and half nodded. Then I poked my finger into the plastic bag to get the last little bit of salt.

"I got something else." Kirsten handed me another bag, this one full of berries, but when I opened it, prepared to gorge, she pulled it out of my hands.

"You can't eat these," she said. "They're ones from the creek. You know, for dyeing my hair."

"Now?"

"We can't do it during the day."

"I don't want your parents to get mad at me."

"I won't tell them you did it," Kirsten said. "And they get mad at me all the time, so who cares?"

We put the berries and some water in a metal cup and balanced it on the fire to boil down to glop. While that was cooking, Kirsten braided her hair into two plaits, which would be easier to hold in the cup. Once the purple glop was ready, she dipped one of her braids while the rest of us stared at the sky and Karessa tried to pick out the constellations.

"You want to do your hair, too?" I asked Karessa.

"Nah, I'm not crazy like Kirsten."

"We're all crazy in this family," Kyle said. "It's how we know we're related."

"The white-blond hair is kind of a tip-off, too," I said. "And the *K* names." No one laughed. (The *K* names were *still* not funny.)

After it had soaked for about a half hour, Kirsten took her plait out of the cup. "Think it's done?"

"Sure," I said, wanting desperately for things like purple hair to matter.

"If the world doesn't end, I want to be a hairdresser," Kirsten said. "Or maybe a makeup artist."

"I want to be a teacher," Karessa said.

"I just want to be a survivor," Kyle said. "And if you all are smart, you'll want the same thing."

We let the second plait soak for roughly the same as the first. Then we dumped the gunk on the ground under a bush, rinsed the cup, and refilled it with a couple of rounds of clear water, which we used to rinse the ends of Kirsten's braids. After that there was nothing to do but wait till morning to see what her hair looked like when it was dry.

Kyle stood up and stretched. "I'm gonna put out the fire."

Karessa pushed herself up to a standing position, then she and Kirsten headed for the cave. "We should all get some sleep."

I lingered to look at the sky. I picked out the Big Dipper and the North Star.

"That's Little Bear, there." Kyle had come up behind me. His breath was warm on my neck. "Can hardly see it when the moon's so bright."

"Where?"

He put a hand on my left shoulder. "There." He draped his other arm over my right shoulder and pointed at the night sky.

"Oh. Right." I had no idea where the constellation was. And I didn't care. The stars had just lost their power to calm me.

I took a step forward, turned, and forced a smile. "It's late. I should really be getting to—"

Before I could finish the sentence, he closed the space between us, placed a hand on each of my shoulders, and bent down to kiss me. I was so surprised I didn't move. Kyle didn't move much, either. We were like two statues with our lips touching. After a few moments, he stepped back.

"Whew!" he said. "Wow."

I didn't say anything.

He ran a hand through his thick, pale hair. "That night at the lookout tower, I thought maybe . . . but then you left."

I still didn't say anything, but he answered my unspoken question anyway.

"We never got our turn."

It took a moment to understand what he meant. And then I got it. He'd made Henry kiss Gwendolyn so that someone would make him kiss me. Or vice versa. But it didn't work out that way.

"I'm glad you're here," he said. "Right now, I mean. But also, in general."

"Thanks." I tried to smile, but I couldn't. "I'd better go in."

He grinned. "Yeah. We wouldn't want to get carried away."

I practically ran back into the cave and burrowed under the bark blanket, half holding my breath in a futile attempt to keep from sneezing.

"Bless you," whispered Kirsten in response to my semi-muffled sneeze. And then, after I murmured my thanks, she said, "I'm glad you and Kyle got some time alone."

I pretended not to hear her.

The sound came in the early hours of morning. Just outside the cave, it was a kind of scratching, and then more of a banging. I sat up, shoving the heavy blanket down.

Was it Henry? Had he finally come? Or was this the Golden Horde, coming to steal our precious supplies?

Another sound came from just outside—an animal grunt.

I tensed. Around the cave, there were murmurs. Some rustling. Footsteps.

And then, a flash of light, and *CRACK!* An animal cry and another gunshot. And then . . . nothing.

An electric lantern flickered to life across the cave. "What in the name of holy heck?" From another corner, a flashlight beam danced across the floor.

A human form loomed at the mouth of the cave: Kyle.

"Bear," he said. "I got her."

Everyone scrambled up and out of the cave. Near the fire's ashes, a black mound lay on the ground. Keanu ran the flashlight over the form and up to the face. The creature's eyes glittered with agony.

"It's still alive," Keanu said.

Kyle raised his shotgun and pointed it at the bear. The sound when he blew a bullet into the poor animal's chest was so loud I screamed. And then I screamed again when Keanu's flashlight illuminated the results.

"What's that bear even doin' here?" Mr. Dunkle's voice shook with anger. "Someone leave food out?"

"Provisions are all sealed up in the barrels," Mrs. Dunkle said. "Checked before I went to sleep."

My stomach dropped. *The trail mix.* I'd spilled bits on the ground and never cleaned them up. It was my fault the bear had come. It was my fault she was dead.

I whimpered aloud and opened my mouth, ready to make my confession, but Kirsten grabbed my arm and pinched.

Mr. Dunkle patted Kyle on the back. "Good job protecting the campsite, boy."

"Just doin' my job." He shot me a grin.

Kyle was the one who snuck out the trail mix in the first place. It was his fault, too, not that he bothered about things like blame.

But I bore most of the responsibility, and I knew it.

Thirty-Seven

THE SMELL OF grilling meat woke me. My mouth watered with
anticipation before I realized that those weren't store-bought burgers
at a cookout.

I was a bear murderer. Okay, technically, Kyle was, but the
whole thing was my fault.

No one else seemed bothered by this crime against nature.
Mrs. Dunkle was outside, minding the fire. She didn't look
happy—smiling was not in her facial repertoire—but she looked
less miserable than usual. Nearby, Mr. Dunkle, Kyle, and Killer
used enormous hunting knives to hack fur and skin off the poor
creature. Mr. Dunkle was whistling.

The bear's head hung at an awkward angle, but her eyes were
open. It felt like she was still alive, her gaze filled with terror and

reproach. She had come to the cave because she was hungry. All she wanted was to nibble on a little trail mix and then find a cozy spot in which to sleep away the winter.

"We should save the head." Mr. Dunkle squatted on his haunches and examined the bear's face. "Nail it to some wood and hang it up in the RV."

"Gotta take the brains out first," Kyle added. "Otherwise it's gonna rot and smell."

Mr. Dunkle took his knife to the back of the animal's neck and sawed at the fur until blood covered his hands. "I always wanted a bearskin rug."

"Can I keep a claw?" Killer asked. "So I can put it on a cord and wear it around my neck?"

Without meaning to, I made a noise, and they both looked up. Mr. Dunkle frowned, but Kyle smiled.

"Bear steaks for breakfast," he said.

"I'm not hungry."

"Won't be ready for a while anyways," Kyle said. "Piece of meat on the fire is pretty thick."

I shook my head. "No."

"No what?"

"I can't eat that," I croaked.

Over at the fire, Mrs. Dunkle grunted with disgust. "You get hungry enough, you'll eat anything."

I was about to protest, but then I realized that she might be right. I couldn't live on weeds and trail mix forever. At some point, I'd have to open myself up to rabbit or squirrel or maybe even bear. But not today.

I crept back into the cave and crawled under my bark blanket.

I didn't think I'd fall asleep, but when the sounds of an argument roused me, I realized that it was considerably brighter outside, so I must have been out for some time.

"Are you out of your mind? You can't just kill a bear because you feel like it! You need a license! And bear tags!"

A man was shouting. His voice was familiar, but it wasn't Mr. Dunkle.

Mr. Dunkle's outburst came next. "It's a free country! Ain't no one gonna tell me what I can and can't do. 'Sides—look around and tell me if you see any park rangers checking for bear tags."

"You work for us, in case you've forgotten." It was Mr. Hawking. I sat up.

"I work for myself," he said. "And my family. No one else."

Kyle broke in, "No one talks like that to my dad."

Mr. Hawking ignored Kyle. "You listen to me, Dunkle. We have been paying you—more than you deserve, frankly—for a year and a half. And we've let you live on our land. Damn right I can tell you what to do."

If Mr. Hawking was right outside the cave, then . . .

I shoved away the bark blanket and hurried into the daylight, trailing bit of grass and leaves.

"Henry!"

He turned. "Daisy! Thank God."

I hurled myself toward him, and he hugged me hard.

"We've been searching for two days."

I stepped back. "Didn't they tell you where we were going?"

Henry shook his head. "We got up in the morning, and everyone was gone."

Mr. Dunkle stood in front of the dead bear, arms crossed over his chest, army fatigues splattered with blood.

Mr. Hawking took two steps toward him. "We have a contract. And that contract states that you will not abandon the property without sufficient notice and a justifiable cause."

Mr. Dunkle sneered. "What ya gonna do, sue me?" (Under the circumstances and considering that Mr. Hawking was a lawyer, it was a decent comeback.)

"We are *one community*," Mr. Hawking said, his jaw tight.

Mr. Dunkle puffed out his chest. "You need us more'n we need you. Heck, we don't need you at all. You go back to your fancy house, see how long you survive on your own."

"We know you lied about being in the Special Forces," Mr. Hawking snapped.

"So?"

"So . . ." Mr. Hawking was at a loss for words, but not for long. "So I feel sorry for your children. Growing up with a father who is a thief and a liar."

Blood-smeared hunting knife in hand, Kyle sprang toward Mr. Hawking. "Don't you talk to my daddy like that!"

"Kyle, don't!" I yelled.

Miraculously, Kyle stopped in his tracks, which gave Mr. Hawking the opportunity to pull out a handgun. Everyone froze. For a moment, I forgot to breathe.

Slowly, Kyle lowered his knife. "Which side you gonna take?" he asked me.

Heart thundering, I looked at Kyle, then at Henry, and then back to Kyle again.

Someone moved near the mouth of the cave. Kirsten and Karessa stood next to each other, each holding a twin. The boiled berries had worked their magic: The ends of Kirsten's hair were a bright, cheery purple. Oblivious to the tension, little Sassy blew me a kiss.

"Can't we all just get along?" I whimpered.

"Too late for that." Mr. Hawking's voice was surprisingly calm considering that a crazed teenage boy with a bloody knife had threatened him just moments before. But then, he was holding a gun, and a gun beats everything. Just ask that poor bear.

Mr. Hawking slipped his gun back into the holster and drew himself up tall. "You will remove your vehicles from our property by sundown." He turned to me. "Coming?"

The tension in the air felt combustible. I hesitated for only a moment before nodding. Eyes to the ground, I joined Henry and his father for the trek back to the house, leaving the Dunkles and the bark blanket behind.

My heart didn't stop racing till we were far away from the cave. I tried not to think about the bear. Or Sassy. Or how I never got to tell Kirsten that her hair looked really good. I was just so grateful that Henry had found me and was bringing me back to safety.

"Do I smell?" I asked Henry. "I really need a shower. And food. I need food."

"You smell like trees." He fished in his pocket and handed me a protein bar. Hands shaking, I ripped open the package and ate it in four dusty bites. Henry handed me a metal water bottle, and I gulped greedily until I had finished the last drop.

I handed back the empty bottle. "Have you heard anything about what's going on out there?"

"Martin drove down the mountain yesterday. Your mother texted back. Said she and Peter are okay and she's glad you are safe in the mountains."

My relief was so intense, it made my legs wobbly, and I had to stop walking for a moment. "Where is she? Did she go to your house?"

"She didn't say anything else, just that they are healthy."

"Well, that's . . . wow." *Peter and my mother are okay.*

"There were no new texts from Sienna," Henry said. "Martin is freaking out."

Ahead of us, Mr. Hawking disappeared over a giant boulder. Henry hauled himself up and turned to give me his hand. I stuck my pink-sneakered foot in a crevice, took Henry's hand, and pushed off from the ground. My sneaker slid out of the crevice, and I began to fall, but he grabbed me under the arm and held me until I regained my footing.

When I reached the top, we both stood up, but he kept his hands under my arms, holding me steady.

I said, "They told me you weren't coming. That you let your parents send me away."

"And you believed that? After everything?"

"I don't know what I believe anymore."

"Oh, Daisy." In a sudden motion, he leaned forward and pressed his lips to mine. My entire face warmed. For the moment, I forgot where I was and why I was here. It was just me and Henry, alone in the universe.

When he pulled back, his smile was gentle. "Now you've been kissed."

I didn't know what to say to that. No way was I going to tell him about Kyle, so I just nodded.

We scrambled down the other side of the boulder and walked along a short path that led to the house, hurrying to catch up to Mr. Hawking. I couldn't wait to get clean and to take a long, long nap in the stuffy bus.

The front gate was open. "So you could get in if you came back," Henry explained.

I picked up my pace. "I never thought I'd be so happy to see this place."

When I got to the open gate, Henry grabbed my arm. "Wait. Something's wrong."

Mr. Waxweiler stood on the front steps, a shotgun poised.

Mr. Hawking came up behind us. "Don't shoot! It's us!"

In his oddly high voice, Mr. Waxweiler called out, "WE HAVE AN INTRUDER!"

A young man stood in the shadows next to Martin's car. I couldn't see his face, but I recognized the way he held his shoulders, the slight paunch around his waist, those long skinny legs. . . .

"Peter!" Overjoyed, I sprinted toward my brother. But Henry ran after me and grabbed me by the waist, holding me back.

"Let me go!" I tried to pry his hands away, but he held tight.

"I don't want you to get sick." His breath was warm on my ear.

"It's *Peter.*"

My brother saw me. "Daisy? Are you okay?"

"I'm fine. Dirty, but safe. And healthy. Are you okay?"

Peter stepped into a patch of sunlight. He needed a shave even more than usual, but that didn't matter because his cheeks bloomed with color. *Peter was okay.*

"I'm going with you!" I called out.

"No!" Henry protested, still holding on to me. "He might be infected."

"He's fine. Just look at him!"

"He's fine now. But he could still get sick. The symptoms come on quickly."

"Where's Mom?" I asked Peter. "Is she still okay?"

"She's fine. She's . . . at home."

From the pause, I guessed that they had gone to Henry's

house. Henry's parents wouldn't like that, but I was past caring what Henry's parents thought about anything.

"Is Mom going to work?" I asked.

"No. Her office is closed till this thing blows over."

"*If* it blows over," Mr. Hawking said.

"Pretty much everything is closed," Peter said. "They shut down LAX this morning." He looked at Mr. Waxweiler, who was still poised to shoot. "Sir? Can you put that down?"

"Only if you promise not to move," Mr. Waxweiler squeaked. "We can't risk infection."

"I won't move," Peter said. "I totally understand why you're freaking out because it's scarier than a zombie invasion out there. They're telling everyone to stay home. This is the first time I've left the house in a week. I've been shut up with my mother and her boyfriend, and no one's sick."

Mr. Waxweiler lowered the shotgun, but he kept both hands on it.

"Randy's still around?" I said, incredulous.

"Turns out he's good in a crisis," Peter said. "Talks a lot, though. It's been a long week."

"What about looters?" Mr. Hawking asked.

"None that I've heard of."

"Not yet, anyway," Mr. Waxweiler grumbled, shotgun still firmly in his grip.

"Is the power still on?" Mr. Hawking asked. "The water?"

"Um, yeah. But it's scary. The news reports? If you get this thing, you pretty much die. But I read on the Internet that they're close to a cure."

"They'll say anything to avoid mass hysteria," Mr. Hawking said. "Even if they've found something that works, it'll take months to get it to market. Years, even."

I said, "Mr. Waxweiler? Please don't shoot, but my brother and I are leaving now. Come on, Peter."

"Daisy, no," Henry said, even as he loosened his hold on my arm.

"I need to go, Henry."

My shower would have to wait until I got home. *Home.* I was finally getting out of here.

But Peter didn't move. "Slight problem," he said.

"What?"

He scratched his scruffy chin. "I drove to the place where we parked last time. I walked a little bit into the woods, but I was afraid I'd get lost, so I went back to the car. But when I tried to start it up, nothing happened."

"The car's dead?"

He nodded. "We're kind of stuck here."

Thirty-Eight

PETER'S DESCENT INTO the bunker wasn't as traumatic as mine for several reasons. One, he got to climb down the rope ladder into the decontamination chamber instead of free-falling into a dirt hole. Two, he knew he was being put into quarantine and how long it would last. And three, over the past few months, Peter had built up an impressive tolerance for spending long hours in confined spaces without daylight. Of course, he couldn't get cell phone reception and there was no gaming console, but Henry gave him a Nintendo one of the Dunkle boys had left in the house, along with a stash of solar-charged batteries.

But still. It was weird watching my brother disappear into the ground. Gwendolyn's dad had opened up the hatch, but then he made a big deal about getting far away before letting Peter approach. From a distance, Mr. Hawking told Peter how to lock himself inside. He made it very clear that if Peter got sick (he wouldn't get sick . . . I couldn't let my mind go there), no one would help him.

That's not true. I would help him. I would never abandon my brother.

Henry and I stood on the edge of the clearing. "He'll be okay," Henry said. "If he was infected, he'd be exhibiting symptoms by now."

"Then why does he have to spend a week underground?" I was still angry at Henry for holding me back when I tried to run to my brother. And I was angry at everyone for treating Peter like he had cooties.

Henry said, "We need to be one hundred percent sure he's not sick. It's community policy."

"Community?" I turned to face him. "Half of your community never showed up, and the other half is gone."

"Do you actually miss the Dunkles?"

"Some of them."

"This is about Kyle, isn't it?"

"What?"

"I saw the way he was looking at you this morning."

"You did *not* just say that."

He checked my face and then looked at the ground.

Suddenly, I was furious. "You're jealous? *Seriously?* Kyle has nothing to do with nothing. I mean *anything.*" (Two days in the wilderness with those people and my grammar was shot.) "It's weird that he kissed me, but I'm just going to pretend it didn't happen."

Henry's eyes widened. In my anger, I'd forgotten that I hadn't told him about the kiss. It used to be that I told Henry everything. All that had changed.

I continued, "I don't dislike Kyle as much as I used to, but I don't *like-like* him. If he *like-likes* me, whatever—I really don't care. I just want to go home. I just want things to be the way they were. Though you and me, our friendship—I don't know if that will ever be the same."

"Maybe it doesn't have to be the same. Maybe it can be something more."

"Is this . . . a new idea?" I asked.

"No. I've thought about it for a long time."

I tried to interpret Henry's expression, but the sun was in my eyes. Not that it mattered. I couldn't read him anymore. Maybe I never really could.

"If you felt that way, Henry, it would have been helpful if you had said something sooner. You didn't even like Hannah, but she went after you, so it was easy. That's what you always do—take the easy way out. I used to think you stayed home from school because you're so smart, you didn't need to go. But really, you stayed home because you knew I'd bring you your makeup work and tell you what you missed. You're just lazy."

On that note, I turned and stomped into the woods, in the direction of the house. When I heard Henry behind me, I started running, at least as much as I could without tripping over a rock or stepping on a snake.

"You're going the wrong way!" he called.

I halted and looked left. Then right. Everything out here in nature looked the same—all, you know, nature-y. Randomly, I chose a direction and ran.

"Stop!" he yelled. "You'll get lost."

I stopped. I waited. I had no choice. I couldn't survive out here on my own. I didn't like Henry much right now, but I needed him.

When he caught up to me, he was breathing hard.

"You mean the world to me," he said. "I don't want to lose you."

I'd always considered Henry the most original person on the planet, and here he was, spouting canned phrases from all those sappy romances I'd made him watch. I didn't say anything, just crossed my arms and waited for him to point me in the right direction. He pulled out his compass and peered at the dial.

"It's that way." He pointed.

I nodded once.

He turned. I followed, keeping half a pace behind. We said nothing.

When we got back to the house, the Dunkles' RV was gone from the front yard. A quick check around back revealed that they had taken the school bus, too. At first, panic seized me—all of my stuff must be gone!

And then I remembered: I didn't have any stuff. And anyway, stuff didn't matter anymore. All that mattered was that my family was healthy and that we would all be together, hopefully soon.

Thirty-Nine

"MY MOTHER TOLD me to give you these." Henry held out beige trousers and a shirt made of some moisture-wicking material.

After a brief hesitation, I took them. "Thanks." I'd pretty much had it with the Hawkings' "favors," but the My Little Pony shirt really needed to be washed. Or burned. One of those.

Henry lingered in the doorway. Since the bus was gone and the Platts weren't coming, his parents were finally allowing me to sleep in the room with the couch.

Henry said, "Dinner's at six. But my mother is cooking, so don't expect much."

Twenty minutes later, clad in my awesome new beigeness, I found Mrs. Hawking in the kitchen, banging pots around and muttering bad words under her breath. When she saw me, she didn't look pleased, exactly, but she looked less displeased than usual. If her opinion still mattered, I'd count that as progress, but at this point I really didn't care what anyone thought about me. I just wanted to go home and hole up with my mother and brother and Randy. Maybe not Randy.

"Dinner is at six," Mrs. Hawking said. "Or whenever it's ready. I'm making spaghetti."

"Okay."

She banged a couple more pots. "I was not supposed to be in charge of cooking. Ever. I have a lot of skills, a lot of expertise to contribute to this community. But cooking—I made it clear from the beginning that someone else would have to take responsibility for meal preparation."

"You want me to make a salad or something?" I offered.

She froze, looking baffled. "Yes. Please. Except. There's no lettuce. Except. I guess. The garden. You can pick something. That would work. Right?"

A broken egg lay in front of the chicken coop. Gwendolyn and her mother stood nearby, bickering with each other and stressing out the animals. Instead of her DRILL shirt, Gwendolyn wore a long-sleeved, baggy gray T-shirt that probably belonged to her father. The stench from the rabbit hutch permeated the air. I held my breath and hurried over to the garden patch without making eye contact.

The first lettuce head I picked was laced with bug bite marks. So was the second. I'd just have to pick through the leaves. Most of the tomatoes were wormy, but I finally managed to find a big juicy one without any obvious tenants, along with a spiky cucumber.

Back in the kitchen, Mrs. Hawking stood hunched over the giant island, sobbing. I tried to sneak back outside, but she had already seen me.

"It wasn't supposed to be like this." Her face was red and puffy, and her glassy eyes looked possessed.

"Can I do anything?"

"Turn back time."

We held each other's gaze. Finally she took a deep breath and drew herself up straight.

"The salad," she said. "You can make the salad."

At dinner, everyone spread out around the enormous plank table, the Hawkings clumped at one end and the Waxweilers at the other, except for Martin, who sat in the middle. I took a seat next to him.

"Your brother's really here?" he asked when I put my plate next to his.

"In the bunker."

He chewed his lip. "Could be worse, I guess."

"Could be better. He could be in the house."

"Yeah." He sighed. "Did he say anything about the outside?"

"He said . . . it's bad."

"How bad?" I wanted to tell him everything was going to be fine, but I couldn't lie.

I said, "People are sick. Dying. And . . ."

"What?"

"Everybody is just waiting for it to be over. Just like we are. Peter said something is going around the Internet about a possible cure, but who knows if that's true."

"Did Peter mention anyone in particular? Who's sick? Or . . . anything?" He looked scared.

I shook my head. "Sorry."

He nodded and jabbed at the overcooked pasta swimming in a watery sauce.

"I'm on lookout duty tonight if you want to hang out." Henry had followed me into the kitchen, where I was attacking the dinner mess by myself.

"I think I'll just go to bed early. I haven't slept much in the past few days."

"I'll bring my guitar," Henry said.

"Okay." I filled the sink with cold soapy water and slid in a pile of dishes.

"You'll come?"

"No. I meant—it's okay for you to bring your guitar if you want. Or not. Whatever. But I'm going to bed."

He nodded and stood there while I picked up another dirty plate and scraped bits of uneaten pasta into a compost jar.

"You shouldn't have brought me here," I blurted out.

"I'm sorry."

Some lettuce and a chunk of tomato went into the compost jar. "People should finish what's on their plates," I snapped. "It's not like this food will last forever."

"You want me to help?" he asked.

"I really just want you to leave."

He stared at me with those sad, dark eyes and then wandered off into the night.

Forty

I SHOULDN'T HAVE bothered cleaning up the kitchen.

When I finished putting away the dishes, I headed upstairs. The house was quiet. No TV tonight. No hanging out or sneaking off into the woods. Instead, everyone had retreated to the bedrooms, eager for the escape that only sleep could provide. After two days in the cave, the stiff couch in my new room felt so luxurious that I fell into a deep sleep the instant my head hit the cushion.

And then.

"Daisy! Wake up!" It was the dead of night. Someone was shaking me. A girl. Gwendolyn.

My first reaction was irritation. If Martin was allowed to sleep through these stupid evacuation drills, I could, too.

"Daisy! Get up! We need to go!"

I squeezed my eyes shut, but she persisted.

"Fire!"

All at once, I smelled the smoke. My eyes popped open. Gray wisps drifted past my open door.

"Gwennie! Come on!" Her father ran over and yanked her arm. Together they fled the room, without looking back to see if I was following. Family first, family second, family third.

I scrambled off the couch. I pulled the beige shirt up over my mouth and nose, grabbed my pink sneakers, and followed the Waxweilers down the wide staircase.

Thick, black smoke gushed from the kitchen. We ran away from it, past the dry fountain in the foyer and out the front door, into the clear, cool night.

"This way!" Mr. Hawking urged, motioning for us to move away from the house, toward the front gate. Martin hopped in his little car, still parked dangerously close to the house, and drove it over to the other vehicles, farther out in the yard.

The house was really burning now. Beyond the dining room window, orange flames thrashed and danced. *Where is Henry?* Panic gripped me until I remembered that he was on lookout duty, safely away from the inferno.

"Looks like it started—" Mr. Waxweiler paused to cough. "In the kitchen."

Everyone looked at me, the last one in that room. This is what I get for doing the dishes.

"Everything was off when I left," I said. But . . . had I actually checked the stove? I couldn't remember. I hadn't done any actual cooking; that had been up to Mrs. Hawking.

"I turned everything off," Mrs. Hawking added. "I always

follow safety protocol. Must have been faulty wiring. We never should have trusted Kurt Dunkle with the electrical."

"What now?" Mrs. Waxweiler's voice quavered.

"We leave." Her husband put his big hand on her little shoulder. "As according to plan. Go to the evacuation location. Reconvene here in twenty-four hours."

"We have to get my brother," I said.

But before anyone could respond, the house's front windows blew out with a flash and a boom. Gwendolyn screamed. Flames spewed out of the windows and slithered up the facade. The blaze had moved upstairs. Orange flames taunted us from behind the upper windows.

"The roof is fireproof," Mr. Waxweiler said, as if trying to convince himself that things weren't so bad. But he'd barely spoken before the fireproof roof collapsed, sending sparks shooting through the night sky and toward the dark, dry, sleeping trees.

"We need to get Henry!" Mrs. Hawking shrieked, all attempt at composure abandoned. She ran for her SUV.

"Head for the road," Mr. Hawking instructed the other family. "We'll get Henry and meet you at the evacuation zone. Dunkle should be there, too, if he follows protocol." As an afterthought, he added, "Take Daisy."

Just beyond the fence, a treetop caught fire like a towering birthday candle with a ghastly wish. The fire spilled onto the next treetop and the next, until a clump burst into flame, lighting the forest with an eerie glow.

The Hawkings' SUV bumped over the gravel and out the front gate, their headlights almost unnecessary in the firelit night.

"Daisy! Get in!" Mrs. Waxweiler yelled from inside the giant pickup truck.

I hurried over. Gwendolyn was in the narrow backseat, strapping herself in. Next to us, Martin waited in his car, windows rolled down so he could hear the plans.

"Who's getting Peter?" I asked, still standing in the dirt.

"The bunker is fireproof," Mr. Waxweiler said. "He'll be safe."

It took a moment for his words to register. "We are not leaving my brother."

"He could be contagious," Mrs. Waxweiler said.

"We are not leaving Peter!" I slammed the door and ran through the yard and out the front gate.

Car lights flashed behind me. A horn sounded. The little blue car pulled up next to me.

"Get in!" Martin yelled. "I'll take you."

We barely made it out the gate before the Hawkings' taillights stopped us. A figure stood next to the car. Henry. He'd come back from the lookout tower. When he saw us, he ran into the glare of Martin's headlights.

Ahead of us, his mother jumped out of the SUV. "Henry! Get back here!"

Henry yanked open the door. I scooted forward, and he squeezed into the backseat. I shut the door before his mother reached us.

"We getting Peter?" Henry asked.

"Not leaving without him," Martin said.

Henry's mother pounded on the car window. She was crying. I couldn't look at her. The Waxweilers' SUV came up behind us, its headlights flooding the inside of Martin's car. Unless the Hawkings continued down the road, all three vehicles were stuck, and the fire was spreading. Mrs. Hawking gave Henry a final, pleading look and then ran back to her car.

The black Expedition lurched forward, and we followed it, traveling as fast as the little car would allow. Its shocks protested with squeaks and groans. Martin stayed silent, his hands tight on the wheel, as his parents followed close behind, their headlights pouring through the rear window like a beacon. Or an accusation.

"I saw him," Henry said from the backseat.

I twisted around. "Who?"

"Kyle. Running through the woods. Toward the house. But I didn't do anything, because I thought he was going to see you."

"When?"

"I don't know. Forty-five minutes ago? An hour?"

Kyle. Of course. In my head, I could still hear him saying, "I burned down a house."

"Did you see him run past you a second time?" I asked.

Henry shook his head. "I could have missed him. I was playing my guitar, so I didn't hear anything, and he could have cut through a different way."

"Your guitar . . ." He had left it behind.

"Doesn't matter. It's just a thing. But Kyle—I should have been paying attention. I could have stopped him. You all could have died."

I reached my hand back between the seats, and he took it. "But we didn't."

At the clearing, Henry's parents turned off the road, and Martin followed. The remaining Waxweilers continued their journey down the road, away from the flames. Henry's parents were already out of the car. Behind us, toward the house, the night sky glowed a sickening orange.

Mrs. Hawking called out, "They can get him, Henry! They don't need you! Come here!"

Henry didn't answer, just ran over the rough terrain with Martin and me, the Hawkings close behind. A flashlight would have been helpful, but for all the time and money spent prepping, they had neglected to bring one along.

The clearing seemed bigger in the dark. I tried to remember where exactly Peter had descended. If he'd had the lights on, little beams would shine through the solar tubes, but it was the middle of the night.

If we'd had to rely on sight, we never would have found the opening. But Henry knew where it was in the way that Henry knew so many things. He darted to a seemingly random spot on the ground, fell to his knees, and pulled opened the hatch.

I caught up with him just as he began his descent and followed him into the darkness. Just a few more moments and we'd have Peter in Martin's car, and we'd all be on our way home.

Was Peter even asleep? He had always been nocturnal. Maybe he was sprawled out on the couch, in the darkness, playing some stupid zombie game on the Nintendo. He wouldn't even know about the fire raging above.

Henry grunted, trying to turn the round latch that opened up to the chamber. "I can't . . ."

Above us, his parents and Martin stood next to the open hatch, ready to help get us back out.

"Is it locked? Is there a key?"

"No, you just turn it to the right and—there!"

He pulled the door open.

"Peter?"

It was pitch-black inside the bunker. Henry fumbled for the light switch. When he flicked it on, the brightness was so intense, I had to shield my eyes.

The first thing I noticed was the smell. With no laundry facilities down here, I might have expected the aroma of dirty socks mixed with cereal dust. Instead, the bunker reeked of sickness and sweat and fear.

Peter was curled in a fetal position on one of the built-in beds at the far end of the bunker, his face pale and slicked with sweat, his eyes open but unfocused.

I ran to him. I didn't make the decision to expose myself to the plague; it was just what my body did. Family first, family second, family third.

His forehead was hot and damp, his breathing shallow.

"Come on, Peter! We have to go!"

He coughed weakly but didn't move. I slipped my hands around his trunk and tried to lift him, but he was too heavy.

And then Henry was there. Next to me. "I'll grab him under the arms, you get his legs."

Together, we hauled my brother through the bunker and out into the decontamination chamber, but there was no way to get him up the ladder.

"Henry?" It was his mother, peering over the edge of the hole. "Is there something wrong with him? Oh my God! NO!"

"He's too heavy for the two of us. We need help."

"I'm coming." Martin was already halfway down the ladder.

"Henry! You need to get out! Quickly! Before . . ." Mrs. Hawking didn't finish the sentence. It was too late to protect her son.

"Put him on my back," Martin instructed. "Henry, you follow behind me, keep a hand on him, make sure he doesn't fall off."

By the time we made it back up to the field, the air was thick with smoke. A few paces away, Mr. Hawking stood frozen, like a statue. Next to him, Mrs. Hawking buried her face in her hands.

Martin said, "We can't carry him any farther, and my car doesn't have four-wheel drive. Can yours make it back here?"

"I think so," Mr. Hawking said, from a distance.

Martin and Henry eased Peter to the ground. I knelt next to him. His breathing came in coughs and gasps.

I stroked his damp hair. "Everything is going to be okay." My words sounded absurd, even to myself.

Martin pulled out the car keys and made his way across the clearing. He stopped several paces away from the Hawkings and chucked them in their direction. They landed at Mr. Hawking's feet. "Now give me yours. I've already been exposed. You haven't."

There was a long pause. Finally, Mr. Hawking took a tissue out of his pocket and used it to pick up the keys. From his other pocket, he retrieved his own set of keys and tossed them to Martin, who immediately took off to get the larger vehicle.

"Come on," Mr. Hawking urged his wife.

But she stayed rooted in place. "Henry, come with us. Please?"

"Get out of here. Call nine-one-one."

Did 911 even exist anymore? Was there anyone to help us other than ourselves?

"I can't leave you," his mother said.

"You have to."

"I can't." She ran across the field, stumbling slightly, and threw her arms around her son. They were the same height, and their dark hair was a perfect match.

Henry whispered something in his mother's ear. Her shoulders shook with what almost looked like laughter. She nodded, wiped her face, and followed her husband into the trees, toward the car.

I stroked Peter's sweaty forehead. He moaned.

"What did you say to her?" I asked Henry.

"That the next time I wanted to get out of school, I was going to pretend to have Mad Plague."

"That's not funny."

"I know. But my family is kind of strange."

Forty-One

MARTIN DROVE THE SUV as if it were a tank, diving into potholes and bouncing back out again. Low-hanging branches clawed the windows. The smell of smoke permeated the air.

The Hawkings had stashed a case of water in the back. I opened a bottle and tried to get Peter to drink, but it just dribbled down the side of his face. We were in the vast backseat, Peter sprawled out with his head on my lap. His T-shirt was drenched.

When we turned onto the state road, our view opened up enough to see flames engulfing the mountainside.

Kyle did that. All because he was mad at me. And Mr. Hawking. And the whole world.

A fire truck, lights blazing, roared past us, and another followed. The significance took a moment to register. If there were fire trucks, civilization had not collapsed, at least not yet. At last, we made it out of the forest and to Casitas Lake. There was a smaller fire truck parked in a lot, along with a paramedic van, and Martin's little blue car.

Martin pulled the big SUV over. A firefighter in full gear strode over to the window. Martin opened it just a crack. "We have someone sick here. Really sick. You don't want to be exposed."

The firefighter shook his head. "I'm good. Let's get him out of there, onto an IV. Medevac is on its way."

"You don't understand," Martin said. "It's the Madagascar plague."

"I know it is." He yanked open my door and helped me out, and then another firefighter helped him ease Peter out of the car and onto a stretcher.

"Aren't you scared?" Martin asked, bewildered.

"For myself?" The man shot a glance up at the burning mountain. "No."

As a female paramedic ran a line into Peter's arm, the Hawkings stumbled over.

"They've found a cure," Mr. Hawking said. "Aspirin, of all things. On its own it doesn't work, but if it's taken early in combination with two different antibiotics, it stops this thing before the infection damages any organs. *Aspirin*."

"So Peter is going to be okay?" I almost collapsed with relief.

Mr. Hawking hesitated. "They're going to take your brother to a hospital. They'll take good care of him there. And we'll go, too, all of us. Because we've been exposed. So they will give us the medication as a preventive measure."

Peter's IV line was in, and the paramedic was giving him oxygen. She looked exhausted.

I pointed to the IV bag. "Is that the antibiotic?"

She shook her head. "Just saline to keep his blood pressure up. They'll start the medication as soon as he gets to the hospital."

"So he's going to be okay?" I pleaded.

She hesitated. "We are going to do everything we can. A helicopter is on its way. They'll get him to the hospital faster than we can. You can either go down with your friends, or you can stay with your brother. Your choice."

"I'm not leaving him."

Henry came over. "They told us to get out of here before the fire gets any worse."

"I'm staying with Peter."

"The Dunkles . . . they haven't found them."

In my mind, there was a sudden vision of Sassy, lost among the burning trees. Would Kyle save her this time? Would someone save Kirsten with her purple-edged hair? Or Karessa, who wanted to be a teacher?

I looked at Peter. The oxygen had helped. There was a little more color in his cheeks, though not much.

"I'll see you at the hospital," I told Henry.

Forty-Two

I EXPECTED THE hospital to be overflowing with plague patients, but almost two days had passed since the cure had been identified. As a night nurse explained, "Either they get better fast or they die fast. If they start the treatment early enough, they're out of here in twenty-four hours."

"Is this early enough for my brother?"

She looked at Peter, ashen-faced and coughing. "Ask me in twenty-four hours."

"You're going to be okay," I murmured over and over and over again as I waited in a chair next to Peter's hospital bed. After all, he had been perfectly fine earlier in the day. He had been sick less than twenty-four hours before beginning treatment. *He was going to be okay.*

The hospital staff let me stay in the room because I had already been exposed and treated. If my mother came, she wouldn't even be allowed into this wing of the hospital, so I decided not to call her, not yet.

Shielded by curtains, Peter's roommate coughed so violently that I didn't think I could fall asleep, but I managed to doze for a few hours, waking up only when an orderly arrived with Peter's breakfast. Sunshine streamed into the room. The dividing curtain had been pushed back. The other bed was empty.

Peter wasn't looking any better, but he wasn't looking worse, either. IV lines snaked from his arms, but he was breathing without help. That was good.

On a metal table next to Peter's bed, the orderly set down the tray of food: scrambled eggs, toast, yogurt, orange juice.

"Doesn't look like he's up to eating," he said. "You can have his breakfast if you want." The orderly was young, with glossy black hair and brown forearms laced with muscle.

I shook my head. "He might want it later."

"Well, the cafeteria's open if you're hungry. First day since this all began."

"Have you been here at the hospital?" I asked. "Through the epidemic?"

He nodded. His eyes seemed older than the rest of him.

"And you didn't get sick?"

"Nope."

"What's your secret?"

His mouth went up on one side in a sad half smile. "Prayer and Purell."

"I can't believe you weren't scared."

His eyebrows shot up. "I've been terrified. Every minute of every day. But you gotta do what you gotta do."

After the orderly left, I got up and stretched, trying (and failing) to get a crick out of my neck. Then I went out to hunt for the cafeteria. I wasn't hungry, but I needed something to drink, preferably something with caffeine.

Just around the corner, Henry sat slumped in a chair. Dark circles shadowed his eyes. When he saw me, he perked up. "Hey!"

I said, "I figured you would have gone home with your parents."

"They're here, too—sleeping in a waiting room, I think. The Waxweilers have left, though. How's Peter doing?"

"Alive."

"Doing better?"

"Yes. No. I don't know. I'm scared, Henry."

"I know."

"Any news about the Dunkles?"

He shook his head.

"So they're . . ."

"They might have escaped. They could have packed up and had everything waiting on a back road. They might have left right after Kyle set the fire."

"Is the fire out?"

He hesitated. "Not yet. But they say it's under control. Whatever that means."

"Kyle saved Peter's life," I said. "Not on purpose. But if he hadn't set the fire, we would have left Peter down there for a week. And when we went to let him out . . ."

"I know. I thought of that, too."

I rubbed my face. I was so worn out with sadness and fear and sheer physical stress. "Okay. Well, I'm going to go grab a soda or something."

"You want me to come with you?"

I was about to say yes, but the truth popped out. "I need to be alone right now. I'm sorry."

"It's okay."

"You can leave, if you want. I'll call my mom as soon as Peter is cleared to leave." Surely Peter would get well. I wouldn't allow my mind to consider any other option.

"I'm not leaving you," he said.

"Okay."

———

It happened later that afternoon. I'd dozed off—my body had no idea what time it was—only to be awakened when a new patient moved into the bed next to Peter's. Someone pulled the curtain shut, and I opened my eyes.

"You so owe me hot Cheetos."

Peter wasn't just alive, he was awake and sitting up with a remote control in his hand. A violent movie played on the wall-mounted television.

He grinned at me.

I burst into tears.

"You know I hate it when you do that."

I sobbed some more. When I could finally speak, I said, "I was so worried about you."

"Yeah, I was a little worried myself. But I figured the universe would look out for me."

"Everything happens for a reason." I tried to smile, but I burst out in fresh tears instead.

Peter shook his head. "You have really got to stop doing that."

Forty-Three

THE NEXT MORNING, Peter was well enough to be discharged. We piled into the Hawkings' Expedition.

"Does Mom know what happened?" he asked. "That I got sick?"

"No. We can tell her later. She thinks you stayed with me at nature camp and we're just now coming down from the mountain."

"She's not going to be happy about her car."

"Wait. You mean . . ."

"You think I was going to take my car all the way into the mountains? It wouldn't have been safe."

"So the Civic cooked?"

"It was time for her to get a new car anyway."

A couple of hours later, Mr. Hawking pulled up in front of my house. It was so weird to be back, so normal, and yet . . . not. Part of me felt like nothing would ever be the same, and part of me felt like the entire time on the mountain had been a dream or just a really bad vacation.

I stood up to scramble around the seats, but Peter said, "Um . . ."

"What?"

"Mom's not here."

With all that had happened, I'd forgotten about sending my family to the Hawkings' house. Fortunately, Henry quickly explained the situation, and if his parents were angry, at least they didn't express it.

Until we actually reached their house.

The Hawkings' front door stood wide open. On the front lawn, cats of every color clustered around three big feeding bowls. A German shepherd scampered up the front walkway and into the house. A tiny white dog followed on its heels.

"What in the name of God?" Mr. Hawking stopped the car with a lurch and left it in the driveway. He and his wife hurried to the doorway, the rest of us close behind.

We found my mother in the kitchen. There were two cats on the black granite counters and three . . . no, four . . . no, six dogs running in and out of the room.

Mrs. Hawking said, "You set up an animal shelter? In our house?"

"Somebody had to!" I had never seen my mother look so furious. "People were abandoning their pets—poor, innocent creatures that have done nothing wrong! And why? Just because they *might* carry fleas that *might* carry a disease that *might* infect someone? Where is the sense? Where is the humanity?"

The fury brought color to my mother's cheeks. She was wearing her favorite yoga pants and one of Peter's old sweatshirts, and her hair swung from a high ponytail. It was like she had gotten younger in the time we had spent apart.

"How many dogs and cats are here?" Mrs. Hawking asked. (Her husband had returned to his former speechless state.) "It *is* just dogs and cats, right?"

"I don't know how many. I'm not good with numbers. And yes—just cats and dogs. I received inquiries about a rat, but with all these cats around . . ." She shook her head. "I blame the media for blowing everything out of proportion. They tried to make us believe that the world was coming to an end! Have you ever heard of anything more ridiculous? But you know what? Everything happens for a reason. Bad times bring out the best in people, and I for one have learned a great deal from this experience."

I started to laugh, which pretty quickly turned into a kind of maniacal sobbing.

"Daisy! I didn't even see you back there! How was camp?"

"Camp sucked," I said through my tears.

She took me in her arms. "You never did like nature."

Three months later

MY HOUSE SMELLS. I'm used to its being dirty, but now every time I open the door and step inside, I am shocked anew by the wall of pet dander, cat litter, and kibble dust that has become the new normal.

Buddy immediately assaults me, rearing up on his hind legs and throwing his full weight against my chest, drowning me in stinky dog slobber.

"Down, boy!" I say. And then I correct myself. "Girl."

Buddy is the fourth dog we've called Buddy since my mother embraced animal rescue as her life's calling and started taking in fosters. Big dogs we call Buddy, little dogs we call Squirt, and cats go by color or pattern: Smokey, Blackie, Snowy, Tiger, Patches.

Buddy gets down, but then she dances around and makes these

high-pitched noises. I don't speak Dog, but I'm pretty sure she is saying, "I'm hungry," or "I gotta pee," or maybe—probably—both.

"Peter?"

No answer.

"Peter!"

Smokey curls around my ankles, and I scoop him up. Immediately, he begins to purr. I fell in love with the first Smokey, and it broke my heart when he got adopted. So now I try not to get attached, kind of like with the Man-Frans.

Speaking of Man-Frans, my mom broke up with Randy. No one's fault, really, but it turned out he was allergic to cats.

Peter is in his room, iPod buds in his ears, bent over a book. When he sees me, he turns off the music.

"You were supposed to pick me up if it's raining."

"So?"

"It's raining."

"It is?" His eyes flit over to his window, which doesn't do any good because the blinds are down. He still hasn't changed the burned-out overhead light, but he moved in a floor lamp from the living room.

The latest Squirt, who is white and not too yappy for a little dog, is passed out on the bed. When Smokey sees her, he jumps out of my arms and bolts from the room. Squirt and Smokey have issues.

"Did you feed Buddy?" I ask.

"Yeah."

"Have you walked her since this morning?"

"No. I've been reading. This is due tomorrow."

Peter has enrolled in community college, and whenever he talks about his assignments, he uses this reverent, hushed voice, as if taking Introduction to Accounting is right up there with joining the Peace

Corps. I'm not sure if he's really that into his studies or if he just sees school as the best way to avoid dealing with the in-house zoo, but I did see one of his papers lying around, and he got an A-minus, so he must be taking his classes at least kind of seriously.

Mom made him get a job to help pay for her new (well, new to her) car. She got some insurance money for the Civic but not a lot since it was so old. Four nights a week, Peter works the Jamba Juice counter at the Brea Mall. He says he hates it, but I stopped by once, and a cute girl from Forever 21 was hanging around, so it can't be all bad.

I say, "Take Buddy for a walk. Like now, or she'll pee all over everything like the last Buddy."

He puts down the book. "Fine."

"I'm going over to Henry's house to study."

He raises his eyebrows. "Is that what you kids are calling it nowadays?"

"Henry and I are *just friends.*"

"Right."

I cross my arms. "I hate you so much right now."

"You can't hate me. I saved your life."

"You did not save my life. I saved your life."

"But my life was only in danger because *I came to save you.*"

"Ah . . . but you *didn't.*"

We've had this discussion before. In fact, we have it pretty often. It's a way to face up to what happened without getting sucked in by the terror of what *almost* happened.

Everything happens for a reason.

Really?

Peter went back to school, and my mother discovered a passion for animals.

Mr. Vasquez recovered, but Mrs. Jessup, the English teacher, is gone. I missed her funeral, but I hear it was standing-room only and everyone sobbed. A fund has been set up to help her little kids.

The yearbook will be dedicated to our classmates who died. Each one gets a page. There's talk of creating scholarships in their names.

The Dunkles were never found. No one reported a burned-out bus or RV, either, but that may not mean anything. Though I hope it does. I hope that every day.

———

When I let myself out the back gate, the rain has stopped, but the path is soaked. By the time I reach Henry's house, mud coats my bright pink sneakers, which were none too clean to begin with.

Mrs. Hawking answers the door. When she sees me, she gathers me in her arms and says, "Sweetheart! It is always so good to see you!"

Ha. Kidding. When she sees me, she says, "Daisy." And then she kind of sighs.

"Henry and I were going to study. Is he here?"

She takes a step backward so I can enter the Fortress. "I'll tell him to meet you in the TV room. You can leave your shoes by the door."

Ever since our time on the mountain, the Hawking parents have implemented a No Girls on the Second Floor rule. By *girls*, they mean me, of course, even though Henry and I really are just friends. I didn't think we could ever go back to the way things were, but weirdly enough, we fell right into our old patterns.

"I hope my mother gets a job soon," Henry mutters when he comes into the den.

The Forever Friends Pet Insurance Company suffered serious

losses from plague-related claims (including hundreds of thousands of lab tests, the vast majority of which determined that the animals did not, in fact, have the disease), and Mrs. Hawking got laid off from her job. It probably didn't help that she disappeared right when the company needed her most.

Now that his mother is home all day, Henry hasn't missed a single day of school. Instead of pulling straight As, he is getting straight A-pluses. It is annoying.

He sits next to me on the beige leather couch, and I open up our chemistry textbook.

"I need to tell you something," he says.

I keep my expression neutral. Winter Formal is in two weeks, but neither of us has mentioned it. Henry can go with Hannah Branson if he wants, and I really won't care. Okay, I will care. Of course I will. But in the bigger scheme of things, dances just don't matter that much.

"I've joined the JV baseball team," he says.

"What?"

"I'll be on the bench this year, but Coach said that if I come to all the practices and then do summer camp, then next year I might get some playing time."

"You hate baseball," I say.

"No, I don't."

"You've always said the baseball stuff in your room is stupid."

He shrugs. "It is stupid. I'm not eight."

"But you never wanted to watch any games on TV."

"That's because watching baseball just made me feel worse about not being able to play."

"But . . ." I am so confused. "If you've always wanted to play, why didn't you?"

"My parents wouldn't let me. Too dangerous. I could get hit by a ball. Or a bat. Though that seems unlikely. But I think they've finally realized they can't protect me from everything. Plus, I asked them, like, five times a day for the past month until they finally caved."

Mrs. Hawking pops her head into the room long enough to see that we are not engaged in any unseemly behavior, then she disappears.

"You like baseball." I am still trying to process this. Does it mean I'll have to go to the school games? Or watch the sport on TV? Will that be payback for all those Nicholas Sparks movies I've forced on Henry?

"So the thing is," he says, "I'll have a new schedule, starting tomorrow."

"Huh?"

"They had to switch my classes around to fit in baseball. We'll still be in AP Euro together, but that's it."

"That's . . . okay," I say, trying to convince myself more than him. "The courses are still the same, right? So we can still do homework together after school."

"I'll have practice after school."

"Right." The textbook feels heavy in my lap.

"But we can study together in the evenings."

"Okay."

He leans toward me, trying to catch my eye. "It doesn't change anything."

"Right," I say to the textbook, thinking, *Of course it changes things. It changes everything.*

But that is the nature of life. Nothing stays the same.

His mother pops her head in for the second time.

"Wanna go for a walk?" he asks me.

The rain has washed the smog from the air. Patches of brilliant blue push away the clouds, and the trees glow with golden light. At the pond, waterfowl outnumber humans for once. Coots dive under the surface, while mallards nap in the shadows by the banks. On the far side, a white egret stands on one leg. In a few months, ducklings will paddle and chirp in the shallows. Seasons follow seasons. Life goes on.

Henry shoves his hands into the front pockets of his jeans. "Mr. and Mrs. Waxweiler are getting a divorce."

"Really? That's too bad."

"My parents said Mrs. Waxweiler couldn't forgive Mr. Waxweiler for leaving Martin behind on the mountain. But I think it's more than that."

I feel bad for Gwendolyn, who kept her spot on the drill squad but looks tense all the time, and for Martin, who was so happy to find out that Sienna hadn't gotten sick—only to discover that she had left him for another guy. And I feel bad for Mr. and Mrs. Waxweiler, too, because I know they wanted the best for the children, even if they went about it all wrong.

"Let's go this way," Henry says, wandering along the pond and then turning off near a feeder stream.

"It's muddy there."

"You're afraid of a little dirt?"

"I'm not afraid of anything." It's a lie, of course. I'm afraid of so much, I wouldn't even know where to begin.

The pond is stocked with fish. At the edge of a tiny waterfall, a metal grate protects the young trout from being eaten by bigger fish below—though not from the opportunistic ducks who paddle on the surface.

A plastic bottle lies in the water, wedged between two rocks.

"I can't believe someone would just throw their trash in the water," Henry says.

I think of the stream near the cave, where Kirsten picked berries so I could dye her hair. How clear that water was, how clean. It was like we were the only people who had ever been there. Or like we were the last people left at the last place on earth.

Henry points at the bottle. "You should grab that. Put it in the trash."

"Why don't you grab it?"

"You're closer."

"Fine." I lean over and pick it up. There is something inside.

"That's weird." I glance up. Henry looks . . . not nervous exactly, but . . . well, yeah. Actually, he looks nervous.

"You should probably open it," he says.

I unscrew the cap and pull out a slip of paper.

Daisy:

1. Will you please go to Winter Formal with me?
2. As a date. (In case that wasn't clear.)
3. I still think that movie was stupid.

Henry

He looks up at the sky. His eyes are so dark. "I almost left a trail of pebbles to lead you here, but I didn't think you'd appreciate that."

"I wouldn't have."

"And then I thought about leaving a trail of bread crumbs instead, but I figured the ducks would eat everything before we got here."

"They would have."

We hold each other's eyes. "So . . . you want to go to the dance?

If not, we can just stay home and watch Netflix. I'll even let you pick the movie."

"I want to go to the dance."

"Good."

"You'll need to get me a corsage."

"I can do that."

"Okay then."

He leans forward and touches his lips to mine. And the earth moves.

No, seriously. It moves.

"Earthquake!"

We jump apart. By the metal grate, a mallard flaps his wings as the water around him swishes back and forth and splashes onto the bank. Around the pond, other ducks awake from their naps to squawk in protest, and a few frightened coots take to the sky. A tiny wood duck rides a wave like a surfer.

The earth lurches. The earth churns. And then it stops.

Like a pendulum, the pond has found its rhythm and continues to move even after the ground has stilled. Back and forth, it sways. Back and forth. If I close my eyes, I can almost believe we are at the ocean.

"It must have been a sign," Henry whispers.

"Of what?"

"I dunno. Of something good?"

"Or something bad."

He takes my hand. "One of those."

The churning in the pond slows and then stops. The coots return from the sky and land in the water, where they resume their paddling and their diving. It is like nothing has happened, and life goes on as before.

Acknowledgments

I'VE WRITTEN FAR too many books to have launched into this one as I did, with a few suspenseful pages and no idea whatsoever where the plot was headed. I owe a mountain of thanks to my gifted editor and dear friend, Kate Farrell, for falling in love with that brief beginning . . . as well as for her honesty a few months later when she told me that the next sixty pages really had to go—but not to worry because we'd figure something out. And it looks like we did.

My wonderful agent, Steph Rostan, has been involved in every phase of every book I've written, and this one was no exception. I am endlessly grateful for her support, as well as for the smart and hardworking crew at the Levine Greenberg Rostan Literary Agency. I am thankful, too, for all the people at Henry Holt Books for Young Readers for turning my messy manuscript into such a pretty book. Thanks to Rachel Murray for her attention to detail; the art department for the gorgeous cover and book design; and the eagle-eyed copy editors whose fact-checking and map-reading skills saved me from tremendous embarrassment.

Thanks to Paul Chiotti and Sue Sefcik for sharing their professional expertise; to Kim Snow for her enthusiastic early reader feedback; and to Tim Scott for backpacking with my husband so I don't have to. Next time, guys, try to remember the matches.

Finally, thanks to my family: Philip, my self-appointed target reader; Lucy, who found a new use for Kool-Aid; and Andrew, who is my everything, always.

GOFISH

CAROL SNOW

What's your most embarrassing childhood memory?
When I was in fifth grade, I had my mother write a note excusing me from playing dodge ball. Actually, I had her write the note in sixth grade, too.

What's your favorite childhood memory?
My family spent summers on Cape Cod, and my friend who lived across the street, also named Carole (but with an *e*), had a boat dock right below her backyard. The summer I was twelve, we spent every day swimming, sunning, rowing, and catching jellyfish. Unfortunately, at the end of the summer, her family moved across the country, and I never saw her again.

What was your favorite thing about school?
The bell at the end of the day. Well—in elementary school, anyway. I loved high school, mostly because I was part of a large and wonderful theater and music community.

What were your hobbies as a kid? What are your hobbies now?
I was a miscellaneously creative kid. I enjoyed drawing, dancing, music, photography, and—especially—drama. I read constantly. I wrote a little. I still take photographs, though now

I mostly use my phone, which is really lazy, but it is so convenient! I also like cooking and entertaining (as in throwing parties, not juggling).

What was your first job, and what was your "worst" job?
That would be the same answer for both: in high school, I worked as a chambermaid at a motel on Cape Cod. Let's just say I do not display a natural gift for cleaning.

How did you celebrate publishing your first book?
By writing a second book! I had dreamed of being an author for years at that point. It just took me a while to realize that I needed to do more writing and less dreaming.

What do you do on a rainy day?
I complain about the rain.

If you could live in any fictional world, what would it be?
I would love to live in Agalinas (or at least spend a vacation there). The conversation would have to get a lot more intelligent, though, or I wouldn't last long.

If you were stranded on a desert island, who would you want for company?
My husband. He's my favorite person to spend time with. But more importantly, he can do anything. So I feel pretty confident that, after building us a shelter and procuring food and water, he'd figure out a way to get us off that stupid island.

If you could travel anywhere in the world, where would you go and what would you do?
I always wanted to live in France, and right now that's what I'm doing. My husband, son, and I are in Strasbourg for nine

months. I spend most of my time writing, grocery shopping, cooking, and messing around with pictures on my iPhone. Which, come to think of it, is pretty much how I spend my time back home in America.

What's the best advice you have ever received about writing?

My friend Michael Grant often points out that writing is something you do, not something you are. You can't get caught up in the mystique of "being a writer" or expect the process to be fun. Writing is work. Obviously, it is more pleasant and personally rewarding than many other jobs out there, and there is nothing else I'd rather do. But if I wrote only on days when I felt like writing, I'd never have finished a single book.

What advice do you wish someone had given you when you were younger?

Stand up straight or you'll have terrible posture when you're an adult

Do you ever get writer's block? What do you do to get back on track?

I never get writer's block, but I definitely have periods when I feel uninspired and unable to produce anything but mediocre writing (at best). Most often, this happens when I am about a hundred pages into a manuscript. Fueled by caffeine and self-loathing, I force myself to write a few miserable pages a day until I get back on track, knowing that I can rework or delete the bad parts when it comes time for revision.

Do you have any strange or funny habits?

That I will admit to? No.

What do you consider to be your greatest accomplishment?
I have raised two wonderful kids. Of course, they might have been equally wonderful had they been brought up by wolves, but I like to believe my husband and I had something to do with it.

What do you wish you could do better?
Speak French. I studied the language for eight years and have now lived in France for five months. I thought I was at least fluent in a French restaurant, but last weekend I went out to get my son a plain cheese pizza. When I got home, he opened the box and said, "Why is there salmon on this?"

FREESIA LIVES ON a beautiful island paradise. But not all is as it seems. Sudden blackouts. Students disappearing. Soon she will have to make a choice that will change everything.

KEEP READING FOR AN EXCERPT.

The signs were all there, but Freesia chose to ignore them. She didn't question the power surges. The electrical blackouts. The sudden departures that bordered on disappearances. Had she been paying attention, Freesia would have noticed that things on the Island had fallen a little bit out of sync. No, more than a little bit: a lot a bit. Nothing so terrible that you'd cry malfunction, but still.

But Freesia never looked for, considered, or even noticed much of anything, good or bad, until she'd had her first cup of frothy coffee, and this morning, for the first time in her admittedly short memory, no coffee smells tickled her nose when she sat up among her fuzzy pink and orange pillows and stretched her toned, tanned arms toward the cloud mural overhead.

The missing coffee? Yes, it was a sign—the second on that day alone—that something in Freesia's world had gone very, very wrong.

The first sign had come a few minutes earlier, when the

two peacocks, Ashley and Jennifer (both of whom were boys), failed to wake Freesia with the latest Chase Bennett song. Instead they just kind of screeched and screamed, which would have flipped Freesia out if she hadn't been so utterly tired from staying so utterly late at Ricky Leisure's pool party. When Freesia was tired, she didn't flip out. She just got really, really cranky.

"Shut it!" she told Ashley and Jennifer as they began their second round of screeching.

Just like that, the peacocks changed their tune. Rather, they started their tune—Chase Bennett's latest, to be exact.

It's another day.
On the island we say, Hey,
Hey, oh. Hey, oh. Hey, oh.
Don't wanna see you frown,
Girl, turn it upside down.
Hey, oh. Yeah, turn it upside down.
Girl.
Hey.

Chase Bennett? Was an artistic genius.

Freesia shooed the peacocks back out to the balcony. The rising sun cast a pink glow on the glassy ocean that lay beyond the island's crystal sand. Graceful waterbirds dove for silver fish, and twenty kinds of flowers released their perfume into the still, cool morning air.

But Freesia didn't notice any of this, because it looked

perfect and pretty and peaceful like this every morning, and besides, *she still hadn't had her coffee.*

"Mummeeeeee!"

Freesia's mother appeared at the door, almost as if she'd been waiting. She looked mom-perfect, as always: nice and trim with shiny brown hair, shiny tanned skin, shiny pink nails. She looked a lot like Freesia, only older. And shinier.

"Sweetie?"

Freesia pointed to her white night table, empty except for her bubble, a solid silver ball cradled in a trumpet-shaped charger.

"Peacocks. Loud. Coffee. No coffee." The very effort of speaking exhausted her.

"Sweetie!" Just like that, Freesia's mother hurried out the door. Just like that, she returned, bearing Freesia's favorite chunky mug, filled to the brim with steaming, frothy coffee.

"It's Tracey's Famous Coffee!" she told Freesia. "Nothing like a coffee cloud to start your day the Tracey way!"

Freesia forced a smile. She adored her mother, but did she have to say the same thing every time she served coffee? And what about that coffee cloud business? It was frothy, sure, but a cloud?

"Would you like an omelet, oatmeal, or pancakes for brunch?" her mother asked.

"Pancakes."

"In here or in the kitchen?"

"Here."

"Should I stay, or should I go?"

"Go."

Her mother turned to leave.

"Wait."

Her mother turned back.

"I love you, mummy of mine."

"I love you too, sweet Freesia." Mummy's skin sparkled with affection.

Freesia blew a kiss. Her mother pretended to snatch it from the coffee-and-flower-scented air and slip it into the pocket of her peach satin robe before heading downstairs to make breakfast.

Alone now (except for the peacocks), Freesia took her coffee, her silver bubble, and a plush pink blanket out to the balcony, where she settled onto a pillowy lounge. Ashley watched her from the corner while Jennifer jumped on the railing and fanned out his magnificent tail.

Freesia's house looked like a fancy cake built into a hillside full of other fancy-cake houses. In the half-moon harbor below, kayakers dipped paddles into glassy water, navigating around quiet white boats and lolling blue buoys.

When she'd gulped enough coffee to clear her cloudy head, Freesia settled her chunky mug on a glass side table and cupped her bubble, which was now a tangerine-sized silver ball, in both of her hands. Soon, the bubble began to emit a greenish light, and her hands grew warm. As she drew her hands apart, the bubble grew larger, first to the size of an orange, then a grapefruit, then . . . something larger than a citrus fruit. Like a honeydew melon, maybe. Deciding that honeydew-melon-sized was perfect, Freesia balanced the silver bubble on her knees and reached for her mug.

"Enemy check," she commanded, sipping her cooling brew.

The bubble's green light changed to blue. Soon names emerged on the screen, followed by messages.

CHAI COTILLION . . . NOT TRANSMITTING
TASER LUCAS . . . NOT TRANSMITTING
DARE FIESTA . . . NOT TRANSMITTING

Dash it. Freesia only had three enemies, and as many times as she had tried to catch them at weak or ugly moments, they only used their public bubble settings when they were being especially luminous or triumphant.

"Fine. Friendlies check, then."

A long list of names appeared on the orb. Freesia tapped the edge of her pink-polished fingernail onto **RICKY LEISURE**. Just like that, Ricky, curled up in a yellow blow-up raft and still wearing his swim trunks from last night's pool party, came into focus. The raft was out of the water, lying in a patch of sun near the pool cave entrance, just down from the steps that led up to one of two waterslides.

"Ricky? Ricky, wake up!"

After a few more *Rickys*, he lifted his head up and rubbed sleep out of his eyes. If Ricky had any enemies, they might enjoy seeing his blue eyes all puffy, his golden hair sticking up at strange angles. But everyone liked Ricky, and besides, even at his worst, he looked utterly de-vicious.

Ricky groped around the raft until he found his own bubble, which he didn't bother enlarging from its original size. Now Freesia could choose between two views: the panoramic she'd started with or face-to-face. Ricky wasn't wearing a shirt. She chose panoramic.

"Freesia! Where is everybody?"

Freesia laughed. "Party's over, Ricardo."

"What time?"

"Dunno. I left around two, but a few people were still there. Cabo, Ferdinand . . . Chai."

She checked Ricky's face for a reaction to Chai's name. Nothing. If Ricky and Chai ever linked, she'd just—ugh.

Not that Freesia wanted to link with Ricky herself or anything. She liked him too much. And everyone knew that if you linked with someone and it didn't work out—it never worked out—you wound up on their enemy list, whether you found each other noxious or not. After Jelissa Moon, Ricky was her best friend. Freesia couldn't risk losing him.

"You going to cultural immersion?" Freesia asked.

"Dunno. What's the language today?"

"Korean."

"Too hard. And I don't like kimchee."

"Well, you better come tomorrow for Spanglish. We can share nachos."

A maid in a white uniform, one of Ricky's many serfs, appeared at the edge of Freesia's bubble and handed Ricky a glass of pale green liquid.

"Kiwi mocktail?" Freesia asked.

Ricky shook his head. "Happy juice. If you come over, I'll share."

Freesia laughed. "I had enough happy juice last night. And anyway, some of us get into trouble if we miss class."

Freesia's parents added shells to her personal bubble account every time she went to class. If she skipped, she got shells taken out. Freesia needed shells for clothes, coffees, conch burgers—everything, really. For her, more shells equaled more fun: simple. But Ricky was lucky. His parents lived on the mainland and kept his account full no matter what he did or didn't do.

"Bubble me later?" Freesia said.

"Come see me," Ricky said. "After class. I'll be dressed by then."

"Don't get dressed for me." Just because they were just friendlies didn't mean Freesia couldn't appreciate his sinewy brown arms and his rippled abdomen. Ricky rarely did anything but lounge around drinking happy juice, yet he was all muscle.

She said, "After immersion, I'm going shopping with Jelissa. I want something new for the dance. And then I've got music class."

"What's the dance theme this week?" Ricky asked. Every Saturday night, there was a dance in the Rotunda's grand ballroom. Students from the Advanced Event Planning class chose the theme and dress code, plus they took care of the decorations, the music, and the food.

"Sweet Seventeen. The girls are to wear girlie dresses. The boys have to dress all in white or all in black."

"Come over tonight, then," Ricky said. "I'll throw another party."

"All righty." Freesia blew Ricky a kiss and then tapped her bubble three times. Immediately, it turned back to silver and shrank to its original size.

Another party at Ricky's house. That was something fun to look forward to. Freesia liked looking forward to things.

● ● ●